You Make Me Wanna

You Make Me Wanna

Nikki Rashan

www.urbanbooks.net

Urban Books, LLC
97 N18th Street
Wyandanch, NY 11798

You Make Me Wanna Copyright © 2009 Nikki Rashan

ISBN 13: 978-1-60162-587-8
ISBN 10: 1-60162-587-1

First Mass Market Printing March 2014
First Trade Paperback Printing August 2009
Printed in the United States of America

10 9 8 7 6 5 4 3 2 1

This is a work of fiction. Any references or similarities to actual events, real people, living or dead, or to real locales are intended to give the novel a sense of reality. Any similarity in other names, characters, places, and incidents is entirely coincidental.

Distributed by Kensington Publishing Corp.
Submit Wholesale Orders to:
Kensington Publishing Corp.
C/O Penguin Group (USA) Inc.
Attention: Order Processing
405 Murray Hill Parkway
East Rutherford, NJ 07073-2316
Phone: 1-800-526-0275
Fax: 1-800-227-9604

Acknowledgments

I'm so grateful to the circle of friends and close family that have consistently remained by my side and loved me, even when I'm sleepy and crabby or hungry and grouchy. If you didn't leave me then, I know you'll leave me never. All of you have been an amazing support to me, and I appreciate each of you.

Dawn: How many books have you been in now? Love ya, girlie.

Bo: Hmm- Did you read the revised DPDP? I love you anyway.

Pat: Love, joy, peace, and enlightenment always.

Brandy: You're the best ambassador ever.

Bernell: Success to you always. We're going to make it to a Sparks game in L.A. one day.

Shenay: Cousin, thanks for the many, MANY e-mails. You know I could write another book.

Pam: By the time this book is published, I really hope we've CELEBRATED!

Acknowledgments

Alta: Thanks for bringing some fun into the workday.

Larry: You're the sweetest friend around.

Monique: Thank you for your hard work and fierce determination while promoting DPDP.

For Those Who Believe

You Make Me Wanna

CHAPTER 1

Where We Left Off

To change and to improve are two different things. This famous proverb blared like trumpet horns in my ears as I awoke this morning. Gently, I shook myself awake and re-familiarized myself with unfocused surroundings. I stretched a kink out of my right shoulder, and accidentally bumped against Angie's short, curly locks.

Fast asleep in the white T-shirt she wore to the club last night, Angie clutched her pillow like a toddler would a teddy bear. One would never guess this domineering lioness purred like a peacefully sleeping kitten when she laid her head to rest. It was moments like these when I found myself most tempted to succumb to her persistent, yet humble requests to claim me as her own.

On far too many occasions I'd been left with the duty of declining Angie's sincere desire to scoop me under her wings and care for me like a newborn bird. It's not that she wasn't a good catch. Actually, she was one of the most successful women I'd met in the city of Atlanta. She held a master's in computer technology from Georgia Tech and owned a very successful consulting business.

While some second bedrooms are furnished as guest-rooms or filled with various exercise equipment, Angie's additional room was the home of AAA Information Technology Services (AAA standing for her initials, Angela Ann Adams). Angie's office contained every amenity needed to run a business from home. The small space was complete with a large oak wood desk, a flat-screen computer monitor and keyboard, adding machine, file tray, and pencil and penholder filled with every colored pen under the rainbow. Pictures of her parents and baby niece, Lauren, were perched next to her framed diplomas, which proudly sat on her desk, as opposed to hanging on the wall. A fax machine that also served as her printer, scanner, and copier sat next to her desk, as well as a file cabinet with the names, numbers, and work orders of her many clients throughout the metro Atlanta area. Every night her cell phone, her lifeline, was placed in a holding tray on top of the three-foot-high table just inside the room.

Angie was by far one of the most sought-after lesbians in the community, not only for the slammin' burgundy Lexus GS300 she drove, or the fact that she made well over six figures, but she knew how to treat a woman. An admitted player in her twenties, Angie hung up her pimp hat and tossed her cane aside when she hit thirty, vowing to commit herself toward two main goals in life. The first of establishing herself as an entrepreneur was already achieved. The second was to find an equally motivated and drama-free woman to share the rest of her life with. So why she settled for every-other-week dinners and once-a-month bedtime sessions with me, I still haven't figured out.

My carefree, non-committal attitude had been apparent since the day I set foot on this Georgia red clay I now called home. I was determined to start fresh, leaving behind the confused, vulnerable, indecisive Kyla I had been for far too many years. I shed my uncomfortable exterior and developed a strong backbone to support my growing wings. My move to Atlanta was to leave the past behind and to begin a new life, focused and determined to live the way I wanted.

I'd be telling the world's greatest fib if I said I hadn't dived headfirst and sunk deep into Atlanta's notorious gay scene. More than once, I found myself caught up in an unexpected, and short-lived, whirlwind romance. In fact, since my arrival seventeen months ago, I've had one, two, three . . . well, let's say, I've had a few affairs with women who resembled the confused, secretive Kyla I was when I'd first met Steph, the only woman I've ever fallen in love with, and for whom I ultimately left my dedicated fiancé, Jeff.

Though I had always been shy in the company of women in the gym locker room, lesbianism hadn't been a thought. I didn't think that feeling awkward around nude women qualified as a hidden fear of being gay. In just the few short months that I had known Steph after our initial meeting in class, her fascinating hazel eyes and alluring charm and personality permanently altered my heterosexual lifestyle, and the longing to be with her settled in the forefront of my mind. Being with her became my greatest wish and greatest fear at the same time.

Fear had delayed my straight versus lesbian inner trial, and by the time the verdict was reached and the gavel had struck, Steph had fallen back in love with her ex-girlfriend, Michelle. Although I was crushed, I couldn't have been angry with her. I had waited too long to admit my love for her, and during the time of my internal debate, she was given a new opportunity with an old love. I missed my chance and lost her.

"Happily ever after" wasn't my destiny with Jeff either. I revealed my love for Steph to him even prior to revealing it to her myself. I had informed him, my mother, father, sister Yvonne, and lifelong best friends, Tori and Vanessa, of my newfound revelation while gathered in my mom's living room on a cold February day back home in Milwaukee. David, my cousin and confidant, was also there for emotional support and to make sure I didn't shy away from announcing my pivotal awakening.

Jeff's response was natural; he was hurt and angry. I had still been scared and in shock at the severe fury and aggression he vented at me. Unbeknownst to me, he had already been aware of my feelings for Steph, yet he had enough belief in me that with time, my heart would lead me back to him. On that winter day, he learned that he was wrong.

Nearly a year had passed before we spoke again, and even then our conversation was limited to short and cordial e-mail exchanges.

My mother was dumbfounded and distraught that I opted not to marry the son-in-law of her dreams to pursue a relationship with a woman. In her eyes, I had just made the most horrifying mistake of my life. Although my father was saddened by my decision, the majority of his discontentment derived from worry about me. Although my parents were divorced, I was certain that my father had to spend many days consoling my mom on what her oldest daughter had done. Yvonne was least shaken by my admission, even though she was still stunned that I chose Steph over Jeff.

Tori and Vanessa took opposing positions in response to my announcement. Vanessa attempted to remain a loyal friend, but after her numerous messages went without response, she eventually withdrew, and the calls ceased. On the other hand, Tori was repulsed and outraged that I was attracted to, and in love with, a woman. She hesitated none in letting me know how disgusted she was by way of a slew of insults left on my voice mail. We bumped into each other once before my departure south in which the degradation continued. My twenty-plus-year friendship with both of them dissolved instantly.

Back to my affairs. Sharon, one of the most timid and nervous I had entertained, was a quiet, shy, older woman I met while walking to the front of the congregation to deliver my offering at a church David and I had frequented at least twice a month at his urging. Since our dual move to Atlanta, and after watching me transform from hesitant and inhibited to sexually liberated, he was adamant that I needed God's supervision for my wanton bedroom behavior.

While I generally enjoyed the sermon and clapped and sang along with the choir, it didn't take long for me to uncover the inconsistencies and inability of church folk to practice what they preach. I found a wicked pleasure in spying the rows of starstruck women as they sat in exalted admiration for the suited-up, Escalade-driving, womanizing pastor in the pulpit. There they sat squirming in their seats, bodies in heat, with absurdly loopy grins plastered across their faces whenever Mr. Preacher spoke words of enlightenment in their direction. At the height of each sermon, just as I thought he'd collapse in exhaustion after his twentieth run across the platform, he'd point to one of the bedazzled women, nearly igniting her afire with an invisible blaze from his fingertip. She'd jolt from her seat in response, waving her hand in the air, singing songs and praises to God the Savior or to Mr. Preacher; it was hard to tell. But who am I to judge, right?

Anyway, when I smiled and said hello to Sharon, she blushed a rainbow red, giggling an unintelligible response before proceeding in the line ahead of me to deposit her contribution. I noticed the strange manner in which she walked, one foot tripping over the other, and I realized my presence made her nervous. I figured she understood the meaning of the rainbow pendant that hung delicately against my collarbone.

When depositing my envelope into the weaved basket, I closed in on her backside.

"Oops," she squeaked when she accidentally dropped hers on the floor. On the way up, her eyes focused on my legs, in discreet admiration.

After church, Sharon stood next to my car, waiting for me.

Quietly we rode to my apartment, stripped naked, and fucked all afternoon. I realized I was her first, from the goofy way she sucked my nipples, like a baby would a bottle, and the unskilled way her fingers fumbled between my legs. Why she chose me that particular afternoon, I'll never know. But by the time I dropped Sharon off, she had learned how to touch my sweetest spots, and I had found her most pleasurable places as well.

However, when I attended services again several weeks later, Sharon sat in the second pew, avoidant of my eye and deep in prayer, apparently repenting for her abominable sin.

On the opposite extreme, there was another set of women I had discovered. These women knew what they wanted, but were unwilling to risk their corporate husbands, 3-ct. wedding rings, Mercedes trucks to haul their two kids in, and the social status they spent years building just for a romp in the sack with a woman. They concealed their hidden passions, unleashing them only when opportunities arose, skillfully maneuvering their schedule to allot for morning, afternoon, or evening escapades. These women had mastered the art of deceit, cleverly disguising a four-hour hotel stay at the Wyndham as an afternoon spent shopping and lunching with friends.

"Here, look what I bought for you," they'd drawl, flashing a new golf shirt or new Kenneth Cole watch in the direction of their leading man.

Not only would there be no questions asked, he'd likely toss a new gold credit card in their direction as a treat—like a bone to a faithful dog.

My fondest yet scariest memory of entertaining this type of woman was of Charlotte, a stunning minx in her early thirties whose frosted blonde hair and Barbie sea-green eyes (yes, I went there), were complemented by her naturally browned skin under the steamy Georgia sun. She was the perfect Charlize Theron imitation.

Each morning before I went to work, I'd stop at a little cafe nearby for coffee to support the caffeine habit I'd acquired. Charlotte would sashay into the cafe a mere five minutes after

I did, leaving her stroller outside and carrying two-year old Edward on her hip. For a woman who had just walked five blocks to drop her older child off to school while traveling with a temperamental two-year old, she always looked pretty damn refreshed and energetic.

Charlotte would smile and say hello while we stood and added cream and sugar to our tall, slender cups. Eventually she advanced the smile and hello by adding a stare. Not a casual stare as if admiring the silk blouse I had on, but a testing stare. One I have since mastered myself. Her eyes would intentionally linger on mine until I finally broke the gaze. When Charlotte advanced to lowering her skim to the chest level, smiling deliciously at my cleavage, I knew what her deal was.

So the next day I purposely arrived early, retrieved my java, and stood outside waiting for her to turn the corner. Only slightly caught off guard, she looked pleased to see me there. With my eyes glued to Charlotte's nearing frame, I visually stroked every angle of her body, from her Reebok walking shoes, up her slender legs, and around her waist. Her nipples hardened through her white T-shirt as my eyes devoured each breast one at a time. Finally, my eyes met hers, and the always composed, fiercely dominant Charlotte looked as if her knees would give in at any moment.

I smiled deviously as she stopped in front of me to release Edward from the stroller. For a white girl, she was built. She possessed a curvaceous ass, trim muscular legs, a taut, firm belly, and round breasts enhanced by C-cup implants received after Edward was born. Only later I came to learn that her successful plastic surgeon husband had molded her into his idea of flawlessness.

I could practically feel the heat simmering off Charlotte's body when she passed me and went into the cafe. Satisfied, I left my business card on the stroller and walked to my car.

I had been at work three short hours before a thick-Southern-accented woman responded after I answered my phone.

"Hi, is this Kyla?"

I knew it was her immediately by the high-pitched voice that matched her high energy level. Even though I had been the aggressor in initiating conversation with Charlotte, I quickly learned that she was anything and everything but passive. She called the shots—what she said was how it went.

Our first meeting occurred the following Wednesday. Charlotte invited me to join her for lunch at the Palm restaurant inside Buckhead's Westin Hotel. She failed to mention that lunch was the appetizer and I was the main course.

To make a long, heated, and spicy story short, Charlotte's caged hunger for making love to a woman was released, and what followed was an afternoon of vigorous lovemaking. Afternoon dessert became a twice-a-week routine we both anxiously anticipated. Charlotte loved to eat my pussy. She'd suck on my clit and stretch her stiff tongue into me as far as she could. It didn't matter if I was on my back or sitting on her face, she craved my sweetness, bringing me to climax after climax.

And what I loved about Charlotte was the unabashed excitement she displayed the first time I pulled my favorite Doc Johnson strap-on dildo from my purse one afternoon. She marveled at how real it looked, touching and even tasting it. Charlotte fell into a frenzied state, her eyes fixed on mine, screaming my name as I pumped in and out, fucking her just like her husband would, only better. Like most lesbians who enjoy penetration, she was thrilled by the masculine thrust contrasted against soft, smooth, feminine skin and touching breasts.

Charlotte and I engaged in our affair for about two months before the disapproving comments I received from David, "You reap what you sow," became too frequent, and riddled me with guilt. While seeing Charlotte quickly became an event

I very much looked forward to, inside I knew it was wrong. Even though I had all the freedom in the world to sleep with whomever I chose, Charlotte didn't. She was committing adultery, and I was her ever-willing accomplice.

Ending the relationship proved more difficult than I anticipated, as Charlotte wasn't a woman who accepted rejection with ease. It seemed she dialed my work and cell numbers every free waking moment she had. I finally had to threaten to ruin her "happily married" facade by exposing myself as her undercover lover. Soon after, I switched my morning cafe run and never heard from her again.

I wasn't fazed though. I knew it would only be a matter of time, short time at that, before my newest lover would appear, a previously unknown face in a crowd, whose life would soon intertwine with mine in a lustful fury, even if only for one night.

Which brings me back to my opening statement: To change and to improve are two different things. In my two and a half years post-heterosexual life, I obtained a successful, fulfilling career, and developed into a strong, determined, outgoing woman living in one of the hottest metropolitan cities in the country. I worked hard and diligently, paid all my bills on time, and remained close to my family despite the states that separated us.

On the downside, smoking cigarettes, although not heavily, was a habit I'd picked up when my body hungered for a lunchtime meal I was unable to grab while buried underneath mounds of paperwork. Bed-hopping, my other vice, had become my number one release, to unwind and relieve stress. I was a full-blown lesbian now. And in this short time I'd fulfilled damn near every lesbian fantasy created, though I wasn't proud of all of them.

Once upon a time I was the committed girlfriend to a wonderful man in a monogamous relationship. And now buried heartbreak and unhealed wounds masked as contentedness had become my day-to-day life as I dined with and then slept with an unimaginable number of women.

But is this the life I'd envisioned for myself? Was my life heading down the path I was destined for? Sure, I had changed. I had grown and I was happy, yet a part of me yearned for the missing link. Deep inside I knew I wanted to love again. But how?

I sighed and rolled over, and began small strokes across the nape of Angie's neck, admiring the smooth lining against her tiny black curls. She roused slowly and reached for my fingers, bringing them to her mouth. She kissed and nibbled the tips of each, the heat of her breath warming them instantly.

With my fingers still warm and moist, I lowered my left hand and lifted her T-shirt, and next her sports bra. I grabbed hold of one of her breasts and squeezed gently, then a bit more aggressively. I pinched her stiffened nipple between two fingers, and she moaned. She liked it this way.

Though Angie's demeanor was softhearted and nurturing, her sex was bold and unrestrained. With her, I let my wildest side free. In her bedroom, or whatever room we ended up in, we each shed our professional exteriors and revealed the raw, brash side of ourselves. Rarely was there a moment of silence; we talked to each other the entire time, pornographic words flying about the room nonstop.

"Fuck me harder, Angie," I told her, my fingers disappearing in and out of my heated body.

Fucking me from behind with her strap-on, one of her hands at my waist, the other holding a fistful of my hair, she said, "Your pussy is so good."

"You like that shit, don't you?" I lifted my ass and pressed into her hips.

"Come for me, baby," she said, going deeper.

***

This morning was no exception. I lowered my hand once more and reached inside Angie's boxers and began a firm rub against her clit with my middle finger. One of the biggest turn-ons about her was, even though she was a "soft stud," she knew she was a woman and let me fuck her the same way she fucked me.

"Make me come, Kyla," she commanded.

Within minutes my finger was slippery wet, yet I remained focused on Angie's now bulging clit, rocking it back and forth with my finger.

"Ah, that's the shit right there." She groaned, just before her body lifted slightly off the bed and her body trembled as she came.

Angie wasted no time, rising up and turning me onto my backside. My naked body was exposed as she stared at me, her eyes poring over my toast-colored skin. She leaned forward and devoured each of my breasts, one at a time, then together, darting her tongue from nipple to nipple. She used her teeth against my skin, sending minor shots of pleasurable pain through me.

I felt a small rush escape my body. I spread my legs, and she placed her first and second fingers inside me, rapidly moving them in and out, using her third and fourth fingers to pound my clit with each entry. My body rocked against the strength and rhythm of her motion.

As the tightness in my belly increased and the spasms became more frequent, I had just one request of her. "Fuck me harder, Angie," I said.

And she did.

CHAPTER 2

Heaven on Earth

Kyla, could you come here for a moment please?" Gary, the divisional manager and my boss requested when I finally answered my phone after ignoring it three times.

It wasn't that I was intentionally neglecting the phone, but it hardly seemed worth the search-and-rescue effort, considering it was hidden underneath stacks of inventory files and shipping orders. "No problem, Gary," I said. "I'll be there in a second."

I pushed aside the catalog of the latest women's trendsetting fashions and picked up the folder detailing October's financial plan. Gary was surely calling me in for it, since I had yet to report the numbers to him. Well, at least I could scratch it off my to-do list now.

Gary's office fell at the end of what seemed an endless hallway. One would think I worked for an upscale magazine, with the decorative walls of models sporting the season's most recent must-have shoe, or extravagant evening gown by the most sought-after designers. Through the glass windows I could see him tapping his pen against his palm to the beat of whatever pop CD was playing in the compact disc player on the desk.

At forty-two years old and married with three children, Gary's life revolved around three things: his family, his job, and the pop phenomenon. At least he had his priorities in the right order. His particular fascination was geared toward the manufactured teen delights of Christina Aguilera, Mandy Moore, and his ultimate fantasy girl, Britney Spears. However, on occasion I'd noticed an *NSYNC, 98 Degrees, and even New Kids on the Block CDs stacked next to the player. Today he was treating his ears to the tunes of Hilary Duff, one of the latest blondes to hit the scene.

"Here you go, Gary," I said, handing him the manila folder.

Dressed casually in a short-sleeve plaid top of reds, blues, yellows, and greens only he could pull off stylishly, Gary lazily flipped through the papers briefly and then set the folder atop his pile of financial plans from all of the other buyers in the women's department. He hummed and closed his eyes, his light eyelids a stunning contrast against his reddened, tanned skin. I assumed Gary sat imagining he was singing on stage right along with Hilary.

"So you're a Hilary Duff fan now, Gary?"

He smiled broadly without even a hint of embarrassment. "Yes, she's quite a talented little lady." He picked up the CD cover and admired her innocent, youthful photo. "I hear she may be coming to town soon, so I'm keeping my ears open for the concert announcement. Missy would love to go."

Missy was Gary's 18-year-old soon-to-be high school graduate. Ever since the Spice Girls domination in the late '90s, Missy had been Gary's excuse to wait hours in line to obtain the best seats for the teeny-bopper concerts he adored so much. Luckily, the fascination seemed hereditary, for Missy appeared twice as excited as he did when a pop sensation announced their future arrival date to Atlanta.

"Sit down, Kyla. Talk to me." Gary motioned toward the chair in front of his desk.

I anticipated his invitation and had already mentally prepared for a minimum fifteen minutes of chitchat.

Gary unashamedly tried to get me to divulge details about my personal life to satisfy his raging imagination. His hands clasped together, index fingers touching, his elbows resting on his desk, inquisition-style, he dove right into it. "What'd you do last night?"

Shortly after I had joined his team, I found myself leery of Gary's sudden interest in my personal life.

He'd noticed my reluctance and attempted to ease my hesitation with soothing words. "Kyla, I hope you don't feel I'm being too forward by wanting to get to know you better," he'd said that day in his office. "You've been working with us for a couple of months now, and you've made yourself comfortable and already established yourself as a strong asset to our store. It's my nature to maintain an open-door policy with my people, and I want you to feel relaxed enough to talk to me about anything, anything that's on your mind, whenever you like."

At that time I knew neither of two things: one, he meant that he wanted me to be relaxed enough so he could talk to me about anything, anytime. And, two, he had already spoken to my co-worker, Megan, who had heard from a friend of a friend that I was out at a club cuddled up with Dana, my companion that particular evening. Word got back to Megan, who quickly shared the unbelievable gossip about the new girl. It didn't take long for the news to travel down the hall to Gary's office.

"Well, Gary," I started, "last night David and I rented a couple of movies and shared a bottle of wine."

A hint of disappointment shadowed his face.

It seemed he expected a detailed narration of a romantic evening spent gazing into the eyes of my latest interest, a young woman by the name of Tiffany, who I'd literally bumped into as I ran into the bank recently, trying to catch the security guard before he turned the lock. Tiffany, obviously on the same mission, unbeknownst to me, was trailing two feet behind my heels when I suddenly stopped in my tracks and turned back toward my car, realizing the check I needed was sitting inside my console, and she and I collided forehead to forehead, chest to chest, and knees to knees.

After a temporary moment of painful blindness, my eyes focused on a lovely woman dressed in a navy business suit, looking as if she might black out as a result of our impact. I reached and held her elbow to steady her wavering stance.

"I'm okay," she said, finally opening her chocolate brown eyes.

"I'm so sorry. I didn't know someone was behind me."

"That's all right." Then her eyes deepened in thought. "Hey, you look familiar. I've seen you somewhere."

I studied her face for recognition but found none.

"Ahhh, yes," she said, a smile creeping at the corners of her mouth. "Yes, you shared a dance with a friend of mine at the Velvet Room one night. Her name is Nicole," she stated, waiting for me to respond.

Now, the only reason I remembered Nicole was because she was a looming barracuda of a woman who asked me to dance about ten times in a two-hour time span. I figured the best solution was to surrender to one song and get it over with. When the song thankfully ended (it just had to be the extended version of Prince's "Erotic City"), I shook her hand firmly and headed back to my table, where David was near tears in stifled laughter.

"Sure, I remember her. So she's a friend of yours?" I asked hesitantly, afraid she might try to reconnect me with the Amazon.

"We hang out from time to time, but that's it. By the way, I'm Tiffany." She held out her hand.

"Kyla," I said, taking hold of her soft fingers.

"So," she said, smiling shyly, "is there any chance I can have the next dance?"

And that's how my relationship with Tiffany began. In between Angie and a select few, she'd been sucking up the majority of my spare time since our collision two months ago.

No longer thrilled by my presence and not wanting to listen to a boring Kyla and David story, Gary suddenly found the urgent need to begin reviewing the financial report he'd tossed aside five minutes before. He picked up a folder and ran his finger down the page, focused on the numbers. "Hmmm," he hummed, seemingly concerned.

"I'll let you get to work, Gary, okay." I stood to leave.

"Yeah, sure, sure." He waved his hand, too fixated on the report to look in my direction.

A few minutes later after I left the women's restroom and walked for a smoke break, I saw Gary casually sitting atop Nancy's desk, another senior buyer, chatting animatedly. Perhaps I would have a more exciting story for him another day.

When I got back to my desk, I punched speed dial 7 and called Nakia, the manager of the Misses Better Sportswear department, for which I was the buyer. Nakia and I took the fast road to friendship shortly after I joined the store. Nakia was a rarity in Atlanta, meaning, she was actually a native. Born and raised in Decatur,

Georgia, she was witness to the emergence of Atlanta as a major city in the world.

We became friends just after I started, and our relationship strengthened when I was quickly promoted from assistant buyer to buyer only five months after my initial hire. The other assistant buyers weren't the only ones surprised by the move. Although grateful and appreciative, I was taken aback as well. The can-you-believe-she-got-promoted stares lasted about a month, until I proved I was capable and competent enough to handle the job.

Nakia's support and constant don't-worry-about-what-they-say comments assisted my transition into my new title.

She would linger hours after her shift ended, chatting with me as I attempted to complete the shitload of tasks upon my desk. Apparently digging through shit was my niche, since it was only nine months later that I was again promoted to senior buyer.

My sexuality didn't bother Nakia, and it was never a topic we had to tiptoe over from the beginning. The news hit the sales floor even before Gary's office, yet Nakia's attitude didn't change, and she never once questioned my chosen lifestyle. I could talk to her about anyone I was involved with, and she listened and offered advice as if she were talking to a straight woman. She empathized with what I had gone through, and it felt good to form a new friendship with a woman since my departure from home. I was doubtful that anyone could ever fill the shoes of Tori and Vanessa, but in Nakia I knew I'd found a true friend.

She was two years older than me, about two inches taller, and two sizes larger. She wasn't a woman a person could walk past with a glance. Her mere presence demanded your attention. Her frame, although tall and built, was a voluptuously shaped size twelve. Even though she had short, curly hair managed with just moisturizer and a brush, a feminine aura surrounded her. Sleek-fitted skirts and daring low-cut blouses filled her wardrobe, and in three-inch heels she towered over me like a mother to a child. I had grown accustomed to her delicate fragrance of musk that lightly awakened one's senses when she walked by.

"What time for lunch today?" I asked when she finally picked up her line.

"Oh, Kyla, damn! I'm sorry," she said. "I can't make it today. Fred Jr. needs new shoes for basketball, and I promised to take him over lunch. I'm sorry, girl."

Fred Jr. was Nakia's ex-husband's son whom Nakia refused to divorce, even after she did his father. Although Fred Sr. and his first wife, the mother of Fred Jr., shared joint custody, Nakia, with little protest from either parent, spent entire weekends with Fred Jr. She attended his sports games, celebratory dinner outings, and spent occasional holidays with him as well. In the event she remarried, Nakia would have happily had children of her own, but firmly vowed that Fred Jr. was in her life to stay.

"All right, Kia, but you owe me one," I said.

Nakia laughed lightly. Thank goodness. For her laugh was just as large as her presence. If she had belted out her usual roar, a painfully loud sound that ranged anywhere from a dog's bark to a rooster's cuckoo, I might have heard her from my office two floors above. I tried to avoid comedy movie outings with Nakia, and on those unusual days when I was feeling especially brave, I attempted to make sure we attended the first showing of the day in which there would be the least amount of people that asked for their money back because some loud-mouthed lady in the audience prevented them from actually hearing the movie. Even though I jumped as if a fire alarm had gone off the first time I heard Nakia belt out a laugh, I easily adjusted and had grown to love this unique trait of hers.

"Okay, I'm going to call David and see if he's free for lunch then. Stop up before you leave tonight?" I asked her.

"Yep," she said and hung up.

I leaned back in my chair after pressing speed dial 1, which was David's cell phone. He answered out of breath.

"What's the matter, David?"

"Nothing, girl, just playing hide and seek with MJ."

"Oh, so I take it you're not free for lunch then," I said, a tad disappointed. Even though David and I shared an apartment together, he spent the majority of his time at his boyfriend Marlon's house, MJ's father.

"Well, baby, you can come over here. I was just about to make me and MJ some tacos."

Working such long days allowed me the luxury of extending my lunch as long as I wanted. So long as the work got done, Gary never hounded me down, even if I was gone two hours at a time. I looked at my watch. It was 11:45. "I'll be there in an hour," I told David.

"See you then, darling," he said, and went back to kidding with MJ before the phone clicked.

Just two trips, one to interview with the department store, and the next to apartment-hunt, preceded my and David's venture down South. Our three-day weekend spent prowling for an apartment proved well worth the sore feet and shin splints, because we lucked upon a beautiful mid-rise community in Midtown. Our $1,300 monthly rent was easily affordable between two, and allowed us the additional luxury of furnishing our home with the best quality furniture the rest of our paychecks could buy.

The fenced-in dwelling resembled a gated community, with trees lined at the courtyard entrance. An Olympic-size swimming pool decorated the back of our building, which had separate entrances either back to the apartments or to the fitness center, nail salon, and dry cleaners on the first level. As I dashed out to work each morning, I often stopped for a cup of sliced cantaloupe or small bag of grapes at the minimart on the first floor before strutting over for my morning coffee pick-me-up.

Marlon's apartment was nearby, on the opposite side of Piedmont Park. It was Piedmont Park that brought David and Marlon together. While I choose to hit the snooze button every seven minutes, three times every morning, David opted for crack-of-dawn walks through the park for what he considered his meditation time. The touch of moist morning dew upon his face, the songs of birds in the trees above him, and a hint of light as the sun peeked above the horizon was what drew him to the park each morning.

About a year ago, David returned from his morning walk and raced into my bedroom to tell me about the beautiful man he had just encountered. After veering from his usual course, David locked eyes with a gentleman in his mid-forties with a light salt-and-pepper beard covering his brown skin. A brief nod and hello from this stranger left him breathless and eagerly anticipating seeing this man the following day.

Strolling down the same path, David came across his knight again, only, this time, he smiled broadly and spoke first. "Good morning," he said.

The runner slowed his pace and jogged in place, while eyeing David. "Care to join me?" the stranger asked.

David, having prayed all night long for this response, was geared up for his run in tennis shoes, shorts, a T-shirt and headband. "Of course," he answered, taking off next to his partner.

And they've been running mates ever since.

Marlon and I shared an instant connection because we both had spent the majority of our individual lives in heterosexual relationships. It was only five years prior to meeting David that Marlon admitted his true sexual identity to his now former wife. Marlon was for twenty-plus years a brother on the "down low."

As Marlon explained to me, after years of falling in and out of love with other married men, and too many close encounters with having been found out, he threw in the towel on a day that, if scripted, would have made a Lifetime movie producer feel as if the screenplay of a lifetime had landed before him.

While Marlon was in the kitchen sipping on brandy to loosen his tensed nerves, his wife, Brenda, was in their bathroom taking a pregnancy test. Finally, at 38, after countless disappointments, she was going to be a mother. Quickly her world crumbled before her as a teary-eyed and overwhelmed Marlon disclosed his surprise first.

Eight months later, after an emotionally agonizing pregnancy, Marlon Junior was born and promptly delivered to the doorway of Marlon's new apartment. Brenda washed her hands clean of any memory of a life once shared with him, which included taking back her maiden name, a relocation to Phoenix, and leaving behind the child that at one point she'd so desperately desired.

In addition to the transition from a "DL" brother to an openly gay man, Marlon became a single, full-time father. After unsuccessful attempts at love, he found David four years later, and although nine years his junior, David was all that Marlon had been praying for.

The ride from my store at Lenox Mall wasn't too rough on my nerves today. Adjusting to the congested traffic had been the one difficult hurdle to overcome after I'd moved. That's why I quickly traded in my outdated Toyota Celica for the drop-top, 5-speed Mustang that cruised in and out of clogged traffic with ease.

MJ greeted me in the hallway after David buzzed me into Marlon's building, located in a prime spot just across the street from the park. Each time MJ ran smiling into my arms, I was filled with flashbacks of Steph's son, Jaron, and his happy beam every time he saw me.

David easily recognized the anguished look on my face as I held on to MJ's embrace, eyes closed, reminiscing upon a time and place so far away, yet so close to my heart.

"Hey, young fella," I said after our hug.

"We're having TAAAACOOOOS," he sang in his almost five-year-old pitch.

"Good, 'cause I'm hungry," I replied.

David, who had the day off, was lounging in pajama bottoms and a wife-beater when I entered the apartment. He looked exhausted. After pulling a double shift at the bank, where he was a lead security officer, and now taking care of MJ, I understood his overextended state.

When David had first told me about the security officer position, I'll admit I was a bit concerned that he wouldn't be taken seriously. Although he stood five-ten with a slender, toned body, one look at David's flip of the wrist, and an outburst of "Honey," or "Girl," and was a dead giveaway to his orientation.

"I dare them HR folks not to hire me because I'm gay. Don't you know that's discrimination?" he scolded me when I expressed my concerns.

I backed off as he went through the interview process: a personality survey, background check (including credit), and drug test. He passed all, and with his natural charm, he had those HR folks eating out of the palm of his smooth hand.

"Hey, baby," he said from Marlon's oversized couch.

David didn't get up to greet me, and with the worn-out expression on his face, I knew he was glad I was there to entertain MJ for a while.

MJ and I fixed our taco plates and ate in the kitchen while watching some public television show on sea animals. Through his taco-filled bites, MJ managed to scream, "Look, Ky, look at the fishes!" pointing at every multi-colored swimming object that moved across the screen.

"Very pretty, MJ," I answered between my own munches.

Having spent time with Jaron and admiring the acceptance he had of his lesbian mom, I often wondered if MJ would grow up with the same adoration and respect for his gay father. Is society less accepting of a gay father than a lesbian mother? At this point in his young life, MJ loved his father unconditionally. Only time would tell if he'd grow up supportive of his dad's homosexuality, or humiliated by it.

Getting MJ settled for his afternoon nap was an easy task. MJ crawled under his navy comforter and welcomed the resting period before him.

David, who had taken a quick snooze of his own, awoke with a jerk when I nestled my head against his shoulder when I sat on the couch.

"Is MJ sleeping?" he murmured, barely lucid.

"Yes, he's in bed. Don't work yourself so hard, David. You look beat."

"And this is coming from the woman who pulls twelve-hour days on a regular basis?"

"I know, we need to quit wearing ourselves out like this." I stared out of Marlon's picture window overlooking the park.

David didn't answer, and only when I glanced in his direction, did I notice he had fallen asleep again. Better let him rest before MJ wakes up, I thought.

I gathered my purse and immediately reached for the pack of cigarettes inside the zipped pocket. More than once I'd made the mistake of leaving a pack in David's view, only for him to swiftly snatch them right out of my purse and toss them into the trash can beneath our kitchen sink—only after soaking them wet under the faucet to ensure their death. I was pissed the first few times this happened and resorted to hiding my cigs.

As I walked down the cement stairs outside of Marlon's brownstone and deliciously inhaled my first puff, I caught sight of a tall, slim woman pushing an elderly lady in a wheelchair headed in my direction. Dressed in light-colored jeans, a fitted white T-shirt, and walking shoes, the woman smiled tenderly as the elderly woman gabbed between coughs so raspy and body-racking, I thought she would surely keel over that very moment. The woman just smiled and gently laid her hand upon the elderly woman's shoulder until the spell subsided.

Immediately, and I guess instinctively, I dropped my cigarette to my side and casually stepped on it before continuing to my car. Hypnotized best described how I was feeling at that moment, as if an invisible magnetic charm circled the woman's body, attracting entranced stares of those around her. A radiant glow shimmered about her and sparkled underneath the sunlight. As cliché as it may sound, if heaven sent angels down to earth, she was one of them.

Jet-black, silky straight hair delicately blew against her smooth, cocoa-brown skin. Her eyes, nearly as dark as her hair, stared straight ahead as she walked slowly and listened intently to the old woman tell a story. Her lips, glossed in a light shade of pink, were parted slightly in an amused grin, displaying the indent of a bashful dimple on her right cheek. She looked at me, her eyes connecting with mine for a moment, a soft smile on her lips. Then she returned her attention back to the old woman.

Snapping myself out of my awestruck gaze, I managed to get in my car and fiddle with the radio, pretending to find a suitable station, just so I could absorb this woman's presence as long as possible. To my surprise, she stopped right at the entrance to Marlon's building. With obvious trained professionalism, she patiently assisted the old woman out of her wheelchair and up the four steps to the front door. She eased the woman inside, leaving the wheelchair on the sidewalk.

Should I help her? Maybe take the chair inside myself? Wait a minute. I didn't have a key to the building, and I didn't know which of the eighteen units belonged to her or the old woman. I could get out of the car and peer through the small octagon window of the door, but what if the moment I began to step onto my tiptoes to look through the glass, she suddenly flew the door open from the inside and knocked me down the short flight of steps to the ground? What if I crashed into the wheelchair and it smashed into pieces?

My mind-wandering stupor was interrupted when she quickly came back outside, expertly folded up the wheelchair and whisked it back inside, catching the door just before it closed again. I leaned back into my leather seat and exhaled, only then realizing that I had been holding my breath while eagerly awaiting her return. So long had it been since I was thoroughly captivated by someone just at sight. I suppose, since Stephanie.

"Who was that?" I screamed into David's ear after I dialed his number the second I thought he was awake from his nap.

"Kyla, who? Who are you talking about, girl?" he asked, sounding bewildered.

For some reason, I presumed he'd witnessed the woman's entrance into my life earlier that afternoon.

"David, there's a woman I saw going into Marlon's building when I left today, dark brown skin, long hair . . . she was pushing a woman in a wheelchair."

David paused for so long, I figured he must have been reviewing each tenant unit by unit.

"Baby, that doesn't sound like anybody in this building. I don't know. I'll ask Marlon tonight."

Briefly I felt a twinge of impatience, but it passed as swiftly as one might be when awaiting the FedEx man. What else could I do but sit back and wait?

"Okay, David, call me as soon as you find out. And tell Marlon I'll be by to see him soon."

"Yeah, I bet you will now."

Caught in my scheme, I laughed aloud before hanging up.

Later that night as Tiffany seductively removed her bra and panties while I sat on the edge of my bed, I heard a light tap on my door. A sweet kiss on her cheek asked her to hold on a second when I got up to see what David wanted. He glanced inside, noticed Tiffany standing naked. Before backing away from the door, he whispered in my ear, "Asia. Her name is Asia."

Asia, I repeated in my head. I winked a thank-you to David before closing the door and returning to Tiffany. I wrapped my arms around Tiffany's inviting waistline and brought her hips to mine. I closed my eyes to kiss her neck. Only, it wasn't her skin my lips touched. Asia, I thought once again.

CHAPTER 3

Chance Meeting

Crossing from one side of town to the other on a Sunday afternoon was an easy mission back home. It took all of twenty minutes to get to any destination. However, in Atlanta, on Sundays when I spent time with my "little sister" Lisa, the entire afternoon needed to be blocked off on my date book, primarily for travel time.

About six months ago I'd taken on the additional responsibility of spending time with a twelve-year-old girl whose mother had died just two years earlier. Devastated and longing for a female presence in Lisa's life, her dad enrolled her into the Big Brothers Big Sisters program. Participating in the program was perhaps my way of contributing to the social services field I'd reneged on due to heartbreak over Stephanie, not wanting to see her at school. Because my schedule left so little room, I committed to one Sunday a month with Lisa.

Our initial meeting was a little awkward, considering I was the second "big sister" in her life. The first woman, a delicate lady in her mid-thirties had believed she could empathize and relate to Lisa, since her own mom had passed away when she was a young girl. Yet dealing with Lisa's still wounded heart reopened unresolved issues within herself, and she found the task greater than anticipated. After two afternoons with Lisa, she left the program and entered therapy.

Understandably hesitant, Lisa held back any indication of taking a liking to me during our first few encounters. Unsure how to move forward with our next date, I consulted with Nakia, who had experience dealing with adolescent children. At her suggestion, on our next Sunday gathering, she and fourteen-year-old Fred Jr. joined us, and then it became our ritual to get together every last Sunday of the month.

Tall and lanky with a mouth full of braces, Fred Jr. melted Lisa's ice barrier when he spoke of the challenges he faced traveling from household to household, with "three parents." And although Lisa had lost one of her own, discovering that someone her age also felt some form of suffering was comfort enough. She began to welcome our time together just as much as I did.

As I wove in and out of traffic en route to Marietta to pick Lisa up, I yakked away on my cell phone to Yvonne, who, now six months pregnant, was overly emotional, extremely uncomfortable with her body, and incessantly needy. In fact we talked more during her months of pregnancy than we had in two years time living at home.

"My back is really starting to hurt, Ky."

"Try sleeping with a pillow between your knees," I offered, retrieving that information from some website I'd found. Just after Yvonne's pregnancy announcement, I found myself surfing the net, gathering information so I could best understand what she was going through. That was about the wisest advice I had to offer, beyond telling her to suck it up and just deal with it until the baby arrived.

"I have. It doesn't help."

"Check with your doctor, Yvonne, especially if it's that painful."

"Well, it's not that bad. Just the extra weight, I guess."

She knew why her back was hurting, and after all, it wasn't that bad, so why was she complaining?

"She's due around Christmas, Ky," she reminded me for the hundredth time. "You are going to be home, right?"

"How do you know it's a girl, Yvonne? I'm going to have a niece?" I asked, excited.

"Byron's sister said I'm carrying low, so it must be a girl."

I didn't remember reading that bit of information online, but I kept quiet.

"Are you going to be here, Ky?".

Asking Gary if I could have two weeks off during the holiday season was like asking if I could have his Jessica Simpson concert tickets. He simply wouldn't have it.

"Kyla, your sister only has her first child once! Don't you want to be here?"

I heard the all too familiar crack in her voice, which was sure to be followed by a sea of tears. At that moment I wasn't sure if I ever wanted to be pregnant. "Don't worry, Yvonne, I'll see what I can do. I promise," I said, feeling guilty for saying anything just to avoid a crying spell.

Still, she managed to sneak in a few sniffles between her words. "I-really-want-you-here, Ky."

"Yes, Yvonne, I know. I'll be there," I said, feeling like I put my career on the line.

"Thank you," she said, giggling suddenly, instantly feeling better.

Wow! "How are mom and dad?"

"They're fine," she said, sounding sad again. "Everyone is looking forward to seeing you."

Since my move to Atlanta, I hadn't been home for even one visit. E-mails and unlimited long-distance calls were what held me in contact with the Midwest. Inside I was anxious to see everyone. I wanted to see Yvonne and touch her belly. I wanted to hug my mom and smell her latest perfume. I wanted to wrap my arms around my dad and feel the warmth of his embrace. During the summer months I missed the lakefront festivals, and on occasion, though rarely, I missed sitting by the fire watching the calm stillness of a winter night as snowflakes clothed and blanketed the ground.

"Don't worry, Yvonne, I'll do the best I can," I said with a bit more determination.

She talked on a while longer until I reached Lisa's home, a beautiful three-bedroom, two-and-a-half-bath brick home that easily would have cost twice as much in Wisconsin. In Nakia's mind, that was one reason so many snowbirds migrated South. The value of a dollar spread farther than in most other cities.

Lisa emerged from the large entryway, looking solemn, if not ill. As she approached the car, I caught sight of just what had her face shadowed with such gloom. A huge pimple. Not on her cheek or near her hairline, but dead smack between her eyebrows, probably the most dreaded place for one to surface. Her eyes were lowered as she got into my passenger seat, like not looking at me would somehow erase the red bump on her face.

"Hey, sunshine," I said, extra chipper, hoping for even a slight grin in response.

"Hi, Kyla," she said, looking straight ahead.

"Ready for some bowling?"

"Do we have to go anywhere? Can't we just go back to your place?" she pleaded to my windshield.

"Nakia and Fred Jr. are already at the bowling alley waiting for us."

"No!" she gasped. "I don't want Fred Jr. to see me like this!"

"Like what?" I asked gently.

"Like this!" she shrieked, facing me and pointing a pink fingernail to her forehead.

Casually I viewed the pimple and then focused on her eyes. "Lisa, sweetheart, it's not that bad."

She exhaled an exaggerated stop-lying-to-me sigh and shifted angrily in her seat. I understood her frustration. It was bad. I might have stayed in the house too if I had it. But I wasn't going to shatter her already fractured self-image and agree with her.

"How about this, Lisa? How about we stop at the drugstore and pick up some acne medication?"

She moaned at my mention of the word acne.

"We can put a little bit on right away, and that way, at least, it's being treated. It'll be gone in no time, you'll see."

Lisa sat still.

"Is this your first pimple?"

"Yes! And today of all days. Do you think Fred Jr. will notice?"

I looked her squarely in the eyes. Nothing worse than talking to a person who keeps staring at your pimple. It would only make her more self-conscious if I did. "He might notice, but he'll know that you're still Lisa, pimple or no pimple. Besides, haven't you seen a pimple or two on his face? You guys are teenagers; it's going to happen sometimes."

"Yeah, I suppose. You're right. Fred Jr. had a pimple last time we were together, and I still liked him."

I started the car. "What was that?"

"Oh, nothing."

"Mm-hm, sure."

I laughed, and she laughed too. Finally!

Nakia and Fred Jr. had already completed a game by the time we arrived, thanks to our pit stop and search for the proper acne cream for Lisa's young skin.

"I beat her," Fred Jr. told me with a hug. "One hundred eight to fifty-seven. I'm the man."

"Let's see how much you're boasting and bragging after this next game," Nakia said, though I had yet to see her bowl over 70.

"How are you, Lisa?" Fred Jr. asked.

Lisa stared at her foot, tracing a speck of hardened gum in the worn carpeting, replied softly, "Good."

"Let's go get your shoes," he said, walking toward the front desk.

"Here, Lisa," I said, handing her a ten-dollar bill. "Grab me an eight and a half."

I wanted to commend Fred Jr. on a job well done ignoring Lisa's pimple like it simply didn't exist. By the time Lisa and I finished our first game and she had beaten Fred Jr. by three pins, it appeared she had forgotten about the atrocity herself.

Nakia and I excused ourselves to order lunch from the bar and allow Lisa and Fred Jr. time to bowl a final game of their own. One game was one too many for me anyway.

"I talked to Yvonne on the way here, Kia. She's not even about to let me not come home at Christmas," I said.

"You got hell to pay either way. Damned if you do, damned if you don't."

"Thanks, Kia, like I didn't already know that."

"If you can get that assistant buyer of yours to get off her ass and do some work, you might be able to swing it."

"Tell me about it," I replied.

Amy, my assistant buyer, to my constant bewilderment, had maneuvered her way into the position of working under me. As wrong as it was, Nakia and I had nicknamed her LALA (lucky-ass lazy Amy) and no one, not even Gary, suspected she was the target of our snickers and jeers when we mentioned the pseudonymous LALA.

"Get that girl off her flat ass and make her do some work," Kia said.

"I will. I do want to go home for Christmas."

"Girl, yeah, you've been here how long and haven't been back to see your family?" She shook her head.

"Don't remind me," I said, wondering what my family must be thinking of my two-year absence. "I think I've been scared, Kia. I'm not the person I used to be."

"Whoever in the hell you used to be doesn't matter, Kyla. You're still your mama and daddy's baby and Yvonne's big sister. You better take your ass home and see your family."

"Damn! Okay. I said I was."

"You better," she said, slapping one of her King Kong hands against my shoulder.

I winced in pain, and a roar of laughter escaped from Nakia. Out of the corner of my eye, I thought I saw a bowler drop his ball.

Lisa and Fred Jr. joined us just after Lisa's second victorious game. By the occasional glances and giggles between the two of them, I could see the formation of a crush on both their parts. I'd have to watch them carefully.

The ride home proved to be a major improvement, with Lisa's sullen demeanor transforming into giddy conversation and laughter.

"When will I see you again?" she asked when I pulled up in front of her house.

Her question was unexpected, since she was aware of our last-Sunday-of-the-month routine. I was curious if, hidden beneath her inquiry, was the real question, "When will I see Fred Jr. again?"

"Next month. Why?"

"I was hoping we could do stuff together more. Shopping or something. Can you help me pick out my first lip-gloss color? My dad said I can wear color now."

"Of course, Lisa! Maybe your dad can drop you off one day at my store, and then we can stroll the mall."

Lisa wrapped her arms around my neck. "Thank you!"

She skipped from my car to Gene, her father, who was outside just about to start his lawn mower, and gave him a hug before running indoors.

I waved and gestured for him to come over.

"Hey, Kyla, how's it going?" he asked.

"Great, Gene. We had a good time today. Your daughter is so beautiful."

Just then, I noticed she had left her bag of acne cream. "Hey, give this to Lisa. We had to make a stop today. Seems like her pimple had her a bit down."

Gene glanced over his shoulder to determine Lisa's distance from us. She was already back outside, sitting on the front stoop, phone in hand, talking someone's ear off. "Yeah, I didn't know what to do with that girl this morning. After she looked in the mirror, she got back in the bed and swore she wasn't leaving the house ever again. So dramatic she can be." He laughed.

"Well, tell her to keep using this, and it will help."

He took the bag from me and smiled gratefully. Within seconds his smile faded and was replaced with a reminiscent daze. "If only her mom could see her now."

"She can, Gene. She's somewhere watching over Lisa and you every day."

No response followed. I wasn't sure if he was lost in a daydream or had simply tired of uninventive reassurances.

"See you in a few weeks?"

"Actually, Lisa and I were hoping to get together before then. Can you bring her by the mall one day for some lip-gloss shopping?"

"She would like that. Call us with a good day for you."

"Sure. See you soon." I released my brake and put my foot on the clutch.

Gene tapped my hood and walked to Lisa and gave her the plastic bag. She waved excitedly, and I tooted my horn to her beaming face and swollen pimple.

Arriving home to a quiet and still apartment was expected. I knew David worked the evening shift most Sundays, which kept him away from six in the evening until three in the morning. When he got off work, he'd quietly creep into the apartment, slip out of his security uniform, down a tall glass of ice water, and crawl into his bed. The next day he'd always question, "I didn't wake you up, did I?"

I'd tell him no, even though my body had adjusted to the brief middle-of-the-night interruptions, and I'd readily fall back asleep the moment his bedroom door closed. It was comforting to know he returned home safe and sound, even if his arrivals home were becoming less frequent.

After I changed into a cozy cotton pajama set and went to pour myself a glass of Merlot, I found David's note taped to the refrigerator door.

Asia—home health nurse to soon-to-be-deceased Mrs. Garfield. Mrs. Garfield was just taken in by bitch daughter, who has no time to take care of her sick mother. Asia is on call around the clock and has nursing assistants to fill her shoes when she attends to other patients. Pleasant, charming, bright, and successful. Is she family? Don't know yet. Thank Marlon for this information—He made his move for conversation when Asia strolled on another walk with the ill-fated.

Smooches!

I kissed the paper back and thanked my lucky stars for Marlon's intrusion. Marlon could gossip and invade privacy like a nosy, old retired neighbor with nothing to do besides peek through curtains late at night, excusing their meddlesome nature as "neighborhood watch" duties.

I picked up the phone and dialed Marlon's number.

"Hello," he answered in his gruff, rugged voice.

"Hey, handsome, it's Ky. I got David's report on Asia, but I want to hear it from you."

"I bet you do." He laughed. "Mrs. Garfield just arrived last week, which is the reason we've never seen Asia before. It was easy to talk to her. I caught her the other day and just introduced myself as a tenant and asked, was she new to the building. That's when I got her name. Today Mrs. Garfield had fallen asleep in the wheelchair, so we had a minute to talk. She told me about Mrs. Garfield moving in, and I already knew about that stank-ass daughter of hers. She doesn't speak or even acknowledge your existence if you pass her in the hallway. And I thought I saw her snotty ass looking at MJ like he was the devil's child one day. But Asia didn't even wince at the mention of that hellish woman. She just smiled and talked on about her job and praised Mrs. Garfield for her positive attitude. She asked some questions about me, but out of kindness, I believe. I could tell it wasn't a romantic interest kind of thing."

"Well, good. At least we know she wasn't taking a liking to you."

"Right."

"Thanks for checking her out, Marlon. I just had to know more about her. What are my chances that she even swings in my direction?"

"Find out for yourself. I invited her over for coffee Wednesday afternoon. She's stopping by after her walk with Mrs. Garfield. She said she could bring the monitor with her to listen in on Mrs. Garfield."

"A monitor? Like a baby monitor?"

"I suppose, girl. Could be some fancy high-tech doctor machine, for all I know. Anyway, just be here on Wednesday."

I hesitated. "Don't you think that will be a little obvious?"

"Well, what do you suggest? This is much less intimidating than you outright asking her on a date. You can quickly find out if she has a man. That includes a boyfriend or a husband, you hear me? You are leaving attached women alone, aren't you? I know you have a sensitive spot for them and everything, but you don't have to be their guinea pig experiment either."

"Hey, hold up now. Don't get me started on you!"

He laughed hard. "I knew that was coming. That's how I know it's a dangerous situation, sweetheart."

"I know. But where would I be if Stephanie had never given me a chance?"

"Let's not even worry about that, because you're where you are now."

Good point. No sense in me still dwelling on what might have been.

"So you'll be here Wednesday, right?"

I thought about how odd it would look for two guys, a couple at that, to invite two women over for coffee at the same time. Pretty obvious, if you ask me. But, hey, Asia's vision was stuck on the forefront of my mind, and I would surely go crazy wondering more about her, as opposed to just finding out.

"Yep, I sure will."

After we got off the phone, I immediately began searching my closet for one of my best suits to wear on Wednesday.

I nervously tapped my fork on the wooden table inside The Cheesecake Factory.

Nakia asked, "What in the hell is wrong with you, Kyla?"

She hadn't noticed that my right leg, repetitiously bouncing up and down underneath the table, was right in time with the fork. I had the jitters from nicotine withdrawal. Ever since that eye-opening day when I saw Mrs. Garfield hacking away and suffering from what I assumed was terminal lung cancer, I vowed not to pick up another cigarette again.

"Ooh, Kia, girl, I have nicotine withdrawal," I said, exaggerating the symptoms by dabbing my forehead with a paper napkin.

"'Bout time you kicked that habit. That shit ain't cute."

Nakia took a bite into a barbecue chicken wing. "What made you quit?"

"I thought you'd never ask," I said with a bit too much enthusiasm, which Kia instantly recognized.

"Oh shit! Who's the new babe?"

I put my hand to my chest in playful jest. "Why, Kia? What on earth makes you think there's a new lady in my life?"

"Because there always is a new lady in your life every other damn day of the week." Nakia didn't even laugh as she said it.

Damn! Had I really gotten that bad? Why was I asking that question? I already knew the answer.

"Anyway, Kia, I don't even know her. Never even met her. I saw her one day at Marlon's apartment, and I just have to know who she is."

"Well, did you ask Marlon?"

"Already taken care of. She's going to Marlon's for coffee Wednesday afternoon, and I'll be there too."

"Hold on, Ky. You're telling me that Marlon invited a strange woman to his apartment just so you can meet her? Damn, girl, times gettin' that hard?"

"Fuck you, Kia," I said, still fidgeting with my fork, feeling worried about the setup all over again.

"Kyla, do you know if this woman is gay?"

"Well, no. I was hoping to find out on Wednesday."

"All right, let's say that on the chance that she's straight, 'cause there are a few of them left out there, in case you've forgotten. Let's say she's straight and here comes you in your rainbow accessories inside your gay cousin's boyfriend's apartment. Don't you think she just might be a little pissed off if she finds out this was a setup so you could get into her panties?"

I laid my fork on the table. "Damn, Kia! Why do you have to say it like that?"

"Because that's been the case with every woman you've met. It's not about a relationship or commitment. You hang out, get busy, and then move on to the next victim."

"They just weren't the right one."

"You tossed them aside so fast, you didn't even give them a chance. How could you have known they weren't the right one?"

"It's there, or it's not. I just know."

"So even if it's 'not there,'" she said, mocking me, "you still like them enough to lay down with them. That's okay?"

"It takes two."

"Yeah, but the other half of the two doesn't know she's about to be dropped like a hot potato either."

"That's not true, I'm up-front with everybody. They know I'm not looking for a relationship."

Nakia was silent while she finished the last bite of her final chicken wing.

"Whatever, Kyla, that's been your excuse and your crutch ever since we met. But, tell me, really, why are you so afraid to settle down?"

Up until this point, Nakia had been sitting back quietly, watching me skip from bed to bed, "relationship" to breakup, without question. Suddenly I felt exposed, as if the mask of contentedness had fallen off and I was left to deal with the truth. I had to face the reality of my behavior the past two years.

"Why are you doing this to me, Kia?" I asked weakly.

"I'm not doing anything to you, girl. If you tell me you don't want to settle down because you like getting your rocks off with as many women as you can, then so be it. I won't bring it up again. But if there's a chance that it's something else, and judging by your reaction I see that it is, then let's talk about it."

I exhaled loudly, blowing my paper napkin across the table. "I'm scared."

Again Nakia was quiet, maybe waiting for me to elaborate on what I knew was an all too common and flimsy excuse.

"It took a long time for me to get over Stephanie. I mean, even though I was too afraid to love her until it was too late, she had taken over my heart completely. Then I lost her. I'm so frightened to let that happen again."

Nakia nodded. "Well, do you plan not to settle down, out of fear, for the rest of your life? Don't get me wrong, I understand what you're saying, but you can't hide behind that loss forever. You remember how you felt when you were with Stephanie, right?"

A doleful look covered my face. "Yes, I do."

"If you want to love like that again, Kyla, you've got to let go."

Had I been hiding behind the hurt, pain, and sadness I felt over my loss of Stephanie? I never really had Stephanie in the first place, did I? I shared a moment, just a fraction of a lifetime with her, while, at the same time, sharing a portion of my life with someone else. Still, there was no minimizing the grief I felt when Steph walked out of my life forever. Was my overindulgence in feminine ecstasy nothing but a protective cover-up for my broken heart? Nakia was right. If I continued to shun every potential mate that entered my life, I'd be a sexually satisfied but emotionally empty woman. I reminded myself of Tori and the numerous sexual encounters she embraced.

"I know Kia. I'll let it go."

Nakia laid her hand atop mine, pleased with my response. "So, tell me about this new lady."

"Well, her name is Asia, and she's a nurse taking care of an elderly woman in Marlon's building. She's beautiful, Kia."

"All the women you date are beautiful."

"This is different though. I've never said one word to her, but I just know she's a beautiful person on the inside also. It's hard to describe," I said, searching for the appropriate words. "There's this glow about her that makes me want to step inside her world."

"What's your action plan? How are you going to figure out if she's a lesbian?"

"I don't have a plan. I'll talk to her and see what kind of vibe I get and take it from there."

"Girl, you better come straight to see me when you get back from this mission." Nakia reached in her purse for her portion of the bill.

"I will," I said, laying down a fifty. "I got you."

"Thanks." She smiled, and then her grin faded. "Kyla, don't be too let down if this doesn't work out the way you hope. Don't shut yourself down to future possibilities in love."

"I won't, I promise. Thanks."

After three days of frequent trips to my closet, my black Jones New York pantsuit was the final decision for my Wednesday meeting. Before my selection, I had stood there and flipped through the row of suits I'd collected since starting my buyer position.

Once, I overheard LALA talking to another assistant, who suggested I had advanced solely on my ability to coordinate an outfit and look the professional part. Then I realized just how much I needed to prove I had business savvy as well. Did they forget I had ten years of retail experience? That I spent a ridiculous amount of time in college taking courses that eventually led to my long-awaited degree? I didn't let those young bitches bother me though. Especially LALA. I often wondered how many dicks she sucked in ground floor fitting rooms before her promotion to the office level.

All morning I tried to focus on my reports, but my eyes kept shifting to my desk clock, which moved slower than on a Friday afternoon before a three-day weekend. Finally, at one o'clock, I couldn't take it anymore. I grabbed my Gucci purse (when had I gotten so materialistic?) and headed to the Misses department. I rocked side to side anxiously, waiting for Nakia to finish assisting a trainee with a return item.

Nakia approached me and grabbed my fidgety hands. "What the hell, Kyla? You going to be all right?"

"I'm about to head to Marlon's."

"I know that, but you look like you're about to pass out, girl. Are you nervous?"

"I think I am. I don't know what it is about this woman. I haven't felt these knots in my stomach since—"

Nakia cleared her throat to shut me up. "Go on and get out of here before you make me nervous too. Everything will be just fine."

A grateful smile managed its way to the corners of my lips. My nearly full pack of Virginia Slims tempted me as I pulled my car keys from my purse. Even though I hadn't placed a long, lean, flavor-filled cig between my lips in over a week, as the yearning to calm my nerves increased, they called my name louder and louder.

"Hand them over," Nakia ordered. "I thought you quit."

"I did. Just didn't throw them away yet," I said, reluctantly handing the pack to her.

Promptly she tossed them in the wastebasket beneath the register counter. "Well, it's official now. And you don't need them anyway. Just go and be yourself."

I inhaled and exhaled to gain my composure and wondered what in the hell it was that had me so on edge. I'd been through how many women the past couple of years? Asia wasn't like the others though. I just knew it.

"I'll call you later," I said when a customer approached the counter.

Kia, mumbling obscenities under her breath, was left to assist the jittery trainee with another transaction. Inside I laughed and recounted the numerous times I had to remind Nakia that those endless customers gave us both our jobs.

The ride to Marlon's was harmless. My over-active nerves didn't interfere with my ability to alternate clutch then gas, clutch then brake, as I drove through the early-afternoon traffic.

Sprinkles of nervous sweat formed tiny beads around my hairline when I parked my car and set the brake. *What in the hell, Kyla?* Why was I so nervous over someone I didn't even know? Using a leftover food napkin, I wiped my skin and brushed a fresh coat of almond powder over my face.

"Ready?" I asked myself as I took one last glance in the rearview mirror.

Marlon's door was ajar when I got out of the car.

"Hey," I whispered to him when I located him at the kitchen counter.

He turned around to greet me. "This isn't a library, Kyla. Why are you whispering?"

"Oh, right," I mumbled, not realizing I was speaking as if I had a sleeping baby in my arms. "Where's David?"

Marlon checked the clock over the stove. "He should be here any minute. He had some last-minute paperwork to complete. One of his staff members was sailing his way into being terminated, and today his ship crashed in."

I placed my purse on the wooden table and reached into the cabinet to retrieve four coffee mugs. "Do you think this is going to work, Marlon?"

Suddenly, warm heat soothed my back, and I turned around to find Asia standing just inside the doorway holding a cup of sugar in one hand and a silver monitor in the other, a pleasant smile on her face. I was fearful I would faint at that moment.

Marlon swept past me and retrieved the sugar from her.

Dressed in uniform, her white pants and white jacket provided a stunning contrast against her dark, glowing skin. Beaming attentive eyes sparkled in my direction as she walked toward me.

"Asia," she stated, offering her hand to me.

Inconspicuously, or so I hoped, I wiped my moist palm with my thumb before taking her hand in mine. "Kyla," I responded, trying to conceal the shakiness in my voice.

Marlon observed the exchange, humored, as if he himself were Cupid the matchmaker.

"Is your coffee maker not working?" Asia asked unexpectedly.

Marlon and I glanced at the shiny top-of-the-line coffee maker he'd received just a month earlier from David for his birthday.

"No, it's working just fine," he said.

"Oh, I thought I heard Kyla ask you about something working." Asia looked back and forth, from me to Marlon.

"No, no, no, Asia, it was nothing." Marlon gave me a quick squint of the eye. "Have a seat, ladies. I'll bring the coffee out in a few minutes."

Asia headed through the swinging door, and behind her back, I looked at Marlon and wiped my right eyebrow, relieved to survive the close call we'd just had. After I followed Asia into the living room, I noticed no wedding ring on her left hand.

"This is a lovely apartment," she said when she sat down and placed the monitor on the table that separated us.

"Yes, it's very nice. Great location. So close to the park," I said, unable to deliver more than fragmented sentences.

"Mrs. Garfield enjoys going for walks through the park." Asia's smile faded, and her glow dimmed.

"How is she?" I asked.

"Not well,' she said sadly. "It won't be much longer."

"Oh, I'm sorry."

"Well, she's heading home to her Maker. At least she'll be at peace."

Oh shit! Was I about to hit on a good ol' Christian girl? The miniature devil on my shoulder laughed. *You've had them too.*

Asia's brilliant smile returned, and she placed her elbows on her knees to lean forward. "So you and Marlon are friends or relatives?"

For the briefest moment, I thought a flicker of amusement flashed through her dark eyes. "Um, no," I answered, desperately wishing Marlon would fly through the swinging doorway Mrs. Cleaver-style and place steaming coffee mugs on the table. But he didn't.

Asia simply sat there waiting for me to elaborate.

Why was I scared to tell her? I was acting like there was something wrong with it. "I know Marlon through my cousin, David. Where are you from?"

She appeared not to mind my changing the subject.

"Originally from Texas. Dallas, actually. I've been in Atlanta for four years now."

"I've been here just about a year and half myself. How do you like it?"

"I suppose I'm used to big-city life, so it's not much different than Dallas to me. Nice change of scenery though."

"What made you leave?"

"Oh, just looking for new opportunities." Asia appeared to eye the door with the same longing I had only seconds before, yet her smile remained intact. "Wow! where's that coffee?"

I didn't know if Marlon had walked to Colombia for the beans, or if he was being sly and giving us time to get to know one another. Whatever the case, I had to take full advantage of the opportunity because I didn't know if there would be another.

"So what do you like to do?" I asked, breaking into a fast sweat underneath my blouse. I was glad I hadn't removed my blazer.

"My schedule is so busy, I don't have very much free time," she answered without answering, very much Kyla style, not knowing I was the master at vagueness.

"Yeah, my schedule is pretty hectic too." I tried to look her in the eyes when I spoke. A sincere spark of interest shined, further luring me in. "I work long hours, but unwind in a few ways—at home in front of the TV, going out, hanging out with friends."

"Oh? Where do you go out?"

I cleared my throat gently, thinking, It's now or never, Kyla.

Just as I was ready to tell her that I spend some Friday nights at a very popular female gay bar, David walked in, dressed in uniform, carrying a white box. "Doughnuts to go with the coffee?" He quickly dropped the box atop the entertainment center and flew over to Asia. "Hi, sugar. I'm David. So glad you could make it today," he said, shaking her hand. He turned to me. "Hey, baby girl," he said and kissed my cheek.

"Well, Asia, this is my cousin I just told you about."

"It's really nice to meet you, David." Asia spied the way David's wrist hung daintily at his waist.

"Same here. Marlon and Ky said such nice things about you."

Asia raised her left eyebrow. "So everyone dropped by for coffee?"

David glanced at me then at the empty coffee table. He probably realized I hadn't gotten too far into my conversation with Asia. "I'm going to check on Marlon," he said quickly. "Be back."

With the swinging door still in motion, Asia said, "I must say, it's interesting of you to say nice things about me before us having met."

I cleared my throat once again. "Um, well Marlon told us that you'd be here because, uh, we had plans for coffee already. He spoke so pleasantly of you, and I told David about it."

"I see," she said, granting me permission to slide on that transparent fib. "So, tell me, where is it that you go out?"

"W-well, er, I visit Traxx pretty often."

Asia's everlasting smile widened as she sat up abruptly, staring at me intently. "Really now, I've been there with friends a time or two myself," she said, leaning back in the seat.

My heart fluttered. And then I quickly thought, *Does "with friends" mean that she was a straight girl tagging along with her gay friends, similar to my initial venture out with Stephanie? Or does it mean she hung at the popular bar with a group of gay girlfriends? Or is it code for with my girlfriend, and she really was in the life? I had to find out.*

Before I could muster the courage to ask her on a date, she beat me in asking a question first.

"Have you been gay your whole life, Kyla?"

Now where did that come from? The question flowed with no sarcasm, no hint of irritation. Just a straightforward question, whose only requirement was an honest answer, like she knew I had a story to tell. How did she know I hadn't been gay my whole life? That I hadn't grown up kissing my Barbie and playing doctor with my little girlfriends? What about me told her that once upon a time I had the American dream in the palm of one hand while the other was weighed down by an unexpected, uncontrollable, inescapable love for another woman?

Once again, that little voice in my head reminded me that I had this moment to seize every opportunity with the amazing bright-eyed woman who sat before me. Nervously twirling a loose curl around my finger, I said, "I'll be happy to tell you over dinner."

Suddenly, coughing spasms and deep groans boomed through the monitor. In response, Asia leapt from the loveseat toward the kitchen. "Be right back," she said without turning around.

David and Marlon, who miraculously appeared two seconds after Asia's departure, found me collapsed on the couch, drained from my five-minute conversation with Asia.

"Baby, you okay?"

"I think so. I don't know what's wrong with me, Marlon. Women don't make me this nervous. There's something about her . . . like just being around her will make everything all right."

"Tell me how it went. The coffee has been ready, girl. I was just giving you some time to talk to her."

"I figured that, thank you. It went well, I guess. So far, I know she's been to Traxx a time or two, as she put it. But, just when I was about to ask her to dinner, Mrs. Garfield started hacking through the monitor."

"What do you think she was going to say?"

"I hope yes. Why don't you bring the coffee in here? I need something to calm me down."

"Yes, you sure do. You're going to scare that poor child away, acting so silly. She's special honey, but she's just a person." Marlon headed toward the kitchen and returned with a cup of roasting-hot, freshly brewed coffee.

He was right. I was acting like a freak, like Asia was a superstar and I was her number one obsessed fan.

Approaching sirens drew us to the front window, from where I saw paramedics racing into the building with a stretcher and speeding down the hall to the witch's apartment. "Well, damn," I said, witnessing the event.

"Next time, baby," Marlon said, giving me a hug. "I'm sure I'll see her soon."

"I hope so," I said, falling into his embrace.

"Baby girl, I haven't seen you like this in a long time," David commented.

"I haven't felt like this in a long time." I took a sip of coffee to refrain from adding, Since Stephanie.

"Well, if it's meant to be, it will be," David added. "She won't slip away so easily."

"I know."

We sat together for just a few minutes while I gulped down the hot coffee, allowing it to sting my chest.

There was no sign of Asia when I glanced toward the open apartment door when I left. Sulking like the last pair of BCBG sling-backs had just been sold, I crawled behind the wheel of my car and started the rumbling engine.

Just as I released the parking brake, Asia jetted out of the apartment building. "Kyla!" she called loudly, waving a small piece of paper in her hand.

I lowered the window.

She hurried to the passenger side door and said, "I'd love to have dinner."

At that moment the paramedics came running out with Mrs. Garfield, flat on the stretcher, oxygen mask over her face, and rushed her into the ambulance.

"Gotta go," she said before dashing to her car. One fast turn on her feet and she yelled, "Don't lose my number!" She got into her truck and sped off behind the ambulance.

Oh I won't. I immediately put her number into my phone-book in my cell phone.

Before putting my car in first gear, I looked up and saw Marlon and David waving wildly and smiling at me from Marlon's apartment window. I waved back, smiled even bigger than their smiles put together, and took off for work.

CHAPTER 4

Out with the Old,
In with the New

You look beautiful tonight," Angie said as we exited the parking lot of Brio Restaurant on Peachtree Road, where we had just eaten dinner. "That blouse really brings out your eyes," she continued, referring to my violet-colored Nanette Lepore chiffon blouse. "I had read somewhere that purple accents the brown in eyes."

"Thanks, Angie," I said, blushing slightly. Even with the simplest words and compliments, Angie always made me feel special.

It had been a week since I left Asia a message the evening after our meeting at Marlon's, and I had yet to receive a return call. It was a Wednesday night, and I had already clocked nearly thirty-five hours in three days, and I was beyond irritation. I had been so sick with anticipation the last seven days that I had snapped at

Nakia and nearly bit LALA's head off (although that was deserved) for not completing a simple assignment, all because I was anxious, irritable, and pissed off because I hadn't heard back from her. So when Angie called me in the midst of hustling back and forth between phone calls and Gary's office, I happily accepted her offer for an Italian meal.

Angie took hold of my hand and brought it to her side while she drove. I knew what was coming next. It was a conversation we exchanged on a regular enough basis that we could record it and replay it for future usage.

"Kyla, what's going on, for real?" Angie turned sideways to glance at me. "Why won't be you be my lady?"

I looked over at Angie, dressed in a brown pantsuit with a deep olive turtleneck, looking sexy in a soft masculine way. She never wore heels; Franco Sarto designed her favorite slide-on flats. Her natural curls were slicked back with gel, and a small, simple silver hoop hung from each ear. A CD of soft jazz played through the car speakers, filling the space before I responded.

I thought about Asia and why I was so drawn to her, someone I didn't even know. Why I had been contemplating severing ties with all the women I knew if I could have just one date with her. And even though I hadn't heard back from her, a nagging from the inside was nudging me to alter my usual response to Angie. I knew that if I was going to move forward with Asia, I had to end the sweet ride that Angie and I had been riding.

I squeezed her hand gently. "Angie, you and I have shared some unbelievable times together. You know that, right? I mean, you make me feel ways that other women don't. You're so generous and kind, and I always enjoy being around you."

"Uh-oh, this isn't sounding right, Kyla."

"Truth is, if we were going to be together, we would have been by now. Come on, we're grown women, Angie. We know what we have isn't a strong basis for a relationship. I like you, you like me, and our sex is amazing, but I think you and I will always make better friends than partners. Neither one of us should keep pretending that one day we're going to settle down together, because that's not the case, and we know it."

Angie was silent, only a brief sign of disappointment across her face, as she slowly nodded her head. She brought my hand to her lips and kissed it. "Well, you can't blame me for trying, right?" She smiled.

I smiled too, grateful for her response and honored to know such a sweet woman. "You're going to make some woman really happy one day, Angie."

"I was hoping it would be you, Kyla, but I understand. You've been laying down reasons for a long time about not wanting a relationship, and when I was in your shoes, I did the same thing. After I decided I wanted to find someone and settle down, I started looking and I found you. But if I'm not the one for you, then okay. When you find her, Kyla, whoever she is, you'll settle down too." She kissed my hand again.

"Thanks, Angie. But I know you're not trying to tell me that you don't have a long line of women to choose from."

She laughed coolly, and I knew the line was probably longer than I thought.

"I might have one or two ladies I could pick from."

"So, tell me, anybody I know?" I asked. If we were going to be strictly friends, why not?

"Now I don't go asking who you're entertaining when you're not with me, do I?" she said playfully.

"Ahh, excellent point," I said, not wanting to divulge any names and praying they weren't the same.

"See, I knew that would shut you up quick."

We both laughed.

"Let's just say, I'm not necessarily hurting, when it comes to finding a woman. I wanted her to be you, but I hear you loud and clear."

I simply nodded, and we rode in silence.

Instead of turning onto my street, Angie pulled into a lot at the park across the street. She parked in a corner space, many feet away from the light post, though a dim glow flickered across her face. I watched the expression on her face transform from sweet and tender to seductive and sensual. The hoods of her eyes lowered, and her eyes filled with desire. My body immediately heated. No Angie, not now.

Angie unlocked her seat belt and reached for the back of my head, bringing my mouth to hers. We kissed hungrily, her tongue entwined with mine.

We kissed like that for five minutes, until my neck became sore and my lips numbed. She reached under my dress and tugged at my underwear, which was already moist.

"Kyla," she breathed into my ear, well aware that was one of my weakest spots, "let me eat your pussy one more time."

If words could make me come, I would have come right then and there. I was so tempted; so tempted to let Angie soothe my body and ease the aggravation I had been feeling. So intrigued by the thought of Angie climbing into my seat, opening my legs, and devouring my clit one last time. And yet, another less lustful and more heedful part of me was aware that even though I'd find myself physically gratified, I would again find myself lacking the meaningful companionship I still had not found and was now searching for.

"Angie," I said, trying to part from her.

Angie stopped nibbling my ear and fondling my crotch to look at me.

"I can't."

"Why not? We always do. And you always enjoy it." She attempted to kiss my ear.

"I know, Angie. I always love our time together, but we can't let it end like this. It just kind of cheapens everything, doesn't it?" I said, as if sex wasn't the primary foundation of our relationship.

Angie retreated to her seat.

"I'm sorry," I said, feeling guilty.

"No, no, no. It's all good."

"Are you mad at me?" I asked, not wanting one of her last memories of me to be negative.

"I'm not mad, Kyla, for real, I'm not. I guess I was looking to dignify what we had, and at least by making love one more time, I would have felt that I at least meant something to you. I know we didn't spend all that much time together, but you're ready to end it out of the blue. I wasn't expecting this, that's all. I wasn't trying to disrespect what you already told me. Just hopeful you could show me something. What, I don't know . . ."

"I think we're looking at it different. I thought being honest was showing you the utmost respect, because that's what you deserve. To me, if we have sex now, it seems like sharing ass is all we were ever good for, and I don't want to go out like that."

"I feel you, Kyla. It's cool. You know I still love you, girl."

"Aw, you're so sweet," I said, reaching for a hug. "So special."

We held tightly for a moment before Angie put the car into reverse and drove to my apartment.

Outside the complex we were quiet, certain the moment was the last curtain to our noncommittal relationship.

"Good night," I said, taking hold of my purse and briefcase.

"Bye, babe." Angie leaned forward and kissed my lips.

I couldn't help but to kiss back.

Once outside the car and inside my apartment building, I watched her drive away through the small window in the door. A minor wave of disappointment swept over me, and I briefly questioned if I had done the right thing. Though I felt I had, I took a solemn stroll up to the second floor to my apartment.

David was sitting on the couch engrossed in a Queer as Folk episode. He loved the Showtime series and could watch rerun after rerun.

"Hey, David," I said in a low voice.

"What's up, sugar?" he asked, not taking his eyes off the TV.

I took my shoes off and walked to give him a kiss on his cheek. "Not much."

David recognized the somber expression on my face. The one I had been carrying around every night for a week. "No call yet, baby?" he asked, referring to Asia.

"No, she hasn't called yet." I headed to my bedroom. I didn't even feel like talking about what had just happened with Angie. "Night, sweetie."

"Night, baby girl."

Inside my bedroom, I removed my dress, tossed my shoes into the closet, and pinned my hair into a heap at the back of my head. I washed my face, applied nighttime moisturizers, and snuggled under my comforter, whispering to the heavens, "When, when, when?"

"What in the goddamn hell fucking time is it?" I grumbled as the musical ring tone of my cell phone interrupted my Thursday night sleep.

Another bad habit I had developed was the merging of various curse words together in unusual formation when I was severely frustrated.

I got up and retrieved the phone from its charger. The phone said ASIA. Humph, I scoffed. A week and a day later she finally decides to return my call? At midnight, on top of that? Clearing the sleepiness from my voice and forcing an instant attitude adjustment, I answered the phone as calmly as I could, "Hello."

"Kyla," Asia said softly.

All the annoyance I felt was easily replaced with the excitement of hearing her voice again. "Yes."

"I'm so sorry," she said a bit louder. "This last week has been so crazy."

"That's okay," I lied.

"We buried Mrs. Garfield today."

Oh damn, damn, damn! I smacked my forehead. In all my selfish emotional distress, I hadn't once considered the old woman. "Asia, I'm sorry," I said, embarrassed.

"She passed the other day, just after I saw you. Between dealing with my other patients and Mrs. Garfield's daughter, I haven't had time to call."

"Marlon told me about her daughter."

"Yeah, well, she's no piece of cake. May Mrs. Garfield rest in peace, but I'm sure as hell glad that I don't have to deal with her daughter anymore," Asia said angrily.

For the first time I could tell that her Miss America smile had disappeared.

"Anyway, Kyla, when do you think we can get together?"

"Tell me when you're free. I can work around you."

"Well, how about now?"

I was so damn tired and desperately needed to rest my eyes and body, but I wasn't about to decline Asia's invitation, even though, only a minute before, I was bitching that she was just now calling.

"Sure." I glanced in the mirror above my dresser to see how bad I looked after only a couple hours of sleep. "Where do you want to meet?" I asked.

"Where do you live?"

"Near Marlon, on the opposite side of the park."

"I'll come by you," she said. "Let's meet at the Waffle House off of Greenview."

I looked at the clock. It said 12:30 a.m. At least we would beat the after-the-club crowd. "Okay. I can be there in thirty minutes," I said, hoping I wasn't underestimating the time it would take me to get ready.

"I'll beat you there. See you soon, Kyla."

"Bye, Asia."

How in the hell do I get ready for a one a.m. date? I had gotten ready for 1 a.m. arrivals to my apartment, which required nothing more than a quick shower and scented candles. I decided not to overdo it. We were, after all, only going to the Waffle House.

After selecting a low-rise pair of Diesel jeans and a Gap favorite tee, I hopped in the shower and then brushed my teeth. I opted against a full face of makeup and settled for M·A·C pressed powder, black mascara, and clear lip-gloss. Surprisingly, my nerves remained untroubled on my short drive to the all-night diner.

When I pulled up, I spotted Asia sitting at a table along the window. She waved as I walked past and entered the near-empty eating-house.

"Thanks for coming at such short notice," she said after I sat down. "I didn't want you to think I forgot about you."

Asia had her hair pulled back in a French braid, a dash of black eyeliner, and two small diamond studs in each ear. She was stunning.

Hmmm, is she flirting with me? "I was beginning to wonder."

"I kept wanting to call, but then I'd get interrupted and then when I'd have a chance again, it was late at night. I just couldn't go another day without calling. I was feeling pretty bad."

"It's okay. I'm just glad you did."

"Are you hungry?"

"Yeah, I'll have a waffle of course," I said, eyeing the all-in-one menu and paper placemat.

With a quick review of the meal items, she said, "Yeah, me too."

I ordered a small milk, and Asia asked for decaffeinated coffee.

After our sleepy waitress lazily wrote down our orders and walked away, Asia wasted no time picking up right where we had left off back at Marlon's. "So how long have you been gay, Kyla?"

"Before I answer that question, Asia, I have to ask why you're phrasing the question like that—how long? Why do you ask that?"

Asia rapped her short, manicured fingers against the table. "Just a hunch, I guess."

"I hope you can't read everything about me that easily."

"That might not be such a bad thing."

I laughed. "Yeah, for you, not for me."

"So?" she asked, not letting up.

Damn, she really wanted to hear my story. "Okay, you're right. I haven't been out all that long," I said, quoting the word out with my fingers. "When I was twenty-six, I met and fell in love with a woman for the first time. Before her, I had never been attracted to a woman. At that time I was still with my boyfriend, who'd proposed to me a few months after I met her. It took me a while to decide what I wanted to do, but I eventually made the best decision for me."

"And that was to be with women."

"Yes."

"What happened with the woman?"

My eyes closed, suddenly I was back on Steph's couch, my heart crushing with her every word. "She, um, she got back together with her ex before I made my decision. By the time I told her I wanted to be with her, it was too late."

"Hey, you okay?"

I opened my eyes to her concerned expression. "Yes, yes, I'm fine."

"Do you feel like you made the right decision still?"

"At first I wasn't so sure, but it didn't take long for me to know that I had. So, yes, I made the right decision."

"How do you know?"

"Because no man has ever made me feel the way a woman does. No man ever will."

"But how do you know that for sure, Kyla?"

"Because I want to be with a woman." Why was she challenging me?

"So you're not receptive to the idea of being with a man again?"

"I love women, not men, therefore, no, I'm not open to the idea of being with a man again."

Asia considered my response for a moment.

"What's it like for you, being with a woman, I mean?"

Aw shit, I got my ass up in the middle of the night for this?

She sure was inquisitive as hell. That was a straight-girl question. "What exactly do you mean, Asia?" I asked, trying to conceal my disappointment.

"Not sexually, I mean, emotionally."

I sighed. "Well, emotionally I feel like I can open up and express myself to a woman in ways that are understood. As women, we're nurturers and have a natural sensitivity to each other's needs and wants. Emotionally and physically, I connect with women in ways I never imagined until a few years ago."

Why was I pretending like I had emotionally connected with any woman since Stephanie? Sounding like I had actually had a real relationship?

"So how many relationships have you been in since you've lived in Atlanta?"

Asia's intuition must have kicked in again.

"Well, I've dated several women over the past couple years," I said coolly.

"So none," she said with a smile.

Asia sure had me penned correctly, making her all the more appealing.

"No, just friends."

Asia laughed aloud.

"Why is that funny, Asia?" I asked, barely able to stifle my own laughter. I knew good and well what "friends" meant.

"You know why. You won't commit to the women you date, so you classify them as friends, even though I have a feeling that you do things most friends don't do."

"What happened this past week?" I leaned forward and placed my elbows on the table. "Did you take a crash course in Kyla 101 or what?"

"So I'm right?" she asked, more as a question than triumph at chipping away the layers of my protective shell.

Damn, did she set me up for that one? "Let's just say, I haven't found the woman who makes me want to commit."

Seemingly satisfied with my answer, she adjusted her seating position, curling one leg under the other, and searched the restaurant with her eyes as the waitress delivered our food.

"Is the interrogation over? Do I pass?" I buttered my waffle and drowned it in maple syrup.

"I haven't decided yet," she answered playfully.

For a straight girl, she sure knew how to flirt, even in its subtlety.

"Is there anything you want to ask me?"

Suddenly my mind drew a blank. The one and only question I wanted to know was painfully obvious, yet I couldn't bring myself to ask it.

"So how do you like your job?" Great, Kyla. Real original. I'm sure she dragged you out in the middle of the night to talk about work.

"I love it. Aside from losing patients from time to time like Mrs. Garfield, I love every aspect of what I do," she answered before taking a bite. "Is that what you really want to know?"

Why was she being so evocative? I wasn't up to being shot down by a beautiful woman at this time of night, but what the hell.

"Why did you agree to have dinner with me . . . well, breakfast, as it turns out? What made you want to come?"

"I found you interesting," she said casually.

Damn! Another straight-girl response. This was the what's-it-like-to-be-gay conversation. Still, there was something different about Asia's questions. Yeah, they weren't as stupid as the ones I used to ask Steph.

"What do you do?" she asked, switching gears once again.

"I'm a buyer at Rich's, Rich's-Macy's now."

"Ah, that explains the designer suit," she said with a grin.

"As hard as I work, I may as well treat myself," I said, justifying the two-hundred-dollar outfit.

"It looked good on you."

"Thank you." I tried to control the heat that flushed my cheeks. "Asia . . ." I said, playing with my napkin.

"Yes," she said, her seductive almond eyes on mine.

"Are you flirting with me?"

"Do you think I am?"

"But you're not, are you?"

"I'm not. Am I what?" she asked, amused by my inability to ask the question I was dying to know.

"Are you gay?" I asked quietly.

"Why are you whispering?" she asked, a glint of humor in her eyes.

"Because I don't want to offend you if you're not."

"Well," she said, toying with her fork between her teeth, lightly licking the surface from the tips, "what do you think?"

"Um, honestly, I hoped you were," I admitted shyly. I thought I'd left that shyness at home.

"To answer your question, yes, I'm gay. Like I said, I've been to Traxx."

"I know, but you know I couldn't assume that meant anything really. I was once a straight girl in a gay bar myself."

"Yeah, been there, done that. I mean, dating those women, that is. Never again, no offense. That's why I asked the questions." Asia frowned. "Straight women complain all the time about not being able to find a man, but finding a compatible woman is just as hard."

My mind briefly wandered to Angie, and I found myself unable to fully agree. Even though I had remained single for so long, it wasn't because I hadn't come across any decent women.

"Yeah, I guess it can be," I said.

"Not for you, huh?" She laughed.

"Never mind that," I said with a smile. "So . . . is it possible we can turn this breakfast into a dinner sometime?"

"Absolutely. I won't keep you up all night next time either."

It was challenging, but I held back the impulse to respond with a sexy remark, which would have been inappropriate for our first meeting, but she read my mind once again.

"At least for now."

"Yes, just for now," I repeated.

Soon we finished our waffles that turned cold, ignored in our conversation.

"Can I ask you some questions now?"

"Be gentle," she said.

"Why did you move from Dallas?" I asked, sensing there was more to the blanket answer she'd given me.

This time, uneasiness swept over her face. "I left Dallas because I fell in love with the wrong person."

Sipping on my milk, I waited a second for her to continue, but she didn't. "So what happened?" I asked, pressing her just as she'd done me.

Asia set her fork down and placed her hands flat against the table then leaned forward. "I got taken advantage of financially by the woman I was living with," she said. "She tried to take me for everything I had, and I was too blind to see it. It started off small, with her needing money to pay her light bill. That upgraded to me paying her rent. When that got to be too much, she moved in with me, saying she was going to start her own business. She asked me to help with the up-front money, and because I loved her, I believed her." Asia rolled her eyes. "Well, everything seemed to get in the way, with the business actually getting off the ground. She'd need money to file some papers, or money for a particular license. Really, they were all bullshit excuses to keep asking for money. My friends, who then could read people better than I can now, always told me she didn't seem right, but I wouldn't listen.

"Finally, after she started asking me for my school money, I said, 'Hell no. No more.' I did some checking around and found out she had another girlfriend in an apartment across town and my money was taking care of them and the other woman's daughter. I kicked her out the same day I found out."

Asia looked at me sitting there across from her, speechless. "Crazy, right?" she said. "Trust me, I'm a smarter woman now, and I will never, ever let that happen again. I'm still a nice person, and I don't mind helping others, but draining my bank account for the sake of love . . . oh, I won't be a fool twice."

"I'm sorry that happened, Asia."

"No need for sympathy. I'm all right now. After I graduated, I packed my bags and came here to start fresh."

"Sounds like we have something in common."

"Unfortunately, you're right." She diverted her eyes from me and scanned the small restaurant.

We sat a few moments in silence.

"Kyla, I know it's late, but I'm not ready to leave you just yet," Asia said in the sweetest tone

I'd ever heard, her eyes conveying her not-so-subtle plea to extend our meeting.

Elated on the inside, I asked, "What would you like to do?"

"I don't know. Anything really. I just want to keep talking to you."

Though I knew Friday would be a busy day, I wasn't going to let work or lack of sleep interfere with spending more time with the angel that sat before me. "I don't want to leave you either, Asia. Follow me back to my place and go for a ride?"

"Yes, absolutely." Asia reached for her small wristlet wallet and keys. She insisted on paying the small bill in reparation for waking me out of my sleep and for having waited so long for our date.

We walked outside to our individual cars, and Asia followed me to my apartment. She waited outside the complex while I parked my car in its underground spot and exited through the iron-fenced gate.

"It smells good in here," I said after I hopped inside Asia's truck and settled into the dark gray leather seat.

"Thanks. It's some cherry something or other I picked up when I had the car detailed the other day."

"It's nice. So, where to?"

"We can just ride, I guess," she said, putting the Lexus in drive.

"Hey, you're not too sleepy to drive, are you?"

"No, I'm fine. My company is too good to fall asleep on," she smiled. "So, tell me, did you give the ring back?"

I laughed. "You're the first person to ask me that. Yeah, I gave it back. Not to him though. He really had no interest in seeing me, so I gave it to David. Jeff, my ex, picked it up from him."

"David is your cousin I met the other day, right?"

"Yes."

"And Marlon is his boyfriend, right?"

Again, I laughed. "How did you know?"

"Come on, Kyla, you're kidding, right? I remembered you as soon as I saw you. Did you think you were that inconspicuous that day I took Mrs. Garfield for a walk? I saw you sitting in your car when I came back for the wheelchair."

"Oh my God! Are you serious? I'm embarrassed now," I said, turning my head toward the window.

"Aw, don't be. You looked nice that day. And I thought about you that night, actually. You know how thoughts run through your mind at the end of the day? I was thinking you were pretty cute, but didn't think I'd see you again. Soon as you turned around in Marlon's kitchen, I was like, okay, something's up. I knew it wasn't just a coincidence."

"Well, I'm not about to tell you the conversations I had after I saw you. I felt crazy pulling that stunt on you, but I really wanted to get to know you."

"Why? What was it?"

"I don't know. There was just something about you. I couldn't help it. But the coffee meeting wasn't my idea. Marlon concocted that on his own."

"Well, I'm grateful he did." Asia reached for my hand and kissed the back of it gently before taking hold of the steering wheel with both hands and continuing to drive the semi-quiet streets of Atlanta.

We were everything but quiet as we began talking about how we each grew up, and some of our dating experiences. Comparing our backgrounds, although states apart, Asia and I grew up in amazingly similar atmospheres. Her mom, a nurse by profession also, worked in the same hospital as did her father, who was an emergency room doctor. They met much older than when my own parents had united, as her parents were currently in their sixties and my parents were both fifty. Asia's older brother arrived when her mom was thirty-three, and Asia entered the world just after her mom's thirty-sixth birthday. Born premature, Asia spent two months under hospital care before being discharged home to her parents. I guess that's why she carried such a glow about her. Surely the guardian angel that touched and healed her underdeveloped organs and bones continued to follow her through her every waking day.

Asia, and her brother, Jason, whom she was close with, attended a Catholic school from kindergarten until they graduated high school at the top of their classes. Attending college was never an option for her and her sibling; it was a requirement. Opting to attend school in another Texan city, Asia left home with a lifetime savings in the bank, courtesy of her parents. In college she explored her sexuality with a boyfriend, who attended Texas Southern University, and with several women on her own campus, eventually defining herself as a lesbian.

News traveled swiftly back to her parents after Asia confided in her brother of passionate love affairs she shared with female classmates. Asia had thought nothing of sharing these encounters with her brother, since he'd initiated such conversations with her about his own campus indiscretions. Asia's parents, overcome with disappointment, insisted she begin visits with a counselor to determine where they had gone wrong. Surely, the counselor would fill in the missing piece of the puzzle.

At Asia's adamant confirmation that love and sex were better with a woman than with a man, her parents gave in to the idea that their daughter was bisexual, just going through a phase. Once she got it out of her system, men would resurface.

After Asia nearly went broke supporting the gold-digging cheater while in school, her parents realized only a woman in true love would so willingly give so much of herself and her checkbook. They came to terms with her being a lesbian. Approving of her move to Atlanta, her parents gifted her with a new Lexus LX to aid in a smooth road trip across the South.

Since her stay in Atlanta, Asia met and dated only a handful of women, nothing compared to the dozens of women I had entertained. After a brief stint with a Columbus woman whose constant demands of unreciprocated late-night drives had taken its toll, Asia had temporarily given up on finding a woman. She wasn't desperate enough to consider a relationship with a woman who hadn't made any effort to drive to see her in two months.

Only a few days separated Asia's breakup, and the first time I laid eyes on her.

"What's her name?" I asked cautiously, mentally trying to retrace my steps of a weekend in Columbus and a young woman who I met and spent some quality time with.

"Her name was Deidra," she said, eyeing me sideways. "Why? You think you know her?"

"Deidra? Hmmm," I teased, mentally scrolling through the numbers in my phone. "Nah, not her. But, anyway, you just said that you were done dating. So, tell me if I'm wrong, but this is a date, right? I mean, you called me in the middle of the night asking me out and all."

"Of course, it's a date. I didn't ask you all those questions just because I like asking questions. In my heart I know I want to love, but I'm tired of meeting women that I don't connect with. I figured I needed to get the fundamentals out of the way, especially if you want to be with a woman, because there are plenty of women out there that really just don't know."

"Who are you telling? I mean, I admit that I was once one of them, but I've dated enough women torn between a man and a woman to know there are a whole lot of them struggling with that issue."

"Let's not even go there, because I know we could be up all night talking about that one," Asia replied. "You know, earlier you said that we had something in common about both of our hearts being broken. And I'm thinking that we have something else in common too."

"What's that?"

"We're both scared to love again," she stated.

This, by far, was the most personal I had gotten with any woman on a first date. Hell, since I got to Atlanta, considering I only opened up to Nakia a few days prior. "Interesting you should say that. I just got up the courage to admit that recently."

"How much longer do you plan to hold on to that fear?"

I stared at Asia intensely, trying to determine why she was digging so deep into my heart so quickly. So fearlessly. Like a woman seeking the antidote for her solitude, she left no territory unexplored. "I want to it let go," I said softly.

"But are you ready to let go?"

"Are you?"

"I asked you the question, Kyla, but I'll answer first if you don't know your answer. Yes, I'm ready. I've been ready for a while. That doesn't mean I'm not scared, but I can't let my fear run my life either," she said, echoing Nakia's words of wisdom.

"Yes, Asia, I'm ready."

Asia smiled. "I'm almost convinced."

"Can I prove it to you?"

"Yes, please do."

"May I?" I asked, gesturing toward an empty lot we were nearing.

Asia pulled in and parked between two yellow lines.

"Come here." I opened my door and went to the back seat.

Asia followed.

"I think this was meant to be," I whispered in her ear. I didn't worry that I had taken this first date too far.

"I think you're right."

I leaned forward and placed my lips on Asia's slightly parted mouth. Thank you I said to myself and to the stars that aligned our paths so perfectly, destined to cross at a time no sooner and no later than designed.

When we separated, Asia seductively licked her lips. "Tasty," she said.

"You're beautiful."

"Back to you." Asia kissed my lips.

We kissed, and kissed, and kissed. For a moment I felt like a frisky high school girl, having spent two evenings in a row smooching and cuddled up in a car. Asia laid me down, her slim and delicate body on top of mine, and we kissed some more, until our bodies commanded rest.

We dozed in the back seat of Asia's car, my body snuggled next to hers, and her arm wrapped around my waist. When the sounds of passersby leaving a nearby club stirred us, we awoke, kissed one more time, and got back into the front seat of the luxury vehicle.

While Asia drove back to my apartment, we didn't say much, mostly sharing affectionate smiles and glances. Outside of my building, Asia pulled next to a car parked at the curb. It was still dark, though the moon had begun its descent into the blue night sky.

She leaned forward and rested her head sideways against the steering wheel, looking at me with amazingly beautiful sleepy eyes. "Thanks, Kyla. I had a great time."

"Me too."

"I'll talk to you soon?" she asked.

"Of course. I'll call you later, okay."

"Okay."

We smiled at each other, trying to say goodbye, even though we didn't want to. It almost felt like we were about to tell each other, "I love you." We embraced over the console that separated us and exchanged one last kiss before I exited the car and walked to the locked gate.

I turned to wave and found Asia staring at my backside. My knees trembled a little. She grinned when we caught eyes, and waved back.

Inside my apartment, my body collapsed on my bed in exhaustion, but the inner joy I felt couldn't be contained. I turned on my laptop.

kyla69: she's the best thing that has happened 2 me. can u believe it?

bottomsup: sometimes it only takes a conversation

kyla69: its real. i can feel it already

bottomsup: i'm happy 4 u baby. treat her right, k?

kyla69: don't worry. i will. this is the same feeling i had before

bottomsup: honey where one luv is lost, another one awaits

kyla69: 4 both of us

bottomsup: yes, 4 both of us

kyla69: time 4 u to make ur rounds?

bottomsup: yep, gotta go

kyla69: see u soon

bottomsup: smooches

Instant messaging with David had become a fun way for us to keep tabs on one another and a useful tool in keeping him awake while he sat in the security office monitoring various hidden cameras throughout the company. Many nights I'd leave a peacefully sleeping beauty in my bed and log on and talk to him. David would harass me about my latest conquest and scold me in bold capital letters across the screen. If my prayers had been answered, those days were finally over.

Even though I was still floating from my meeting with Asia, I opted for a catnap, which did my body wonders, and by 6:30 a.m., I was wide-awake and full of energy, singing along to the latest R&B hits on the radio while searching for an outfit.

A gray pantsuit with a silk pink cami fit my mood for the day. The caressing of silk against my skin reminded me of Asia's gentle brushes of her body against mine and her fingertips down my arm. Just the thought reverted me back to daydreaming of the kisses we shared just a short time before, but my cell phone rang, zapping me out of my dream state.

The caller ID flashed TIFFANY.

Damn, what in the hell does she want this early in the morning? "Hey, Tiff," I said cheerfully, sharing my festive attitude. Except, Tiffany was clueless as to what, or rather, who had me so happy.

"Hey, sexy," she said in her best midnight-love radio voice.

I tell you, that girl could sing me a bedtime lullaby anytime (pre-Asia, of course). So many nights I'd wrap her in my arms and she'd hum a tune, or softly sing a romantic song until we both drifted off to sleep. I'd lay my palm against her chest and feel the vibrations as she seduced me with her lyrics. Yet, even in those most intimate moments, I knew she wasn't the one.

"Where have you been?"

And that was precisely the reason why. Tiffany turned out to be possessive as hell. When I pulled twelve- and fourteen-hour days, she easily left three to four messages "just checking in." In reality she was trying her damnedest to occupy my every free moment and ensure that no other woman was taking up my time. More than once I reminded her that I wasn't ready to settle down. Truth was, she, along with every other woman I had encountered, hadn't sparked the desire in me to want to settle down. Asia was my dream come true. I knew it. She was well worth the wait.

"I had a busy day, Tiff."

"Oh," she said. "I miss you, Kyla. Can I see you?"

Should I? Shouldn't I? Did one date with Asia automatically translate into happily ever after? Was I supposed to cut all ties with Tiffany and the few dawdlers that remained, and profess my newfound monogamy? I knew the answer to those questions, as I had already let Angie go two days prior.

"Why don't you meet me for lunch today?" I suggested.

"What time?" she asked, sounding excited.

"Two o'clock. I'll be outside the store."

"See you later, baby," she said sweetly.

"Um, yeah, okay. Bye."

Shit! Let a woman into your bed a few times (well, more than a few times) and she automatically thinks she's your girlfriend. But what could I say? I felt as if I had fallen in love with Asia the instant I saw her, and we hadn't even slept together yet.

A twinge of guilt crept through my veins as I realized I had lied to Tiffany and to all of the others. Meeting Asia hadn't changed me. I'd always had love to give, and with Asia, my desire to be in love again had resurfaced. I prayed Tiffany would understand that I no longer wanted to see her.

David strolled in shortly after seven while I was sitting at our nook flipping through the most recent issue of InStyle magazine. In my profession, it was a must to stay on top, if not ahead, of what was hot and what was not.

"Hola, chica. Check you out. You look so happy," he said before kissing me on the cheek.

"Pinch me, David. I'm scared to wake up and find out she's not real."

"To have you glowing like that, she must be the bona fide package."

"Yep." I folded the corner of a page as a reminder to review the Ralph Lauren ad displayed on it.

"Guess I won't be seeing her at Marlon's place," he said, referring to the passing of Mrs. Garfield.

"No, not anymore. But I was thinking I would invite her over for dinner next week and cook up something for you, Marlon and Kia also."

"Aw snap! You? In the kitchen cooking? Hot damn!" he shouted.

We both laughed.

"You and Marlon just better have your asses here Tuesday at seven. Bring MJ too."

"Of course, baby doll," he said, loosening his tie and unbuttoning his shirt.

"Go get some rest, sweetie, I'm about to get to work."

"I am, babe. I'm tired as hell."

"Will I see you later?"

"Honey, you know I'm going to see my man."

"Damn, David! I never get to see you any-more." I pouted playfully.

"But you know I still love you, right?"

I smiled and kissed him good-bye before head-ing out the door and driving to work. My mind wandered to and rested on Asia the entire ride. A part of me was still amazed that I had spent the night with the woman I had spent a couple of weeks fantasizing about; first eager to know her name, then jittery about our first meeting, nause-ated that she hadn't called, and finally, overjoyed that our feelings were mutual.

Maybe it was the pep in my walk or the "Happy Friday" I shared with everyone as I walked to my office, because even though I hadn't seen Gary, he called me in to see him within minutes of my arrival.

"Happy Friday, Gary," I said when I entered his office.

Gary sat anxiously on the edge of his desk, hands folded in his lap. "You're awfully chipper today, Kyla. I must not be working you hard enough," he joked.

"That's bullshit, Gary, and you know it," I said, chuckling.

"Who's the lucky new lady?" he asked quickly.

"She's the lady, Gary," I declared, giddier than he had probably ever seen me.

"Well now, never thought I'd hear those words come out of those pretty lips of yours," he said, verging on flirtation.

Because we had a mutual respect for one another, and because neither of us had a remote interest in the other, we could kid on nearly any level without feeling offended or violated.

"I wasn't so sure myself either."

"Tell me about her."

"Not right now, Gary. I have to finish up the presentation due next week."

"Right," he said with a slap against his thigh. "Well, if she's still around at Christmas, bring her to the holiday party."

I cleared my throat. Christmas . . . he brought it up, so I thought I might as well walk through the door that had been opened. "Oh, yes, Gary, I need to talk to you about that. You know my sister is pregnant, right?"

"Yes, I sure do. Congratulations to her."

"The baby is due December twenty-third."

"I see," he said in a more professional tone.

"I haven't been home to see my family since I moved here, Gary. I'd really, um, like to take time to go see them, especially with this being her first—"

Gary held up his hand. "No need for the soap opera story, Kyla. You work harder than mostly everyone in this office. You work harder than me," he joshed.

Maybe he thought I'd laugh that one off with him, but hell, I knew I busted my ass for this company.

"Go ahead. Go home for Christmas. Just get your forecasting reports together beforehand, and we'll be fine. Amy can hold down the fort."

Amy in charge for the holidays? Was he out of his damn mind? Yeah, she was my assistant, but could she handle shit by herself? The thought terrified me, and Gary sensed my apprehension.

"I'll keep an eye on her," he assured me with a wink.

Maybe now he would see how useless she was, just taking up space in the place.

"Thanks, Gary," I said as I walked toward his door. "I'll keep you posted on Asia."

"What a beautiful name."

"It is."

While waiting for Tiffany, I rehearsed my lines. *I met someone else I want to be exclusive with. It's nothing against you, Tiffany. This all happened unexpectedly.* No, I didn't think that would work. *It's not like I don't care about you, Tiffany. I didn't expect this to happen.*

"Hey, beautiful," Tiffany suddenly murmured in my ear, startling me.

"Hi, Tiff," I said, turning around to face her.

Tiffany looked cute, really, really cute, in a J. Crew silk dress with kaleidoscope paisley print and low heels with a small strap and buckle. Her skin shined under a sparkle lotion, and her eyes glowed behind cobalt blue eyeliner and black mascara. One thing Tiffany and me had in common was our love of shopping for sexy, feminine clothing and colorful makeup.

"I got something for you." She giggled, holding up a small glossy-pink bag.

"What's that?" I asked nervously, not wanting anything from her on this breakup lunch meeting.

"It's a little something for an afternoon rendezvous. I thought we could skip lunch and dive right into a mid-afternoon snack. I got something you can nibble on," she said coyly.

Damn! This would be more challenging than I thought. I took a step back to distance myself from her. "Tiffany, let's go grab a smoothie at least. There's something I want to talk to you about."

Picking up on my uneasiness, Tiffany took a step back as well. "What is it, Kyla?"

I took hold of Tiffany's elbow to guide her toward the food court, but she snatched her arm away.

"I don't want a fuckin' smoothie," she yelled, causing several shoppers to pause and look in our direction.

"Not here, Tiffany. Let's go somewhere to talk."

And that's when it happened. Tiffany threw a temper tantrum right outside of my damn job in front of a crowd of onlookers.

"You don't want to be with me anymore? Right? That's what you're going to say? How could you do this to me?" she screamed.

Holy shit. We hadn't been in each other's presence more than sixty seconds, and she was making a fool out of herself and attempting to make one out of me. Once again, I reached for her, and she began to stomp her feet, one heel clicking repetitively after the other on the tiled floor.

"What am I supposed to do with this?" she shouted, reaching into the small pink bag and tossing her new red lace bra and panty set at my feet.

Without answering, I spun on my heels and furiously walked toward the mall exit. That freaked her crazy ass out even more.

"Wait, Kyla, wait!" She followed me, leaving her purchase behind on the ground.

A group of young boys, maybe thirteen, scooped up the items and shot each other high-fives like they had just scored their first lay. It was so embarrassing.

"I'm sorry," she said when she caught up to me. "I shouldn't be acting this way."

Out went the speech I had been preparing., and guilt and empathy flew right out of the door with it. "It's over, Tiffany."

"Kyla, nooooo!" she said, placing her hands over her ears. "Tell me, what did I do? What happened?"

Looking right into her maddened eyes, I responded, "I fell in love, and it's not with you."

Harsh, yes. Perhaps it was a brutal statement to make to someone in such a fragile state. It surely wasn't the delicate manner I had planned, but I needed to smack her with a dose of reality.

"But I thought you loved me?" she whined, her eyes shining with threatening tears.

"I've never said I loved you."

"What about all those nights we spent in your bed? You didn't love me then?" Tiffany began to cry, covering her face in her palms.

I wondered if I should comfort her, but there was no need. Within a bipolar minute, her attitude switched from that of victim to victor.

Smoothing her hair and straightening her overcoat, she said, "If that's the way you want it, fine." She vigorously erased the tears that fell down her cheeks. "I don't have to beg someone to be with me. You don't know what you're missing. You'll be begging me for some of this pussy." She huffed and walked back into the mall and through the crowd of gawkers who had trailed behind us to witness the finale.

She caught up to the group of young boys and snatched her lingerie items out of their hands. "Give me my shit back!"

That is one loony-ass woman. I never would have known. I put on my dark shades and exited the scene of the crime. I immediately used my cell phone and dialed Nakia's number to fill her in on what had just happened.

"Girl, stop," she said at least five times while I was talking.

"Isn't that crazy?"

The more I talked to Nakia, the more I realized I had been ignoring the warning signs about Tiffany's possessive character. As demanding as she was for my time and knowing my whereabouts, I should have known she'd act a clown when both my time and location were taken away from her.

"I'll pray you never run into that girl again," Nakia said.

"Me too. I'll see you when I get back."

"All right, then."

We disconnected the call, and I went to lunch on my own, often peeking over my shoulder and around corners, making sure Tiffany wasn't tailing me. I was grateful when I made it safely and quietly back to my office.

Boney James played lightly through the surround sound speakers in the living room while I slid into the role of head chef in the kitchen. My mother had given me her famous cornbread recipe, which served as a side to the baked ham, cabbage, and corn I had prepared. Good food and easy to fix—that worked for me.

"What's got you in the kitchen cooking?" my mother asked.

"You mean who," I corrected.

"Oh, I see," she responded without inquiring further.

Accepting my lifestyle was still proving to be a difficult task for her. The moment lightened when I let her know I'd be home for Christmas.

"I can't wait to see my baby," she said, sounding tearful.

I had gotten off the phone with her before she made me cry too.

Just as I laid the final plate setting perfectly, the doorbell buzzed. Even the buzzer seemed louder when Nakia chimed.

"Girl, go freshen up," she told me after I let her in. "It's five thirty."

"Okay, just let Asia in when she gets here."

"Yeah, I can't wait to see this wonder woman who has you ready to burn your little black book."

"You're going to love her," I stated confidently.

"Get your lovesick ass out of here," she joked, with a wave toward my bedroom.

When I stepped out of the shower ten minutes later, I could hear Nakia laughing with Marlon and David in the next room. Quickly I slid on my cutest, curve-fitting hiphuggers that accentuated the ten pounds I had gained eating out for breakfast, lunch, and dinner five days a week over the past couple of years. David, who always said I had been too narrow, thought my new hips looked good.

A hush fell over the room when the intercom rang again.

David whispered, "It's her," like the birthday girl had just arrived for a surprise party in her honor.

"Kyla," Nakia belted outside my bedroom door.

"I'm coming," I responded excitedly.

David, Nakia, and Marlon stood side by side like cutout paper dolls when I entered the room, each of them grinning broadly like I was on my way to my first prom, glowing in my formal gown.

"Where's MJ?" I asked Marlon as I ran to the mounted intercom.

"He stayed at the sitter's through dinner. She's dropping him off at eight."

"Okay, good. I want Asia to meet him," I said before heading out to greet her at the elevator.

When the doors opened, she stood smoothing her eyebrows with a compact mirror in one hand, while trying to balance a bottle of red wine in the same hand.

"You can't go springing up on a girl like that." She laughed and put her compact away.

"Hey, gorgeous." I took her in my arms for a tight hug and kiss on the lips.

"For you," she said, handing me the bottle of Leonetti Cellar Merlot.

"My favorite! How did you know?"

"It's my job to know all the things that make you smile," Asia kissed me again.

Had I died and gone to heaven? That time I did pinch myself.

Asia was dressed cute and casual, in white wide-leg jeans with a cuffed hem and a peony puffed-sleeve V-neck top.

When we walked into the apartment, the gang was playing busy by adjusting the already smoothed napkins and rearranging the carefully placed glasses on the table.

Marlon quickly walked to Asia like long-lost friends reunited and gave her a big hug. "I'm sorry for tricking you," he said.

"Tricking me? You two really thought you pulled one on me, didn't you? I knew what was up the second Kyla happened to show up for coffee at the same time I did. Come on now, Marlon, how long does it take to brew a pot of coffee?"

"You don't seem mad by our little stunt," Marlon said.

"I'm far from mad, or I wouldn't be here now." Asia winked in my direction.

"Asia," I said, leading her by the arm, "this is my good friend Nakia."

Ever since my "breakup" with Tori and Vanessa, I vowed never to call another woman my "best friend." We may get along marvelously and share a lot in common, but my "best friendship days" were over. When I looked at Nakia, it was obvious she was drawn to Asia's alluring presence as much as I was the first day I saw her.

Nakia mechanically shook Asia's hand without ever taking her eyes off her.

Asia met her gaze confidently. "Nice to meet you, Nakia. I've heard lots about you."

"Likewise," Nakia replied, just above a whisper.

Marlon, David, and I all glanced at one another in question. Nakia spoke a word that didn't automatically trigger an uncontrollable furrow of the eyebrows from her thunderous voice? What was happening?

Asia freed her hand from Nakia's grasp and reached for David. "Good to see you again, David," she said, giving him a warm hug.

David welcomed her into his arms as if accepting her into the family. "You too, baby," he replied, giving me a thumbs-up behind Asia's back.

"The food is ready," I announced. "We can eat right away."

"Don't hurt us, Kyla," Nakia bellowed, released from her Asia trance.

"If it's not right, you have to take it up with Gladyce," I joked.

"Girl, just because you tell a pig how to fly doesn't mean it can," Nakia roared, clearly amused with herself.

"All right, Kia, don't act like you've never had my cooking before."

Nakia waved a hand at me, dismissing my comment. "I'm just playing with you," she said, eyeing Asia like a piece of cake. "I know you went all out to impress this beautiful lady."

"I'll open the wine," Asia said, trying to seize control of the moment before I could respond to Nakia.

And if my eyes weren't deceiving me, after we were seated, I thought I saw Nakia lean in toward Asia's breast as she bent to pour Kia's glass of wine. David's "take-a-look" slap against my thigh proved that I was indeed not blind.

"Mmm, what perfume are you wearing?" Nakia asked, her nose lingering in the path Asia walked.

"It's just a body spray I picked up at the drugstore," Asia answered with a confused glance into my eyes.

"Really? It smells like a bottle of the finest fragrance on you," Nakia said.

David looked at me like, Will she shut the fuck up already?

Five minutes into dinner, I regretted having placed Nakia and Asia next to each other at the table. Nakia stroked Asia's hair, pretending to be retrieving a piece of fuzz stuck between strands. Then twice she dropped her napkin and bent down to grab it, her head nearly lying in Asia's lap.

"Oops! My napkin fell again." She laughed.

Three times she offered Asia food from her fork, like the meal on her plate was different than Asia's.

"You want to taste my ham?"

"My cornbread is so warm. Want some?"

"You sure you don't want some of my cabbage?"

Asia declined every offer.

Throughout the entire meal, Nakia hung onto Asia's every word as if Jesus himself was reciting the gospel. Marlon, David and I tried our best to divert Nakia's attention from Asia, to no avail. Nakia found any and every reason to relay any story to Asia.

Whether Asia purposely raved over the food to boost my ego, or truly delighted in the meal, I wasn't sure at the time. But a second and third helping preceded her final motion, which consisted of leaning back in her chair, a rub to her belly, and a barely audible burp under her breath. Asia's down-to-earth manners were surprisingly pleasant.

Thanks to Nakia's excessive thirst, three bottles of wine circulated the table, and by this time, she was drunk and louder than usual. I felt another unexpected friendship explosion brewing and I wasn't prepared for that.

Nakia blurted with a lopsided grin across her face, "I like a woman who can eat."

Asia, ever so swift on her feet, replied, "I like a woman who can hold her liquor."

Nakia smiled. "Beautiful, smart, and sarcastic—I like it. You sure Kyla deserves a woman like you?" She laughed.

Confused and hurt, I stood to start clearing the table. "Nakia, can you come help me in the kitchen please?" I asked.

In response, Nakia rose unsteadily from the table, bumping her chair into Asia and almost hitting Asia in the forehead with her hand. Fortunately, Asia was quick enough to duck out of the way of Nakia's swing.

Nakia slowly followed me into the kitchen, carefully balancing herself with each step.

"What's going on, Kia?" I asked, once we were inside.

She leaned on the counter, apparently unable to stand on her own. "I'm just having a good time, Ky. Come on."

"What's the deal with Asia?

"What do you mean?" she asked, her thick speech a clear indicator that she was quite inebriated.

"Why are you all up in her space? What's going on?"

She shushed me with a wave of her hand for the second time that night. "Like I said, I'm just having a good time. You invited me to meet your new girl, so here I am." She said it like I'd brought this on myself by inviting her.

She was pissing me off, acting like she didn't know what I was talking about. "Exactly—my girl—so what the hell is up with you?"

"Girl, please," she said, wobbling out of the kitchen.

David, forever my protector, joined me in the kitchen just after she left. "What kind of stunt is your friend pulling out there?"

"I don't know what the hell is going on, but it doesn't make any sense to ask her now. She wouldn't know what in the fuck she was talking about anyway. And I can't kick her out in that condition."

"It's a good thing you're still being a friend, honey, 'cause she sure as hell isn't right now."

"Just wait until we get to work tomorrow."

The intercom buzzed again.

"That must be Carlotta, the sitter," David yelled through the connecting swinging door. "You can get that, Marlon."

"This is such bullshit." I piled empty plates into the dishwasher. "I thought I could trust her. She's not even into women. I don't get it."

"Has she ever said she wasn't into women?" David asked.

"No, but damn! How long have I known her? You'd think it would have come out by now."

"You and I both know that it's not always easily revealed," he said calmly.

"You think so? But why tonight? And why Asia? I told Kia how crazy I am about her," I said, starting the dishwasher.

David held the door open for me. "Apparently she wasn't listening."

The scene on the opposite side was as if my worst nightmare had manifested. My dinner guests were all standing, Marlon looking petrified, Nakia appeared instantly sobered, and Asia's naturally cool demeanor seemed shaken. Two more steps into the room and a better view of the entranceway uncovered the reason for the restive atmosphere.

Carlotta, holding MJ's hand, shrugged her shoulders. "I didn't know," she said apologetically, after letting an uninvited guest inside with her.

Behind Carlotta was Tiffany, whose appearance, at first sight, seemed professional and composed, but behind her smile was a woman who had fallen off her rocker. Hard.

"There you are, my darling." Tiffany gushed, arms open as she brushed past Carlotta and rested her hands on my shoulders.

If I had grown up a fighting woman, I may have beaten her ass on the spot. "What are you doing here?"

"I'm here to see you, of course," she said smoothly. "You haven't returned my calls in days, so I thought something just had to be wrong for that to happen."

Even with her dramatic departure in the mall, Tiffany had left a minimum of fifteen voice mail messages despite her statement that she didn't have to beg for anyone to be with her.

Tiffany studied the room. "But it looks to me like you're having a party." Her eyes focused on Asia. "Who is the guest of honor?" she asked through clenched teeth.

"Let's go outside, Tiffany," I said.

She laughed. "That sounds familiar, Kyla. Let's go somewhere to talk, right? What? You can't talk to me in front of your guests? Don't they know who I am?" she asked, venom dripping from her every word.

"Not now, Tiffany," I yelled, losing the poise I had silently promised to maintain.

"Oooh, look, y'all," she said to my guests. "Kyla's getting all upset 'cause somebody is finally calling her out. You thought that bedroom turnover rate of yours wasn't going to catch up to you one day, didn't you? Did you think I would just walk away after all I've given you?"

Given me? What was she talking about?

"You look perplexed, Kyla. Open your eyes for a minute and think. While you were out fucking every woman you could, did you consider that some of them actually cared about you—hoping they could be the one to turn you around? And now that you think you found the one," she hissed in Asia's direction, "you just want to kick everyone aside. Did you think I was some sort of ho or something? Just fucking you for fun? I was in this to win your heart, Kyla. I'm supposed to be the one," she insisted, pounding her chest with her index finger.

Was I supposed to feel bad? Should I feel bad? I mean, hadn't I told her all along that I didn't want a relationship? She was cuckoo as hell, but apparently not as stupid as she was nutty. She knew I just didn't want a commitment to her.

"Tiffany," I said, softening my tone, "this is not the time." I eyed Marlon, who then hustled Carlotta out of the apartment, and MJ into David's bedroom.

"I'll go." Asia headed for her purse on the living room sofa.

"No, Asia, please don't go," I begged. Between Nakia's and Tiffany's antics, I was sure I would never hear from Asia again if I let her walk out of the door.

"She said she wants to leave, Kyla, so let her go," Tiffany said, a smug look on her face.

Asia halted in her tracks. "Don't think for one second I'm leaving because of you." She gave Tiffany the once-over. "I have better shit to do than be in the middle of some lover's quarrel." This time her eyes squinted toward me.

"Fuck it! This is some bullshit," David broke in. "You got to go, girl," he directed at Tiffany. "Don't think you can come storming up in my apartment acting like you lost all your damn senses. You're embarrassing yourself and nobody else, honey. Now scoot," he said, forcing Tiffany toward the door.

Struggling with whether to cuss David out, or pick her face up off the floor, Tiffany stared at me with a mixture of contempt, humiliation, and sorrow.

"Karma is a bitch, Kyla. You'll get yours," she said before walking out, feeling redeemed for having gotten the last word in.

A heavy cloud of panic loomed in the air around me. I was fearful of whatever next unexpected event in my evening would follow. A dinner trying to impress couldn't have gone worse.

"You all right, baby?" David asked.

"Yes, I'll be fine." I turned to Asia. "Can we talk?"

Asia looked at David, Marlon, and Nakia, whose solemn faces must have diffused her anger a bit. Hesitantly, she put her purse down and eventually reached for the hand I held out to her.

We walked in to my bedroom, closing the door behind us. Silence ensued as I sat on the bed searching for the right words. She waited, arms folded across her chest while she stood leaning again my dresser.

"I'm sorry, Asia," I said. What else could I say?

"Look, Kyla, we haven't known each other long enough for me to be questioning you, but damn, what in the hell was that?"

"That was Tiffany, one of the women I was seeing. Last week I told her I didn't want to see her anymore."

"I see she didn't take it very well."

"No. She embarrassed the shit out of me in public."

"Did you know she was that crazy?"

I shook my head. "I had no idea. She acted an ass when I told her, but I didn't expect to see her again, let alone show up at my place. I figured she'd stop calling if I ignored her long enough."

"When was the last time you talked to her?"

"Last week. I just told you that."

"When was the last time you were intimate?"

"Not since I learned your name." I got up and stood in front of her.

"And that was when?" Asia reached for my waist and pulled me closer.

"Before the setup." I chuckled.

"I left the drama back in Texas, Kyla." Asia kissed me softly on my nose. "I can't and won't be dealing with any Tiffanys in my life." Then she pecked me on my cheek.

"Don't worry," I replied, responding with a kiss to her neck. "I'll protect you."

"I don't need a bodyguard," she said, nibbling my bottom lip.

I ran my hand down her neck to her chest, and placed my hand firmly between her breasts, so I could feel her beating heart against the palm of my hand. "This, Asia, is what I'll protect," I pledged, sealing it with a kiss on her lips.

Asia took hold of my hand and positioned it on her left breast. Guiding my middle finger, she stroked her hardened nipple. "Is that a promise?" she asked, looking me straight in the eyes.

"It is."

Asia parted her legs slightly and, directing my hand, lowered my fingers across her belly, over her zipper, and down. Her breath quickened as she circled her hips against the palm of my hand. "No more Tiffany," she said between heavy breaths. "Just me."

I unbuttoned and unzipped her pants then slid my hand inside her lace thongs. "Only you, Asia. Only you."

Asia stepped out of her jeans, and I guided her to my bed. I drenched her smooth thighs with kisses and inhaled the womanly scent between her legs. Asia's hands stroked my hair and scalp as I made my way to her belly with its glittering navel ring. Between her soft moans, I heard shuffling about in the living room and the front door close and lock.

"Oh, Kyla," Asia whispered when I took one of her breasts in my mouth.

I continued to fondle her erect nipples after I returned to taste her flavor below. As it is with most first times, it took a moment to find her spot. When she exhaled sharply and her grip tightened around my hair, I knew I had located it.

I remained focused, my tongue intent on stimulating the place that would make her come. She fooled me numerous times, writhing and panting and murmuring how good it felt. Then the wave would subside before building up again. I didn't mind. I felt like I could rest my head between her thighs for an eternity.

Suddenly, her thighs tightened around my head, and her body twitched. And then she sighed a relaxed, "Mmmm."

She spoke after a few moments. "Kyla," she said softly.

"Hmm?"

"Stand up."

I lifted myself from her warmth and stood alongside the bed, admiring the bare lower half of her body. "Yes?"

"Take off your shirt," she said, positioning herself on an elbow for a better view.

Slowly I untied the wrap of the brown shirt I was wearing, and it fell open, revealing my Very Sexy push-up bra.

She eyed my cleavage. "Nice. Let me see the rest."

I removed my belt and unbuttoned and unzipped my jeans. I tossed them aside and kept on my matching bra and panty set.

"You're so sexy." Asia sat upright on the side of the bed and removed her light sweater and bra.

"Thank you," I said, walking to her.

"Turn around."

With my back to her, Asia ran her hands over the Lycra spandex combination of my V-string bottoms. She caressed my skin, kissing the small of my back, and sucking tenderly on my ass. Her short fingernails grazed up and down my spine, while her tongue delightfully moved across my skin. With her other hand, she reached to stroke the embroidery of my underwear from behind. Her thumb stroked my wet lips, until she slid her fingers inside of me.

How did she know how much I loved this?

"Bend over," she commanded, standing up.

When I opened my legs and rested my palms against the cream-colored wall, Asia took hold of my waist and guided my hips back and forth over her fingers. Her lean fingers pressed deep, sending pleasing sensations throughout my insides.

Though I craved more, after several minutes, she withdrew her fingers and laid me down. She straddled my body and looked into my eyes. "I'm going to make you so happy," she said and kissed me gently on my lips.

CHAPTER 5

Revelations

I had almost forgotten what it was like to make love. Countless one-night stands and sexually gratifying, but emotionally vacant encounters, had left me with a clouded perception of intimacy. "Get mine" and "get yours" had become my bedtime theme. Making love to Asia reawakened the sentimental senses associated with touching and being touched. Not only had I been brought to tears by her insatiable desire to please me, but it also renewed my acceptance to the often disputed myth of love at first sight. The stirring Asia caused within me was quickly breaking down the barricades I had built around my heart when I lost Stephanie.

My restored faith in love, however, did little to diminish the anger I felt toward Nakia as I patiently awaited her arrival at work. I positioned myself at the entrance to her office in the rear of the Better Sportswear department. Nakia's

sales associates nervously looked in my direction
while my right foot tapped irritably against the
floor.

Nakia, puffy and red-eyed, eventually turned
the corner and spotted my roadblock to her door.
Apologies began filtering from her trembling lips
before she even reached me. Not anticipating
this particular response from her—I expected
a defensive demeanor—I switched from attack
mode to compassionate listener.

"Kyla, I am so sorry," she sobbed.

Once inside her closet-size office space, just
large enough for a desk to complete her weekly
schedules, I said, "What in the hell happened last
night, Kia? I don't understand."

Nakia sighed heavily and dropped her purse,
which was as large as an overnight bag, onto the
wooden desk. "I'm so embarrassed."

"You should be. You made a fool of yourself
and a mockery of our friendship."

A groan escaped from deep inside of Nakia.
Standing behind her desk, she leaned forward,
fists weighing down on the scratched surface.
"Last night, Kyla, I realized I have to face something I've been hiding for a very long time."

Oh damn! David was right.

"I-I have . . . wanted . . . " she stammered then
gave up.

I knew exactly where she was headed. I had grooved with enough women whose confessions began with those three words as well. I had two choices: continue to be pissed because my friend decided to acknowledge her feelings for women with my new girlfriend; or I could be a supporter, and comfort Nakia as she attempted to express what was awakened inside of her.

"What is it, Kia?"

Nakia lowered her head for at least sixty seconds, saying nothing. Is this how I used to look in other people's eyes, distraught by the thought of admitting I was attracted to a woman?

"Kyla," she finally whispered, "I've wanted to be with a woman for years now."

Nakia exhaled so loudly, I thought she'd pass out from sheer exhaustion of the effort it took to make her announcement.

"Do you want to talk about it?" I asked patiently.

"Not right now. But, you're not mad?"

"We can talk about Asia later." Even with my understanding of the turmoil Nakia felt, I wasn't going to let that shit slide so easily. "How about I call you tonight?"

Relieved, Nakia agreed to talk that evening. I gave her a supportive hug before leaving her alone with her unresolved emotions.

My lunch break was spent munching on grapes and repeating the morning conversation to Asia over the phone. I sat in my office with the door closed and shades down, shielding my view to the parking lot, which was filled with cars and people streaming into the popular mall.

"You're saying you've never gotten that vibe from her?"

"No, I haven't," I said, trying to trace a sign I may have missed.

"She dates a lot of no-good men. That's all I've seen."

"Maybe that's it right there. She could be dating these rotten men, knowing there's no potential in a relationship, so she won't have to settle down."

I'd never thought of it that way, but Kia had never given me a reason to question her dating pattern in the first place.

"Don't stay mad at her. Maybe last night needed to happen so she could finally be honest with herself and with you."

"It was wrong though, Asia," I replied, still hot by Kia's performance. "You weren't upset?"

"Yes, it was wrong, and I hate that it came out this way, but I can't help it that I do that to women."

I laughed. "You did it to me."

"You put a spell on me yourself. Last night was wonderful. I haven't made love in so long."

"Me either. I mean, I've been with people, but not with them, you know? Last night was a rebirth."

"I'm glad I was the lucky participant."

"Me too."

"You will let me know if you hear from that crazy-ass woman again, won't you?"

"Of course."

"You better. Okay, I have to go. My patient is waking up. Good luck with Nakia. Call me later, okay."

"Sure. Bye, sweetheart." I hung up the phone, praying the set of challenges placed before me since Asia's appearance into my life were on the downhill. Only time would tell.

Nakia sat on my couch, rapping her fingers against her thigh, while I patiently waited for her to muster up the courage to reveal her innermost desires. Having been in her shoes only a few years earlier, I understood her struggle and tried not to force her to speak before she was comfortable. But as we neared five minutes of heavy silence, which felt more like ten minutes, I was beginning to feel we'd waste the entire evening if I didn't initiate the conversation.

"Kia, whatever you have to say is all right. Please, tell me how you feel."

Nakia's eyes eventually met mine, wet tears glistening at her lower lids. "I wish it didn't have to come out like this."

"It's okay." Seeing the pain in her eyes set aside the ounce of remaining annoyance I had felt for her actions the previous night.

"Well, I've never been with a woman before, if that's what you're wondering," she said aggressively, like I would have thought less of her otherwise.

I nodded.

"But the attraction has always been there, Kyla. It's the same attraction I feel for men though. I think I've been bisexual my whole life, but never acted on the bi part. Sometimes I feel like I'll go crazy if I don't do something about it soon, just to see if the attraction is really what I think it is."

David was going to love this, considering his disregard toward the bisexual community; he believed they needed to make a stand, once and for all.

"Kia, you know me, I've been in your shoes. Why haven't you ever said anything about this before?"

"I don't know, Kyla. I guess I just wanted to pretend like it wasn't there. And I didn't want you to think I was trying to hit on you."

"But it was okay for you to hit on Asia?"

"No, no, it wasn't, and I'm sorry. I don't know what came over me. You're right though. I can tell she's not like your other women, and I was wrong for the impression I left on her and our friendship last night."

"I'm going to let it slide, Kia, because I trust that was a one-time thing, right?"

"Right."

"So, anyway, do you feel you're ready to explore those feelings?"

"Yes." She then asked, "What if I like it?"

"That wouldn't be a positive for you?"

She hesitated. "I can't be open about this, Kyla, I just can't. I want to explore this with someone who knows what it's like to be with a woman already. They also have to be willing to keep this under cover."

I thought I picked up on a sly plea for help, but I ignored it. "Is this all about sex to you?"

"Right now it is. I'm sorry if that disappoints you. I know it's not just about sex for you anymore."

No, it wasn't. From my experience with Steph, and now Asia, I'd learned that emotional love was what I wanted, needed, and desired.

"Well, Kia, it probably won't be hard to find someone looking for a piece of ass."

Nakia sat quietly for a while.

Had I anticipated her question, I would have interjected with a comment to deter her from asking it in the first place, but Kia went from timid to brave in a matter of moments, the bass in her voice resuming.

"Would it be okay if I watched you and Asia sometime?"

What the fuck?!

"She's beautiful, Kyla. When I saw her, all I could think about was how lucky you are. You're right, she's amazing."

Didn't I just tell her to leave my woman alone?

"It's not like you've never let anyone watch you before."

So this is what I get for sharing my every dirty sexual adventure with a friend? I had no idea my stories were making her panties wet. I was further insulted by her question. I wished I could erase that one regrettable evening I had allowed a husband to watch while his wife tried to figure out if eating pussy was a delicacy she preferred. A rising bout of shame emerged within. Did my careless bedroom practices translate into a free-for-all?

"I can't do that, Kia. Regardless of what I've done in the past, I can't believe you would ask me such a thing."

She appeared disappointed. "I'm sorry, girl. You're right. I shouldn't be asking you any shit like that. I'm feeling desperate right about now. So how am I supposed to go about this then?"

"Well, I can take you out with me sometime."

Nakia's slump in the chair disappeared, and she sat upright. "I am not going to a gay club, Kyla."

"You say it like it's a bad thing. Damn! You're the one trying to get with a woman."

"I know. I'm just saying . . ."

Nakia was tweaking my nerves again. I'd seen a million like her in the club. They might be scared as hell, but at least they made the effort to go after what they wanted openly. "Saying what? You're too good to be in a gay club?"

"No. I mean, I just don't want to be seen. Come on, Kyla, all the women you know, you must know somebody to hook me up with."

Another mortified moment surfaced. I had been with all the women I knew. Surely, I wasn't passing my leftovers on to her. "No," I said simply. "How about a personals ad?"

Nakia considered that idea, and a slow grin crossed her face. "Yeah, yeah, I can do that. That'll work!"

"There are a lot of places to try. You can put an ad in the paper, but these days, online is better. A lot of women put photos out there too."

"I'm sure as hell not," she responded instantly.

"Whatever, Kia. You might not get any responses without people knowing what you look like."

"Not at first. If I find somebody and like them, I'll send a photo, but not until then."

I shrugged. "That might work, I guess."

"When can we get started?"

I looked at the time. It was ten o'clock. "Not now, Kia. It's late."

"You'll look up some sites for me?"

"Sure, I will." I silently wondered what happened to her own Internet service.

"Thanks, Ky." Nakia hugged me. "I'm really sorry if I offended you."

"Thanks. I appreciate that. And keep your eyes off my woman, you hear?"

Nakia barked her unique laugh. "I'll try."

I responded with a fierce look.

"She's yours. It's written all over your face how crazy you are about her."

"She's the one." Nakia rubbed my arm. "I'm glad you finally found her."

kyla69: u won't believe this one david

bottomsup: what did she have to say for herself?

kyla69: she wants 2 b with a woman

bottomsup: i told u that honey. what else?

kyla69: asked could she watch me and asia

bottomsup: OH HELL NO she didn't!

kyla9: yes she did

bottomsup: what did u say baby girl?

kyla69: i said no, what do u think i said?

bottomsup: i know that. just making sure i don't come home to any pools of blood

kyla69: i didn't kill her

bottomsup: that's cuz ur sweet. what did she say about asia?

kyla69: that shes amazing

bottomsup: dayum girl, does she want your woman?

kyla69: i told her to back off & she apologized

bottomsup: all right now. you better watch her still

kyla69: i am. i'm supposed to help her find somebody

bottomsup: how?

kyla69: personals

bottomsup: oh lawd, help the both of u

kyla69: it won't be hard to find someone willing 2 turn her out

bottomsup: i wish i could be a fly on the wall 4 that shit

kyla69:?

bottomsup: can u c her loud ass screamin cuz somebody is eatin her pussy right?

kyla69: lol—stop david!

bottomsup: u know i'm right. i'm glad u didn't go there

kyla69: come on david

bottomsup: babe, it's not like you haven't slipped once or twice

kyla69: i know. why is everyone reminding me of my mistakes?

bottomsup: so u don't make them anymore

kyla69: i'm not. i'm not messing this up david.

bottomsup: good. she's wild 4 u. i can tell

kyla69: and vice versa

bottomsup: ok—gotta go baby girl. mwah!

kyla69: me 2. c u later

"One more time," Asia whispered just as the sun tempted to put an end to an all-night session of exploration, fantasy, and fulfillment.

Aroused just by the warmth of her breath against my ear, I responded with a swift reach under my bed and retrieved Bunny, my softened nickname for the Rabbit, the never-disappointing vibrator and dildo combination.

Guiding Bunny into Asia's heated body didn't take much effort, since she was still moist. I marveled at the silken hair, as she lay still, allow-ing me and Bunny to do the work.

With Bunny circling inside, and its fast-paced flitter against her clitoris, I took hold of her right breast and squeezed tenderly.

Asia's eyes locked onto mine, and her gaze intensified, her eyes widening in a frenzy. Her body jittered lightly. "Ahhhh . . . yes!" And she continued moaning until the waves passed.

After a stillness crept back over the room and settled upon the bed, I said, "You're so amazing, Asia."

She chuckled. "What? You've never seen a girl come once, twice, or a few times before?"

"No, you. You make me want to wrap you up and carry you with me all the time."

Lying down next to her, I wrapped my arms around her waist, and we fell into a peaceful sleep.

A persistent knocking on the door stirred me awake at noon. A flashback of Tiffany's erratic behavior jolted me upright. I know her ass didn't break into my apartment. I hopped up in my birthday suit and cracked the door.

"Ooh, chile, I just ate," David said. "Put some clothes on, baby."

Relieved, I laughed with him and grabbed my velour robe. Even though I didn't necessarily agree with the fashion statement velour was making with jogging suits of various colors, it did feel good behind closed doors, lounging around in my apartment.

Asia exhaled deeply and nestled against the pillow.

"What's up, cuz?" I asked, stepping into the living room.

"Check this out."

David handed me a shell-colored envelope addressed to both of us. The return address was from Wisconsin. And there was no mistaking the street address, since once upon a time, I'd almost claimed it as my own. The wedding seal on the back of the envelope confirmed the contents.

It took about a year after our breakup for Jeff to initiate contact with me. David and I were in the midst of early moving plans when I'd received an e-mail from him. Word had gotten around about my relocation. He told me that he had forgiven me and wished me well. I responded immediately, thanking him for his blessing. We corresponded occasionally, but the frequency had slowed down, and by way of my mom, I had already known he was getting married next year.

I never once thought I would make the guest list. Why was I receiving an invitation so early? Should I be flattered that my ex-fiancé thought about me and invited me to his upcoming nuptials? Or should I be insulted that he thought about me and invited me to his upcoming nuptials? Was this to show me up? A slap-in-the-face reminder of all I had given up? Or did he sincerely want my blessing?

"Open it, girl."

Nervously I reached for the letter opener on the coffee table. Why were my hands shaking? Carefully I released the ivory invitation, trimmed in a burgundy swirled border. A silhouette of a couple, a man and a woman, greeted me. A smaller return envelope and RSVP card accompanied the invite, which read:

Thomas and Claudia Smarczyk request the honor of your presence at the marriage union of their daughter, Julie Samantha Smarczyk, and Jeffrey Terrence Oldham on Saturday, December 27, 2003.

David took hold of my trembling hands as I stared at the cards I held. Between Tiffany, then Kia, and now this, I thought for sure I was given hell for some sort of bad deed on my part. What was next?

"It's going to be okay, Kyla. This wasn't the life for you, remember? Think of the beautiful woman waiting for you in your room." He looked deep into my eyes. "You made the right decision."

"I know I did, David. I know. This just threw me off, that's all. I didn't think I would actually be invited," I explained.

"Well, baby, it couldn't have been better timing. At least you'll actually be at home for it."

"I know. Did he and my mom conspire this shit? I thought the wedding was next year? I can't even use not being at home as an excuse not to go."

"Girl, you don't need no excuses. You better show up at that wedding proud, with your head held high. Don't weaken on me now, sweetie. Look how far you've come."

I rested my head against his narrow chest. "What would I do without you, David?"

David rubbed my matted, sweated hair. "You're about to find out, 'cause I'm not going home for Christmas."

"What?" I screamed, releasing myself from his arms.

"Honey, Marlon, me, and MJ are going to Disney World for the holidays."

"Why didn't you tell me?"

"'Cause you're a grown-ass woman and can handle your own baby, that's why. You can do this."

"Did you know about the wedding date, David?" I asked, suddenly aware that this may have been a surprise to me and only me.

"Yes, honey, I knew. Mama told me."

"Oh, hell, if Aunt Shari knew, my mother knew, which means everybody knew but me."

"Ky, calm down. We figured you wouldn't plan the trip home if you knew about Jeff's wedding. But, baby, it's time. You've been hiding for nearly two years now. To everybody at home it looks like you're ashamed of yourself, and that's not the case, sweetie. You know that, and I know that," he said with a stroke to my cheek. "But they don't know that. So go home and show them what you're made of, darling."

Once again, someone else was right about the direction of my life. Why was I so frequently compelled to these panic attacks? *Get it together, Kyla.* "I'm good, David," I announced with a straightened posture and with self-confidence in my voice.

"All right, sweetheart. Now go take a shower. You got this whole place smelling like twat."

We laughed.

Once inside my bedroom, I leaned against the closed door and admired Asia as she slept. With her straight hair frizzed from the heat of our passion, and a smear of eyeliner down her cheek, she was still magnificent. If there was anything I learned from my tumultuous affair with Steph, it was not to wait to tell someone you love them. When you do, you just do, and there's no reason to pretend you don't.

I snuggled behind Asia, which awoke her from her nap.

"Hey, baby," she said with a stretch of her arms and an attempt at running her fingers through her tangled hair. "Damn," she hissed.

A brief silence followed as the words formed in my head made their way to my lips. "Asia," I said, my voice a little shaky.

Unraveling her finger from her mangled hair, she turned to me. "What is it, Kyla?" she asked hesitantly. "You're not getting rid of me already, are you?"

"No, never. Asia . . . I'm in love with you. I am so in love with you," I said slowly, with emphasis on the so in love.

Through chunky eyelashes and blurred eyeliner, her midnight-colored eyes softened. "Oh, Kyla, I love you too, honey," she said with a hard kiss against my lips.

"It's not too soon, is it?" I asked. "I mean, we've known each other just a month."

"It's never too soon to fall in love. I knew I could love you the moment you walked into the

Waffle House. And by the end of the night, I already had."

I blushed. "You are too much."

Asia jumped up to straddle me at my waist. Slowly she loosened the strap of my robe and stroked my breasts with her fingertips. "I think it's payback time," she said slyly, then lowered her head and took turns sucking each of my nipples in her mouth.

It felt so good. Never in my dreams had I envisioned finding and having a love so satisfying. I couldn't wait to share the new joy and happiness I found with the world. Which gave me an idea.

"Asia?"

"Hmm?" she answered, her mouth full of my breast.

"Um, what are you doing for Christmas?"

The next day I returned the RSVP card with my and Asia's name on it.

We'd spent two weeks deciding which personals site Kia would join. Some nights I searched the net alone and reviewed various sites that promised successful love connections. Other times she and I would close the door to her office and browse different ads to see which sites carried the most promise for her. With her I reviewed the options: whether or not she wanted a free ad or to pay for service, and if she wanted a site specifically for lesbians or one that accepted all lifestyles. She finally decided on a popular site for lesbian and bisexual women, figuring she'd find the most success there. She also paid the required three-month fee so that she could initiate first contact if she chose.

Next, we developed her ad. Nakia worked on the ad as if it were the thesis for her master's degree, calling me numerous times throughout the day for the latest one- or two-word change. Seven revisions later, she was finally satisfied. Leaving subtleness behind, Kia titled her ad "Quench My Fire"—not an ad I would have overlooked, which was her goal, since she insisted on not submitting a photo. Her profile read:

Mature, sophisticated diva seeks another to take me to a place I've never been. Can you do that for me? My curiosity is piqued, will you satisfy my unanswered question: can a woman do it better? If you're clean and, above all, discreet, shoot me a line back and let's talk about it.

To me, nothing about Kia's ad was mature or sophisticated, but that's what she wanted. I didn't think her words would meet the approval of the conservative dating service, but within twenty-four hours, her mission was underway.

Over the next month, Nakia had rejected all of the responses she'd received for various reasons. Several of the women were in relationships and looking for a piece of ass on the side. A few of them wouldn't send a photo unless she sent one first. The others were too old, too young, or just not on Kia's level, according to her.

I feared our friendship was nearing a danger zone as both our frustrations mounted, although for dissimilar reasons. Kia grew more antsy and horny with each day that passed without a successful connection. I was just sick of hearing her whine about the possibility of never getting some from a woman.

Midway through month two, Shanna arrived. Within moments of checking her e-mail, Kia phoned me to her office, so I could review it with her and determine its fate. Would she delete it? Would she reply with a simple, "No, thanks"? Or would she finally be willing to give someone a try? Shanna's e-mail was humorous and creatively answered Kia's question.

"How do I look?" Nakia swirled around in a new snug-fitting knee-length V-neck black dress she purchased for her first date with Shanna, aka "Lickemlo."

It was only after an exchange of several e-mails did Kia learn Shanna's hidden message: "Lick 'em low." Rather than being turned off, Kia was that much more enticed.

For me, this day couldn't have arrived fast enough. "You look lovely, Nakia," I told her. "Where are you going?"

"To that little Indian spot by my house. If all goes well . . ." she said with a smirk.

"Well, call me later, girl," I said with a high-five.

Nakia strolled out of my office like a woman about to find the answer to all life's questions. I prayed the afternoon would prove to be a defining moment for her.

LALA was hunched over the phone, looking exasperated, when I stopped at her desk to review the final details before I left for vacation.

"Yes . . . I will. How much? . . . On the fifteenth? . . . Oh, right now?"

I took two steps backward when I noticed her tear glistened eyes and the shaking hand holding the phone. Times like this I actually empathized with the girl. Numerous times I accidentally intruded on a call from a bill collector as LALA desperately tried to extend the length of time to pay her already past due debt. For that reason, my Christmas gift to her would be a monetary token this year. I hoped the card containing five crisp twenty-dollar bills would aid her in this latest mishap.

LALA held her finger up to me, and embarrassed, continued to beg for leniency to the merciless debtor on the opposite end of the line.

Sitting at my desk waiting for LALA allowed time for my mind to wander to Asia, as it so often did throughout the day. What was she doing? Were we thinking of each other at the same time? Lately my thoughts had ventured to my trip home and bringing Asia with me. Not even Steph had been introduced to my family as my "girlfriend." Asia was the first to wear the official title. Was she as nervous as I was? She knew I hadn't spent hardly a moment back at home since my new lifestyle emerged. As we lay in bed at night, she'd wave off my constant concerns of what would happen when we arrived to the dairy state.

"You're going to make it bad just by thinking it's going to be bad, Kyla. Stop it."

And when I asked how she felt about attending Jeff's wedding, she grabbed and shook my behind. "I'll show him who's hittin' this ass now." She laughed.

Asia may have comprehended my discomfort more clearly had I been more open with the details of the conversation I had with my mother. Instead, I conveyed the message to her that my mother was "fine" with my bringing her home with me, leaving off, "If that's the way you want it," followed by a sharp click of the phone. My daddy, on the other hand, welcomed my visit and the opportunity to meet the woman who stole my heart once and for all.

Asia was to meet me on Christmas Eve, four days after my arrival home. That provided me time to spend with my baby niece, whose birth I missed as she entered the world healthy, yet three weeks premature. Gladyce Marie was the five-pound one-ounce blessing to Yvonne and Byron on December 1st. I had to ask Yvonne why she would torture the child by naming her Gladyce in the year 2003. Her response was that after years of cute names like Amber, Nicole, and Brittney, it was time to bring back the strong and bold old-school names, and of all names to choose, she opted for Gladyce, after our mom. It was that or Aretha, after Byron's grandmother.

"Yes, Kyla," LALA said, taking a seat in front of my desk.

"Hey, Amy," I said, reaching for a stack of folders. "How are you?"

"I'm okay," she answered, pulling at her Barbie-blondestreaked hair.

Briefly I debated on whether or not to press her and see if I could be of any help, but I decided against it, when I remembered that equally lazy-ass boyfriend she allowed to lay up on her couch.

"Good. Here are all the reports you'll need while I'm gone. It's all laid out for you in order. Inside each folder is a memo detailing exactly what should happen with each item mentioned inside and a list of all order numbers and contacts. Everything is all set for delivery. I just need you to follow up, if needed, and resolve any issues that may arise. Does this sound all right for you, Amy?"

"Sure, Kyla. I've been doing this job for quite some time. I know what it is you do."

I know she wasn't getting smart, was she? "I want to make sure you've got this, Amy. I've never left during the busiest time of the year."

"I can handle it," she said, standing up. "By the way, if all goes smoothly, which it will, can you pass that info on to Gary? I think I'm about due for a promotion."

A promotion? I don't think so. People really grew balls when they were hard up for money. "Yes, I'll talk to him."

Satisfied, she left the office with an armful of folders and paperwork.

Good. Maybe this was just the opportunity she needed to get on top of her job. About damn time.

"What about these?" Asia asked, holding up my leopard-print undies.

"Perfect. I'll save them for when you get there." I grinned.

"Can't wait," she said, continuing to search through my underwear drawer. "What are you wearing to the wedding? I need to find something for you to wear underneath."

From my closet I pulled out my already packed garment bag and unzipped it, revealing a black-and-rouge Nicole Miller evening gown, with a scoop neckline that displayed my still firm cleavage. Satin strapped heels, ruby earrings, and a ruby pendant necklace would complement the stunning garment.

I hoped Asia didn't feel I was overdoing it, but I knew I had to knock the socks off everyone's feet at the reception. Not only had the wedding date been kept hidden from me, but so had the details of Jeff's fiancée number two: the biracial daughter of the CEO of a well-established luxury automobile franchise, whose fair skin, dyed blonde hair and fat wallet allowed her access into the most prominent social clubs, parties, and organizations in the city. Her African American mother, who spent her days at the spa for pampering, and evenings dining at elegant restaurants, raised and prepped her daughter for the same lavish lifestyle. I was surprised Jeff had selected such a bourgeois bride, considering his humble upbringing. But if he'd found happiness, I wasn't going to question it.

"You'll blow them away. Now I know just what to bring."

"I love you so much for doing this with me." I gave her a peck on her cheek.

"I want to do this with you. See your home, meet your family, and see all that aided in molding you into the Kyla you are today."

"I couldn't do this without you."

"Yes, you could." She squeezed my hand. "But you don't have to."

"You're the sweetest."

"I know. You're lucky as hell." She laughed.

My cell phone cut short the liplock we shared, and there was no guessing who was interrupting my final evening with Asia for four long days.

"What's up, Kia?" I answered.

"Girl, girl, girl," she mumbled into the phone.

"What?" I whispered back.

"Girl," she repeated.

"What?" I asked, losing my hushed tone.

"It was sooooo good. Oh my God!"

"Well, damn! What happened?"

"I can't really tell you right now," she said, clearing her throat as a hint.

"Shanna's still there?"

"Mmmm-hmmm," she said lustfully.

"Call me in the morning then, while I'm at the airport, okay."

Kia giggled and then covered up the phone. Through the muffled sounds, I heard her say, "I'll be right there. Oooh, I can't wait."

"Bye, Kia," I hollered into the phone.

"Oh, right." She laughed. "Okay, bye, Kyla."

"She did the deed," I announced to Asia as I flipped my phone shut.

"Good for her. All those years of pent-up sexual energy. Can you imagine what kind of release that is?"

Briefly I was back to the Bahamas, leaned against the wall, my heart thumping in my chest while slowly being undressed by Steph, her hazel eyes locked onto mine, her fingers removing the straps to my dress.

"Kyla!"

"Yes, yes, I can imagine what it's like," I said, quickly snapping out of my dreamy state. "Hey, it's eleven. You still want to watch a movie?" I asked, changing the subject.

"No. Come here."

I dropped to my knees in front of her while she sat on the bed. "Yes," I said, like a kid about to be punished.

"Why so many trips down memory lane, Ky? I'm here now. Did you think I didn't catch that daydream at the Waffle House? Why do you fall back into the past so easily?"

Shit. My old tricks weren't going to work with Asia. Was I still living in the past? Was my anxiety about seeing Jeff and flashbacks of Steph translating into a longing for what once was? Surely there was no going back, so why was I reminiscing about lost love?

"Kyla," she said, irritation and concern in her voice.

"There's nothing to worry about," I responded. "I don't wish to be anywhere but here. Not with Jeff and not with Steph, only with you."

"I'm trying to support you by going home with you. Don't get there and then act like you don't want to come back with me."

Why was I so gifted at making those I cared about doubt my feelings for them? Because I always give them a reason to. "Don't say that, Asia. You know I'm in love with you."

"If you're going to be in love with me, you can't be missing the ones you used to love. That shit doesn't fly with me."

Unable to defend my irresponsible and impulsive thoughts, I replied softly, "It won't happen again."

"Good. Now get up so we can watch that movie." And I obliged like an obedient pet.

CHAPTER 6

A Trip Home

As I sat in the airport waiting to board a plane, I was talking on the phone with Nakia, who was telling me every detail of her experience with Shanna. "I never knew, I never knew." She laughed. "I see why you're a lesbian."

"Oh, hell yeah! Never go back either," I responded quickly. "So let me get this straight. You met at the restaurant, ate lunch in an hour, and were in your apartment right after that?"

"Yep. She's even more attractive than her picture, and she's sexy as hell, Kyla. We couldn't get through the meal fast enough. It was just like you see in the movies, girl. When we got to my place, we started taking each other's clothes off right at the door. She was aggressive, but so gentle, just like I imagined a woman to be. She did all kinds of stuff to me first, and I can't lie and say I wasn't nervous when she asked me to go down on her. I had no idea what to do."

My mind flashed back to Sharon, and I prayed Nakia wasn't that bad.

"She was so cool about it though. She told me what felt good and how to move my tongue, and even though it took a long time, she did come."

"That made you feel good, didn't it?"

"I can't even explain it. Men come all the time so easily, and they're usually controlling it, so it's not that big of a deal. But to feel a woman get wet and see her body shake and shiver was fucking mind-blowing. I see why men are always trying to get in our panties, 'cause the shit is the bomb."

"Yeah, it is." I caught myself just as memories of my first time with Steph crept into my mind.

"I have to ask you this because I'm just too curious," Nakia started. "Um, do all women taste the same?"

I started laughing so hard that several others waiting at my gate looked my way and even chuckled at my amusement.

"All right, I'm going to assume that was a dumb question."

"I'm sorry, girl. It just reminded me of some of the crazy questions I used to ask Stephanie, that's all." I wiped my eyes with my fingertip. "To answer your question, no, all women don't taste the same. What makes you ask?"

"Honestly, I was a little thrown off when I first went down there. I didn't know what to expect. Not like it was bad, because it wasn't at all. But it was kinda bitter at first, like licking real, real salty grits."

"Kia, grits? I've never heard that one before."

"That's probably not a good description, but that's all I can think of right now."

"Well, every woman is different, just depends on her chemistry."

"It got better though. And after she came she got real, real wet, but it tasted good."

"Yeah, that's the good part," I said, just as I heard the gate attendant begin calling for boarding.

"Is that you?"

"Yep, I have to go, but I'll talk to you soon as I get back, okay. Enjoy your time with Shanna."

"Oh, you know I will!" She giggled. "But, girl, my tongue is sore as hell today. How long is this going to last?"

I laughed. "Yeah, it's tiring at first. You'll get used to it, don't worry."

"Good. 'Cause I definitely want to try going down on her again."

"Enough, Kia, okay! Have fun."

When I hung up the phone, I gathered my purse, carry-on, and boarding pass and prepared to meet my family on the opposite end of my flight. Before takeoff I quickly called Asia to wish her a good day. She insisted that I kiss her through the phone prior to saying good-bye.

The elder couple next to me thought it was sweet. "Was that your boyfriend?" the smiling, brown-skinned, gray-haired woman asked.

"Um, no, it wasn't."

"Oh, your son or daughter?"

"No, I don't have any children."

Visibly I could see their minds twirling, wondering if I would smooch my mother or father or aunt or uncle through the phone. Both the old lady and old man leaned forward, kind curiosity in their eyes. I didn't want to say I was lip-smacking my girlfriend over the phone for fear of their response. Perhaps they were old-fashioned and conservative, not in agreement with same-sex relationships. Or maybe I was assuming and judging them incorrectly; for all I knew, they could have an adult gay child or grandchild themselves.

"I was just, uh, saying good-bye to someone special," I offered.

The elderly woman was pleased. She patted my hand and gave her husband a warm glance. He leaned his face to his wife's forehead and kissed her with wrinkled lips.

I could only imagine the strength and love in their union after so many years. I closed my eyes and imagined me and Asia forty years into the future, traveling on a plane to some unknown destination, still joyfully in love and happy with one another.

When I awoke, the couple was still engaged in a tender conversation as the plane rolled down the runway.

My entire family was there to greet me just past the security checkpoint when I arrived at Mitchell International. My mother, father, sister, Byron, baby Gladyce, and Aunt Shari stood behind the guarded terminal with visible anticipation. As I approached the ramp, it felt to me more like a tunnel taking me back into a time and a place I had stored away in the corner of my mind.

Temporarily in shock by my three-inch camel-color suede boots and matching coat, Louis Vuitton carry-on, auburn-highlighted hair, and polished makeup, my mother covered her gaped mouth with her glove-covered hand.

No, I no longer looked like I was from the Midwest.

Flurries of panic were cast aside upon seeing Yvonne glowing and basking in motherhood, holding baby Gladyce's hand and waving it at me. Bundled in a pink Eskimo snowsuit with a furry hood, all I could see was baby Gladyce's fat, rosy cheeks, teeny nose, closed eyes, and drooling lips. Overwhelmed with confirmation that I was "Aunt Kyla," I blinked back the tears that surfaced in the corners of my eyes.

Quickly I hugged Byron and Aunt Shari. An initial icy hug heated to lukewarm within seconds from my mom.

Anxious for my father's comfort, I sank into his arms and exhaled in his tender hold.

"I missed you pumpkin," he said, kissing the top of my head.

"I missed you too." I pecked him on the cheek.

"Yvonne, she's beautiful." I reached for baby Gladyce. I instantly fell spellbound, inhaling the scent of milk and baby lotion, and mesmerized by the peaceful way she sucked in air and released it from her slightly parted lips. "Beautiful," I repeated. "You did well," I said to Yvonne and Byron.

"How was your flight, baby?" my mom asked as we walked to claim my luggage.

I couldn't wait to see the expression on her face when she discovered the luggage matched my carry-on. "It was all right. I read most of the way."

"Oh, what are you reading?"

"The autobiography of E. Lynn Harris."

"Who?"

"He's an author. Never mind," I said, not wanting to turn the conversation "gay" already.

Yvonne looked at me sideways and shook her head, obviously disappointed by my avoidance of the topic. Aunt Shari, familiar with the famous author by reading all of David's hot-off-the-press copies, gently rested her hand on my mother's arm before she began to protest my resistance to elaborate.

Riding home in my dad's newly purchased Navigator (Did he buy it from Julie's dad? I wondered) eased the mounting tension, since I was able to sit up front with him, close my eyes, and pretend to catch a short nap while we drove the familiar route to my mom's house.

Please, God, don't let this trip be a disaster. Without the designer clothes and hardened attitude, I'm still Kyla underneath. Don't they see that?

Noticing a wince on my face during my prayer for a peaceful trip, my dad reached across the wide console between us and gave me a comforting squeeze to my shoulder. Roused from a phony sleep, I opened my eyes to his empathetic gaze.

"I'll pick you up at noon tomorrow," he said.

I smiled and nodded my head.

Cries erupted from the back seat when we rolled over the hump in the ground leading to my mom's driveway.

"She cries every time we hit that bump." Yvonne soothed murmurs into baby Gladyce's covered-up ears.

"You know I'll babysit anytime," I said.

Like a needle scratching over a record, putting an unexpected stop to the rhythm of a dancing crowd, a hush fell over the huge vehicle. Even baby Gladyce silenced her cry as if to say, *Huh?*

"No, no, Kyla, that's okay," Yvonne said quickly. "We're good. Thanks for the offer."

"Don't be scared y'all," I replied, understanding the not-so-subtle hint that they didn't trust me with their most precious little one.

"Kyla, when was the last time you took care of a baby?" Yvonne asked.

"Same time you did before baby Gladyce."

She laughed, "Ha, ha!" Then she said, "Very funny. You got me."

"That's all right though. I see how you are."

"Let's just maximize our time together, and you can see Gladyce as much as you want to," she said, politely easing her way out of leaving me alone with my niece.

"Sure, whatever," I said as I hopped to the ground from the monstrous truck.

To my surprise, my dad didn't stay. He waved good-bye and took off after helping me retrieve my luggage from the back. I wondered what was up with that. Even so many years after the divorce, he and my mom had remained constant figures in each other's lives.

Not much had changed on the interior of my mom's home. Once again, the calm side of the teeter-totter rose to the occasion, and I felt all tightness loosen and my muscles relax when I rested on the cozy loveseat. No need to fret, Kyla. This is your family. These people love you regardless, right?

"Baby, what do you want for dinner? Anything, sweetheart, and I'll make it for you," my mother offered from the chair facing me, a practiced smile threatening to crack her lightly applied foundation.

Waves of sadness, love, concern, warmth, and scorn flashed through her eyes every two seconds. Why had my sexuality caused such an abundance of mixed emotions in my mother? It was my battle to fight, not hers. Why did she feel the need to carry the burden? Why did she have to see it as such a burden?

"I'm really not that hungry, Ma."

The forced smile vanished in a split second.

Damn! Wrong answer. Did she really want to cook dinner for me, or was she asking as a courtesy gesture as one would ask a houseguest? Had I become a foreigner to the home I grew up in?

"Well, um, I'm sure I'll be hungry later," I said. "How about some fried chicken?"

"Perfect." She rose out of her chair. "I'll get started."

"Thanks," I said to her back.

"How's my David doing?" Aunt Shari asked after my mother left for the kitchen.

David. How much I needed him now. No, you don't, Kyla. *You can do this. Use him as inspiration.* "He's great, Aunt Shari. We both settled into the Atlanta way of life so easily."

"I'm going to miss him this Christmas," she said. "But I'm sure he's having a good time with Marlon in Disney," she added pleasantly.

See, now why couldn't my mother share in the joy of the love I've found, rather than treat me like my mere presence was a reminder of her imagined failure as a parent?

"Give her some time, Kyla," Aunt Shari whispered, reading my thoughts.

"It's been almost three years since I left Jeff."

"Yes, but you secluded yourself and then ran your tail out of here so fast that no one really had any time to adjust. You hid from all of us, and next thing we knew, you were gone, hardly having said good-bye."

"What about me, Aunt Shari? Doesn't she know how hard it was for me? She acts like it happened to her."

"It did, sweetheart. Whether you want to admit it or not, your decision affected a lot of lives, not just your own. Look beyond yourself for a moment," she said tenderly.

So the traditional four-person household wasn't only a fantasy I had to let go of, but also a dream my family had to abandon as well? I suppose my hiding out in the South did nothing to help the situation.

"What is it going to take?"

"Time and understanding," she replied. "Acceptance will follow."

"So time is what has allowed you to approve of David's lifestyle so well?"

"Honey, now you know David had no qualms about his sexuality. He didn't change the course of his life the way you did. He's always been just the way he is."

"I hope this time home helps us to start getting along better, you know, give us a chance to get to know one another again. I want her to see that I'm still me."

"She will, baby. You're putting a lot on her plate with this first visit back, you know. I hear we're having an extra guest at Christmas," Aunt Shari said.

"Yes, Asia is coming." I gushed then wondered if I should have seen my mother alone, instead of forcing her acceptance on my first visit home.

"David says Asia is wonderful."

"Oh, did he? What else has he said?"

"Not much," she replied with a smirk. "Just that he's happy you're finally settling down."

What else had he told her?

"Don't worry, sweetie. He doesn't tell your business."

Now when did she go developing the talent of reading my mind? "Good. I can't have you passing that info on to Ma."

"Honey, no, I wouldn't do that." She shook her head. "I'm only here to offer assistance when she has questions on how to handle this."

I didn't respond.

Byron and Yvonne descended from the staircase after lying baby Gladyce down for a nap.

It was cute the way the both of them hovered over the baby and did everything together. When Gladyce burped up a bit of milk, Byron unzipped the diaper bag, Yvonne reached and retrieved a baby wipe, handed it to Bryon for clean up, who then returned it to Yvonne for disposal in a plastic baggie, while Byron zipped up the pink-flowered bag again. It was like watching a well-rehearsed two-person assembly line. No wonder they didn't trust me with the baby.

"So what's goin' on in the A-T-L?" Byron asked, trying to mesh his proper articulation with "a hint of street."

Yvonne looked at him lovingly for his effort.

"Everything," I said enthusiastically. "You all should visit sometime. The city is nothing like home. One, it's almost always warmer. Also, there's always something to do. We can try some restaurants, shop, visit historic sites, whatever you want to do."

"We can do dat," he said.

I almost laughed. Just because I lived in Atlanta didn't mean I lost grasp of the English language. There was no need for him to try to sound hip. "Right."

"Why did you do that, Kyla?" Yvonne asked, not specifying what.

"What?"

"At the airport. Why do you get so defensive when anything gay-related comes up? It wouldn't have killed you to tell Mom who E. Lynn Harris is."

"I'll go help your mom," Aunt Shari said.

Behind Yvonne and Byron, Aunt Shari placed her fingers under her chin and lifted her head confidently. "Keep your head up," she meant to tell me.

"I didn't feel like talking about it," I said.

"I know that, Ky, but as long as you don't want to talk about it, she's not going to let up. You have to walk around here like you don't give a damn what anybody has to say because you're proud of who you are. The more quiet you are, it seems like you're ashamed, and you don't have a thing to be ashamed of, girl. You might have to keep talking about it and talking about it until she finally accepts that this is your life and you've chosen to do what you wanted with it. Quit tiptoeing around your lifestyle like it doesn't exist, 'cause we all know it does."

"Damn! Did you and Aunt Shari rehearse your speeches?" I asked.

"That too," she said. "You always make a joke of it. If it's real to you, Kyla, make it real to her too. She'll get it."

"When did you become the big sister?"

Yvonne shook her head at my second dodge of the subject. "I'm proud of you," she said. "That took some serious courage to do what you did. A lot of people would have taken the other route, despite how they really felt."

"And look at me now," I said cheerfully.

"Yes, look at you. You look stunning. And happy. It's wonderful to see you doing so well."

"We have Asia to thank for that."

"Yeah, she may have something to do with it, Ky, but don't be afraid to take some credit yourself. You got to where you are on your own. You did this."

My baby sister's encouragement was doing wonders for my injured spirit. "Thank you, Yvonne," I said, getting up to give her a hug. I noticed the extra bulge in her middle. "I'm sorry for staying away so long and missing out on being here for you."

"I understand why you did it, but no more excuses, okay."

"Okay," I said, and bravely walked into the kitchen. "Need some help?"

My mother turned around, and before she could respond, Aunt Shari handed her apron to me and bolted out of the kitchen.

"Warm up the grease in the skillet," she instructed. "You can finish flouring this chicken too."

Without speaking, we prepared dinner, reaching over one another's shoulder into the cabinet, or standing aside while the other retrieved an item from the refrigerator. Crispy chicken wings and breasts sizzled on a plate, along with buttered rice, French-cut green beans, and rolls before we spoke.

"Thank you, baby."

I responded with a warm smile. "I'm glad I could help."

Although it wasn't much, I felt as if one hurdle in our path to recovery had been moved. Her reach for my hand and brief stroke of my palm assured me that we were, indeed, on the road to a healthy relationship once again.

Darkness fell suddenly as I strolled toward my mom's from an afternoon walk in the park nearby. I looked at my watch—only 3:45—yet looming black clouds raced through the sky. A shiver ran down my spine, and I quickened my pace. As I neared the stoplight, an endless line of cars passed through the street, separating me from a shadowed stranger on the next block. Will this light ever turn green? Three fifty.

A second stream of cars formed at my side, engines purring simultaneously as they waited for the green signal. Unexpectedly the light changed. The two lanes of cars criss-crossed fearlessly through the intersection in perfect unison, pinning me inside the 90-degree formation. The sound of heels tapping against concrete prompted me to spin around as I tried to focus on a second frame coming behind me. Before the long wavy hair became visible, before the freckled skin appeared, were the eyes. Those hazel eyes that once upon a time caused a rousing within the depths of my soul by just a glance.

A fog gradually lowered, blurring the silhouette of a third figure to my left, who was halted across the street by the increasing traffic. At that moment, the silhouette and the shadow ahead stepped into the street, in my direction, walking between the cars effortlessly. Broad shoulders, dark eyebrows, and unforgettable long curly eyelashes appeared through the fog ahead of me.

Then a familiar feminine shadow neared me to my left. Her scent of soft femininity traveled through my air passages like a sweet summer breeze.

"Kyla," they each said together.

Steph's raspiness, Jeff's baritone, and Asia's airy voice combined into one melodic trio. "I miss you," they sang in chorus.

Steph's touch of my back sent electrifying chills up my spine.

Jeff's caress against my cheeks with the tips of his masculine fingers caused a rush of heat to my face.

Asia's stroke down my arm and reach for my hand generated an intense yearning in my heart. For her, only.

Guided by the gentle tug of her hand, I stepped between Steph and Jeff and followed Asia to

*the street, where the cars instantly stopped,
allowing us to pass through unharmed. Through
the darkness, Asia's angelic glow appeared and
wrapped around us.*

*"What about us?" they called from behind,
their voices becoming mere whispers in the dark.*

*As Asia and I reached the curb, she paused and
nodded her approval in my direction. Slowly, but
confidently, I turned to face the treasured gifts
of my past. "Good-bye, my love," I whispered
once. "What's done is done. You both have found
happiness. Now it's my turn."*

*Understanding my need to let them go, Jeff
and Steph parted ways and headed down the
sidewalk in the same paths they had come.*

*I waved to the fading figures as they walked
out of the corners of my subconscious mind,
until they disappeared in the misty air.*

*Stormy clouds gave way to an emerging light
in the sky. Relieved and empowered, I turned
back to the waiting love of my life, and she
welcomed me. Welcomed me to her love. Into
her heart. Forever.*

A light rap on the bedroom door forced my
eyes open to the purple pillowcase that covered
my head while I slept. After removing the pillow
off my face and focusing on the Prince poster on

the door, I caught sight of the wall clock. It was 12:15. Shit!

I hopped out of bed and opened the purple-trimmed white door. "Hey, Daddy," I said, forcing my voice into an alert tone.

"Still like to be fashionably late, I see." He chuckled.

"Sorry. I was lost in a dream." No, I had been found in a dream.

"I'll wait outside."

"Okay."

I rummaged through my suitcase and retrieved black slacks and a gray wool sweater with an oversized turtleneck. It was cold in this city. Quickly, I showered, dressed, applied makeup, and pulled my hair into a single, loose French braid in the back.

With lightly tinted J. Lo sunglasses perched on my nose, I jumped into my father's truck twenty minutes later. Again, I found it odd that he chose to wait outside in his running vehicle rather than sit and chat with my mom in the living room. What had changed?

"Where to?"

"You'll see."

My dad filled our ride time with colorful stories of Yvonne and me as babies, memories that resurfaced with the birth of baby Gladyce. He shared with me the joys of marriage to my mom, and how proud the both of them were of the two of us.

"She loves you so much, Kyla. Her main concern was that you were making life harder for yourself. No parent wants to see their child struggle and hurt."

"I know, Daddy, and I understand now. It's going to get better."

He segued into a conversation on the circle of life and change, and how one must always follow their heart. Momentarily terrified that my dad was going to come out to me, I sat frozen in my seat, bracing myself for his confession that he had passed the gay gene down to me.

"Come with me," he said after parking in front of a jewelry store, whose diamonds on display in the window twinkled underneath the glistening sun.

"Good afternoon, Mr. Thomas," a suited-up salesman said from behind the counter. "Big day for you."

"Yes, yes, it is," my dad replied. "This is my daughter, Kyla."

The salesman smiled at me.

"What's going on?"

"Sweetheart, I know you've got a lot to handle this week, but I wanted to share this with you."

My dad signaled the clerk, who reached into a locked cabinet, all-smiles, and pulled out a small box and handed it to me.

"Open it," my dad said.

I opened the red velvet box and saw an incredible platinum band covered with emerald cut diamonds. "Her name is Evelyn. I'm in love with her, Kyla," he explained to the confused expression on my face.

Stunned, I was at a loss for words.

"Seems like someone is always getting married around you, huh?" my dad joked.

"How come you never told me about her?"

"I don't know about everyone you date, now do I? Just the important ones, no?" He nudged me in my side.

I looked at the salesman, who only continued to smile, obviously envisioning his fat-ass commission check. "But you're ready to marry her? How long has this been going on?"

"Long enough to know I'm making the right decision. But remember, Kyla, there's no time frame on love. You know that."

"Yeah, I know. I'm happy for you." I threw my arms around his neck.

He held on tight. "Thank you, darling. Thank you."

"When do I get to meet her?"

"Well, I was hoping you and Asia could come by Friday night for a while. She's got to meet my oldest baby," he said proudly.

Uncontrollable tears welled in my eyes. "Oh, Daddy." I accepted a Kleenex from Mr. Salesman and wiped my face. "We'll be there."

Mr. Salesman and my dad finished up their exchange, while I stood aside and ogled some of the shimmering engagement rings inside the display case. I imagined which ring I would slide on Asia's finger when we were ready to take our relationship to the next level. It was a shining platinum band with brilliant, emerald cut three-stone diamonds. It was perfect for her. I took a mental snapshot of the ring for future reference.

"You ready?"

"Yes."

We left with my dad delicately holding the beautifully wrapped box in his hand.

"Does Mom know?"

"Of course. I told her a while back. She's all right with it."

"Just all right?"

"Yes, just all right. If you never noticed, Ky, your mom and I didn't always act like a divorced couple. We saw each other pretty often, and well, now that's come to an end."

As I had so many times in the past, I silently wondered what exactly happened to my parents. Neither had been forthcoming in sharing the reason for their divorce, except that they had fallen out of love. I suppose that was reason enough.

"I take it you won't be over for Christmas," I said, after closing the door and putting on my seat belt.

"No, I won't be. I want to be, for you, but Evelyn and I are spending time with her family."

"She has children?"

"Yes. Three adult boys."

"So you'll be with them?"

"Don't go getting green on me, Kyla. You of all people should understand the need to do things differently."

I pouted like a kid. "I know, Daddy. It's just so many things at once."

"Hopefully some Christmas in the future you can spend it with us. Right now, be with your mom. You both need this time together."

"It'll be all right."

"Just all right?" He smiled.

"No, better than all right," I said, self-assured and more determined than ever to show my mother that love existed in many forms, like the way it once did with her and my father, with Yvonne and Byron, and now with me and Asia.

"I'll be thinking about you," he said with a kiss to my hand.

"I'll be thinking about you too. You better call me."

He shook the top of my head like I was a little girl. "Come on, Kyla, you know better."

***

"This is where I attended grade school, middle school and high school." I slowed my mom's Taurus for Asia to view the three buildings that took up a square mile of the small suburban community where I grew up.

We had spent the afternoon driving around my hometown after I'd picked her up from the morning flight we'd booked a few weeks back. We stopped on Lake Drive, taking a moment to park and watch the ice-tipped waves attempt to travel to shore. We lunched at a well-known gay restaurant, following a tour of the downtown area, admiring the many renovations and developments of condominiums that were new to me also.

We hugged. We kissed. We reconnected after the brief time we'd spent apart.

"Right around this corner," I said, pointing forward, "is home."

I carefully pulled into the drive and pressed the button attached to the visor to open the garage.

"Lovely house," Asia commented.

Three and a half months into our relationship, after evenings sharing take-out in Asia's apartment, hovering in conversation with David and Marlon over coffee, and countless nights of

lovemaking, I was about to formally introduce
Asia as the woman in my life, a monumental step
in my adulthood.

Asia and I gave each other a this-is-it look as we
walked through the garage door into the kitchen.
My mom was busy inside making homemade
eggnog when we walked in.

"We're here," I said.

For someone who would be spending the
day preparing Christmas dinner, cleaning and
decorating her home for guests, my mom had
put extra effort into her appearance. Still looking
fabulous in her early fifties, she was wearing
maroon slacks and a cream sweater, her face full
of makeup, and her hair smoothly pulled back
into a bun. Her intent to look put-together for
Asia was obvious. Even her favorite apron hung
on its hook against the storage cabinet, a place it
rarely visited, considering how much she loved
cooking in her kitchen.

I gave my mom a tight hug, and when she
released me, I said, "Mom, this is Asia." I turned
to Asia's smiling face.

"Hello, Ms. Thomas. It's very nice to meet
you," Asia said, extending her hand.

After the swiftest, almost inconspicuous once-
over, my mother took Asia's hand in hers and
squeezed. Yielding to Asia's seducing charm,

she sighed a sweet concession and then smiled. Whether it was Asia's irresistible aura, or the sentimental outpour of feelings shared when my mom had crept into my room the previous night, whatever it was, her welcoming arms accepted Asia into her life.

Just as I was falling asleep the night before, my mother had told me, "I love you, Kyla. There's nothing you could ever do that will ever change that."

"I love you too, Ma. You have to know that none of this was done to hurt you. I had to follow what my heart was telling me."

"I know, baby. I know you wouldn't make the decision without believing you were doing the best thing for you. I wish I had been more supportive to you, Kyla, but it took a while for me to adjust. Just know that I'm here for you now."

I smiled. "Asia's made this whole journey worth it."

"If she makes you happy, then that's all that matters."

An overwhelming sense of serenity soared through my body, my eyes brimming with appreciative tears. Nearly three years of turbulent emotions of worry, abandonment, confusion, and lack of understanding between my mother and I flew out of the window in a moment's time, and for that, I was so grateful.

She rubbed her fingers against my face and stroked my skin, humming a song until I fell asleep, just as she did when I was a child.

The kitchen was scattered with cooking items and utensils. "You need some help?" I asked

"I got this in here just fine, but sit down and talk to me for a while," Mom said, gesturing toward the sitting area.

Asia and I took seats at the oval table and watched my mother add various ingredients into a mixing bowl.

"You had a good flight, Asia?" Ma asked.

"Yes, thank you, it was nice. Next to me was this nice woman coming into town to visit her children for the holiday, and I was telling her this was my first visit to the city. Aside from the winter snow, she had the nicest things to say about Milwaukee. She said the summers are pretty nice."

"Oh, yes, they are," my mom said, agreeing with Asia's flight mate. "There are all sorts of things to do around here. Festivals at the lake and concerts in the park. One summer Kyla took me to an outdoor jazz picnic, and we had such a good time, didn't we, Kyla?"

"Yes, we sure did," I answered, recalling the sweltering day my mom and I sat on a blanket drinking wine and munching on cheese and crackers and listening to the tunes of a smooth jazz band.

"You'll have to come back in the summer." Ma smiled.

Asia and I exchanged soft looks between one another.

"Definitely."

We continued with small talk, my mom asking about Asia's family, job, and hobbies. My mom was surprised when Asia mentioned that one of her favorite ways to unwind was knitting small quilts.

"Is that so?"

"Yes. I actually made one for baby Gladyce as a Christmas gift. I hope Yvonne likes it."

"Asia, that was so sweet of you." Ma walked to Asia and give her a quick rub on her shoulder.

"Thank you. I sent one home to my mom too. She said she likes to lounge around the house with one wrapped around her shoulders."

"Precious . . . just precious. I think the last gift Kyla made for me was a warped pottery cup in the third grade." She laughed.

"Oh my God! Mom used that as the candy dish for years!"

"I still have it somewhere." She began looking through the cabinets.

"No, no, that's okay. I'm not as talented with my hands as Asia."

My mind wandered to Asia's fingers and the phenomenally skillful ways they pleased my body. Just sitting there and observing her fingers clasped together in her lap turned me on.

"Well, girls," my mom began, linking us together as she always did with Yvonne and I, "you two can go ahead and start working on the decorations."

"Will do," I said, giving my mother a quick peck to her cheek.

Grabbing hold of Asia's hand, I led her from the kitchen, once turning around to my mom, whose eyes were focused on the firm clasp of Asia's hand in mine. When our eyes met, once again, unspoken words conveyed silent messages of mutual respect and support.

Late that night, after the gifts had been wrapped, the last piece of garland was hung, and a dozen batches of cookies were baked, I lay comfortably wrapped around Asia's body in our dimly lit hotel suite while she played in my hair. We opted to stay in a hotel room instead of my mom's house, out of respect. We wanted to spend intimate time with one another and didn't want to stretch my mom's acceptance too greatly.

"One down, four to go," Asia said, referring to the number of days before Jeff's wedding.

"I'm not even worried about that anymore."

"No? What brought on this newfound confidence?"

I let them go, I thought to myself, reminiscing about the therapeutic dream I had. "I really needed to take this trip home. Had I known confronting my fears would have eased the relationship with my mom, I wouldn't have waited so long to come back. I feel like I can conquer the world now."

"Good. 'Cause I'm taking you home next," she said, twirling my hair around her finger.

I blushed. "You are, are you?"

"Yeah, girl, you're not the only person who wants to show off."

"Oh, is that what I'm doing?"

"Yup. You know they don't make women like me in the Midwest." Asia laughed. "Besides you, of course." She kissed my heated skin.

"You better fix that." I turned over quickly to pin her underneath me. Leaning forward, I took one of her nipples between my teeth.

"Don't start something you can't finish."

"I know. Who told your period to come?"

"Stop pouting. It'll be gone by Saturday. Then I'll let you have some, if you're good."

"Okay. But in the meantime . . ." I slipped out of my cotton pajama bottoms.

Asia grinned. "I got the hint." She adjusted her head comfortably on the pillow.

My fingers gripped the headboard as Asia took hold of my waist and, from underneath me, guided my hips to her waiting lips.

Once word traveled that cousin Kyla, niece Kyla, or Gladyce and Richard's daughter had brought home her lesbian girlfriend from Atlanta, my mom's home was inhabited with a constant stream of relatives and friends that normally weren't visitors on Christmas. Second cousins, Jennifer and Jeremy, a rowdy set of twenty-one-year-old twins, followed Asia and I around as if we were a scientific experiment, asking questions, analyzing our responses, and conjuring up a follow-up hypothesis for our review, confirmation, or dismissal.

"Asia, did you date men before Kyla?" Jeremy asked, somewhat hopeful, infatuated with Asia.

"Well, not right before Kyla, but a long time ago, yes."

They put their heads together and came to a swift resolve that all lesbians dated men before dating women. To be sure, they asked.

"No, that's not the case," I answered, even though many of the lesbians I knew had dated boys back in high school, if only to appease a parent. "Some lesbians have never dated men."

"Have you ever been cheated on by a woman, Asia?" Jenny asked.

Asia's eyes grew twice their size. "Why do you ask that?" She attempted to conceal her annoyance.

Jenny rolled her eyes in her brother's direction. "Just curious if girls cheat the way so many men do."

Asia looked at me like, Get these two the hell away from me.

"Yes, women cheat too," I answered.

"Really?" Jeremy asked. "All women?"

"No, not all women, but if you mean, Do straight and gay women cheat? yes, some of them do."

"So that means women don't date women just to get away from cheating men? I mean, women who used to date men go to women because their man cheated on them, right? At least that's what one of my roommates told me."

I prayed I didn't say shit this stupid to Stephanie. "No."

Again, they put their heads together.

"Right, right," Jeremy said. "Jeff didn't cheat on you, did he?"

I gave them both my best squinted evil eye and didn't answer the question.

"Okay," Jenny said. "Well, Asia, are you from Atlanta?"

Asia sighed. "No, I'm from Dallas."

After learning that Asia was originally from Texas, they then determined that Atlanta was the lesbian capital of the country and that all gay women must flee their hometowns to a safe haven called Atlanta.

"Excuse us," I said, taking Asia by the waist and leading her to the kitchen for a wine refill. I nearly tripped over the feet of Justine, the fearless twins' mom. She may have been the instigator, since she did little to prevent the interrogation as she sat on the couch surveying the entire exchange.

Aunt Minny, estranged cousin to my mother, was as vulgar and ferocious as they come. Even as we devoured our individual heaping plates of my mom's cooking, Aunt Minny yelled across three heads and across the table, "So just what is it that lesbians do?"

Our attempt at laughing off her inappropriate question didn't put an end to the topic either.

"I need muscle!" she howled. "I need strength! I need somebody to hit it from the front and the back, not some soft-ass titties against mine!" She took a sip from her flask.

"Minny! That's enough," my mother insisted.

Finally I understood why Aunt Minny was seldom invited to family gatherings.

Seeking temporary escape from the insanity soaring through the household, I crept into the bathroom just outside the staircase leading to the second level. With my eyes closed, I leaned against the sink for a breather.

Arms around my waist and a light grind from behind brought a sensuous smile to my face. Responding to the delightful touch, I swerved my hips against the body pressed into mine and reached to caress the hand that was seductively ready to grab me between my legs. Noticing the thickness of the flesh behind me and the decorated, claw-like nails on the fingers of the hand attempting to molest me, my eyes shots open. Lustful eyes and a devious smile peered through the mirror, smugly admiring the hand approaching my crotch.

"What the fuck?" I growled, impulsively jamming my elbow into Shanice's plump belly.

Shanice, Aunt Minny's twice-divorced daughter and mother of five, had inherited her mother's crassness, but apparently not her heterosexual integrity.

Heaved over, she gasped for air. "We're-second-cousins," she explained between breaths.

"Second cousins, my ass!" I stepped past her, leaving her to regain a steady flow of air on her own.

Had there not been a brighter side to the eventful day, I may have been on the edge of insanity after the meeting with my incest-driven cousin. Catrina, David's sister and the closest of my cousins, next to David, treated Asia like they had known each other a lifetime, even introducing her to Brianna, her eleven-year-old daughter, as "Auntie Asia."

"You're pretty," Brianna sweetly told Asia.

"So are you, little lady."

Brianna leaned into her mom's waist and blushed. Having David as a brother and an uncle to Brianna, Catrina was most gracious in understanding the bridges Asia and I were attempting to cross that day.

On more than one occasion, John, Catrina's husband of fifteen years, cleverly intervened with witty comebacks when Aunt Minny's incessant inquiries of the details of lesbian bedroom activities would not cease. "You must want a little bit, Miss Minny," he'd said, "since you keep talking about it."

When he noticed Shanice trailing several seconds behind me from the bathroom, short of breath and wincing in pain, his eyes gleamed with laughter.

Yvonne and Byron were awed by Asia's good-natured personality, laughing and chatting with her about some of my and Yvonne's childhood stories, and taking helpful nursing tips from Asia about sleeping habits for baby Gladyce.

I was tickled pink when Yvonne passed baby Gladyce to Asia's arms within minutes of meeting. To me she whispered, "Let Asia hold the baby, Ky." It was the most pleasant insult I had ever received.

Asia took that opportunity to meet many of my other family members as they all gathered around baby Gladyce to admire her red velvet dress with matching elastic bow around her tiny, almost-bald head. She eyed each new stranger cautiously, and soon tired of the attention and wailed for her parents.

Aunt Shari, just as impressed with Asia's smooth integration into the family, took me aside to hug and congratulate me on finding someone whose love for me shined with each endearing smile she sent my way. Trapped in her embrace, my head nestled in her double D bosom, I temporarily lost the ability to inhale and exhale. But what a fine way to suffocate, by the loving squeeze of a relative.

By far, the most treasured moment came when Asia and I exchanged gifts in the midst of family members, just after Yvonne and Byron opened their presents from each other.

Sitting on the edge of the chair in which Aunt Shari sat, my mom proudly announced, "Asia and Kyla," as if daring Aunt Minny or any of the other nosy, intrusive relatives to protest our open relationship.

Just three short winters ago, I had sat in the same living room, aching in pain, yet drowning in love by the man who'd asked for my hand in marriage. Prior to that occasion, never had I imagined that in terms of the length of a lifetime, would I, such a short time later, be in the same room, thanking the lady love of my life for the much-needed Coach briefcase, whose fresh leather scent permeated the air.

"I love it," I said, giving her a brief hug after I sifted the compartments of the case.

In exchange, I granted her with a cashmere sweater in pale pink, a softer shade of a similar burnt orange sweater she had admired in my closet just a month before.

"Now we can be twins." She giggled.

"That would be cute. I used to dress Kyla and Yvonne like twins," my mom reminisced.

"Don't worry, Asia's just playing," I said, before my mom could ask me to send her pictures of Asia and I dressed alike.

The rest of the gifts were exchanged for those guests with presents, with most gifts given to baby Gladyce. Yvonne and Byron were stunned that Asia had taken the time to make a quilt for her, thanking her repeatedly for her thoughtfulness.

I hadn't been able to wait until Christmas to give my niece all of the pink clothing items and baby toys I had purchased for her before work, during lunch, and again on my way out of the store on so many days.

Later, as candles fluttered in their last breaths and wine buzzes fizzled, the atmosphere quieted as we relaxed and enjoyed an encore presentation of It's a Wonderful Life—always the uplifting reminder that a life trial is supreme to no life at all.

It reminded me of a story David had shared with me many years earlier about a friend of his who caved during his coming out process. His friend's family had immediately banished him, damning him to hell for his desire to love another man. Without the support of his mother and father, he felt no will to live and took his own life by way of three bottles of over-the-counter pills. I wondered what would have become of the man if only he had realized that it does get better.

Throughout the movie, undetected caresses were stolen while Asia and I settled under the fleece blanket on the loveseat. A small river of tears escaped when George and Mary were blessed with the generosity of friends and towns-people. Did I use to cry this much? Perhaps my tears were a release of the tidal wave of emotions I felt throughout the day.

"Aww, babe." Asia quietly kissed my finger-tips, salty from wiping my eyes.

My mom watched the public display of affec-tion with fondness, afterward turning her head upward to the ceiling and closing her eyes, as if deleting all previously held freeze-frames of Jeff and I and storing this visual memory in a new file in her head.

Aside from the mendable pricks and thorns throughout the day, in my favorite dreams I couldn't have asked for a better first Christmas with Asia. A small group of determined tears rolled through my already damp mascara and fell onto Asia's hand.

Looking at me, her own eyes colored red and wet, she rubbed the tear until it absorbed into her skin, a symbolic gesture that my tears were her tears, and what I felt, she felt as well.

We were, after all, a merging of two souls into one perfect union.

CHAPTER 7

Letting Go

Damn, Kyla! How cold does it get up here?" Asia shrieked as frosty wind bit our cheeks while we ran from our rented Cadillac STS toward the hotel revolving door after grabbing a fast-food breakfast nearby.

The rented sparkling silver sedan was our attempt to travel to and from Jeff 's wedding in style. My dad's fiancée, Evelyn, who attended church with a woman whose sister's friend worked for the Smarczyk enterprise, informed us that she heard Jeff and Julie's wedding was going to be a sophisticated affair, attended by the wealthiest who's who in the city.

The night before, while Asia and I dined at Evelyn's with my dad, I learned that she, just like my mom, was a woman devoted to her kitchen. Only days after Christmas with a refrigerator filled with a variety of tightly sealed containers of leftovers, Evelyn still insisted upon whipping up a fresh feast for her soon-to-be daughter-in-law and new girlfriend.

When Asia and I offered to wash dishes and clean, she politely declined, stating the kitchen was her home within her home. My dad chuckled at her words, and winced just slightly when he caught sight of the sly, but curious smile across my lips.

Fit and fabulous in her fifties, Evelyn was another version of Gladyce. So if that's what he wanted, why part from my mother in the first place? Yet, Evelyn was the one sporting the new diamond engagement ring from my dad, instead of my mom wearing a thirty-year anniversary band.

In addition to her homemaking talents, Evelyn was warm, kind, and gracious toward both Asia and me. What I especially appreciated was not once did the topic of sexuality arise. She simply talked to us as human beings, not as some science experiment that needed solving, or sinners that needed repentance. She spoke with sincere interest, wanting to know what Asia did for a living, how I enjoyed being a "big sister," if Asia knew a relative of hers in Dallas, and where I bought the designer jeans I was wearing. She showed us pictures of her sons and grandchildren and informed us that one of her sons was considering a move to Atlanta. She also said she may have to call upon us for information about places to visit and things to do in the city.

The interaction between Evelyn and my dad was sweet and affectionate. She fixed his plate for him; he held out her chair before she sat at the table. He poured her glasses of wine, while she made sure he had continuous warm servings on his plate.

Over dinner they shared the story of how they'd met through a girlfriend of Evelyn's that met my dad at an annual charitable golf outing. The friend asked my father for his business card and promptly delivered it to Evelyn, stating she must call him, that he would be perfect to end her dry dating spell. Old-school and not one to pursue, Evelyn declined.

In response, the friend called my dad and asked if he could meet her for lunch to discuss my dad sitting on the board of the charity organization for which the golf outing was held. When my dad went through the interview process to join the board, he met Evelyn, the board's vice president.

After the interview, Evelyn called her friend and thanked her for the referral, saying that the man she interviewed was so handsome. The friend, also the board secretary, informed Evelyn that the handsome man was the one from the golf outing that she wanted her to meet. Evelyn stated that she felt it would be inappropriate as board vice president to entertain its newest member, although it wasn't specifically forbidden by the board's guidelines.

Evelyn stepped outside her comfort zone and when she called my dad for another meeting to discuss his membership, she told him about her friend's previous suggestion that they connect for a date. My dad, who found Evelyn attractive as well, was in agreement.

"What do you think about that?" my dad had asked smoothly.

"Well, had I met you before the interview, I would have said yes," Evelyn had responded to him. "However, if you become a board member, I'm afraid I'd have to decline."

"Let's fix that. I withdraw my application," my dad told her, and they went out for dinner the following evening.

At the end of sharing their story, they kissed lightly on the lips and smiled at one another. Asia and I grinned. I felt happy that my dad had found such a complementary companion.

It was ten a.m., and Asia and I were dangerously close to a tardy arrival for the 11:30 ceremony. Who in the hell gets married that early in the day? Oh, right, they do. I wondered if Jeff had to lecture the members of his family about being on time for the nuptials.

Laughing out loud, I pictured a stream of "CP Time" folks lined up outside the closed sanctuary doors, putting up a fuss about not being able to get inside to see their nephew, cousin, or friend get married. One thing I knew for sure, I didn't want to be one of them.

Inside the room I clicked the flat iron on for Asia and the curling iron for myself. Asia, who wasn't exactly the neatest person to room with, stripped out of her clothes, wrapped her hair, covered her head with a hotel shower cap, and jumped into the shower.

I picked up her clothes that had been left on the floor right where she stepped out of them. After I folded and put the jeans and sweatshirt in their proper places, a piece of paper slid from the unzipped top compartment onto the floor just as I was closing her suitcase. A familiar name written in Asia's loopy handwriting was jotted on the yellow Post-it note. Nictoria Townsend, with her address and phone number scribbled beneath it.

Tori? What in the hell did Asia want with Tori? Had they been talking? What about? ME? Asia knew how heartbroken I was at the end of the lifelong relationship with my childhood friend. Why would she go behind my back to talk to her?

I began to crumple the paper in my hand when the sound of water against the tub basin slowed and silenced. Quickly I smoothed the crinkles and placed the paper back where it had sailed from. A mounting wave of nausea rose from my stomach to my throat. Had we moved too quickly? Did I not know her as well as I thought I did?

"What's wrong, babe?" Asia asked as she entered the room, her skin sparkling from water droplets clinging to her body. Asia didn't believe in towel-drying. Instead, she opted to lay her naked body on the towel and allow air to cool her freshly bathed skin.

The sight of her sprawled across my bed, drips of water disappearing into her skin, nearly brought me to my knees the first time I witnessed the event. "Nothing."

"It doesn't look like nothing."

"No, I um, I thought I broke a nail, that's all," I lied. I thought I had left my lying days behind? But she was obviously lying to me or, at least, not telling me something.

Asia hesitated a moment before deciding she approved of my explanation. Sighing, she spread the white hotel towel on the bed and lay down. I thought for sure she peeked at her suitcase at the exact compartment where Tori's number was placed, but it could've been my paranoia that had me hallucinating.

"You better go shower," she urged.

Silently, I removed my clothes and entered the damp stall. Of all days, why did I have to find Asia untrustworthy on this one? Angrily I scrubbed my skin, hoping to temporarily wash away the combination of hurt and irritation I was feeling. Trying to figure out why Asia had Tori's number was like trying to figure out why the country was at war. There could be no justifiable, satisfying explanation. Whatever the reason, it had a high probability of fucking up my day, so I resolved to tuck the issue into the pending folder of my brain and address it later.

"Kyla," Asia said, tapping softly against the door.

I turned the water off and wrapped myself in a towel. "Yes." I cracked the door.

"I need to start on my hair," she responded, a concerned look in her eyes.

"Oh, right." I opened the door, allowing the steam to perform its disappearing act as it drifted above our heads.

With a firm hand against my belly and another at my waist, Asia halted my exit through the door. "You sure you're all right?"

An intimidating squint of her eyes had me taken aback. I gazed into her smoky, China doll eyes and nearly crumpled at their intensity.

Mixed with a desire to confront her and a wish to avoid her, I chose the wimpy route. "Is there anything I need to know?"

Asia's eyebrows furrowed, her halo floating away with the steam. "What is it? I don't want to play a guessing game."

I removed her hand as I eased past her and sat on the bed. "Can we talk about this later?"

"Talk about what later? You won't even tell me what it is."

I ignored her while I put lotion on my body.

Risking a run in her silky black pantyhose, Asia kneeled in front of me and took my hand in hers. "Kyla, sweetheart, why do you hold it all in? Don't you trust yourself with your own feelings? Whatever is bothering you, you'd rather pen it up all day and be upset? I don't understand that. Remember what I asked you that night at the Waffle House? I asked if you were ready for a relationship, and you said yes. Are you sure about that? I can't be with someone who won't be honest with me about how they feel and would rather keep their feelings bottled up instead of trusting me with what's going on in their mind. We've had a beautiful time here with your family, and now I feel like the progress we're making is all for nothing. This is silly, Kyla. It's obvious you're upset. So what is it?"

Shamefaced, I lowered my head. She was right. As usual, someone else was always right about my behavior. What sense did it make to keep all day what I had found hidden? Would I really be able to forget Tori's number in her suitcase? Would I be able to smile and share her as the love of my life, with a nagging concern of why my ex-best friend's address was stored in her luggage? What kind of woman was I if I couldn't confront my own concerns?

"Asia," I said slowly, lifting my head to meet her eyes, "why is Tori's number in your suitcase?"

Heavy silence loomed above us, distracted only by the murmur of air blowing through the heat vents. The frustrated grimace on Asia's face spoke volumes, and my mind was immediately filled with visions of late-night phone calls between the two of them, conspiring against me, pitchforks in hand, horns growing from their heads, as they laughed devious roars at me while my spirit weakened and melted away into the muddy soil of the hellhole they lived in.

"Kyla," Asia said, snapping me out of my frightening daydream, "do you honestly think I'd have her number in an effort to hurt you?"

My lack of a response revealed the embarrassing haste with which my trust in her had disappeared.

"This is fuckin' crazy," she murmured.

"What? You're mad now?"

Asia stared at the ceiling. "I understand why you're upset. I really do. But damn! What I don't understand is how little you think of me that you don't trust and respect me enough to even ask what's going on. That's bullshit, Kyla," she yelled.

"What am I supposed to think? You have my ex-best friend's number and address written down in your suitcase. You haven't told me you talked to her. You know what happened between us, and you expect me to be okay with you hiding this from me?"

Asia stood in front of me, hands on both hips, her stomach heaving underneath her control-top pantyhose. "Hell no, I don't expect you to be okay with the number. What I do expect is you not to think the worst of me. How do you think that makes me feel?"

"I'm sorry, Asia. You haven't given me a reason not to trust you. I just got scared, that's all."

"Okay, I understand that too, but that shit is going to get tired with me real quick, Kyla. You're always hiding behind fear. You think you're the only one who gets scared? You have to stand up to it and stop using it as your crutch. Especially if you expect to be with me. I can't have someone thinking negative shit about me. What have I done to make you think I don't have your best intentions at heart?"

Not a damn thing. Was I doomed to fuck up every good relationship I had?

I stood up and took her clenched jaw between the palms of my hands. "I do want this, Asia. I want this more than I've ever wanted anything. Please forgive me for not believing in you."

"You have to trust me."

"I will."

She brushed a light kiss against my lips and started for the bathroom to smooth her hair.

"Asia."

"Yes?"

"Um, aren't you forgetting something?"

A sly grin fluttered about the corners of her mouth. "What's that?" she asked, realizing I wasn't going to let her slide.

"You never answered the question."

"Damn, Kyla! Didn't I just say you have to trust me?" she asked sternly, but on the verge of laughter.

"Come on, Asia."

"Trust me, love," she sang and disappeared into the bathroom, closing the door so I couldn't ask another question.

Worry over the reason she had Tori's number slowly diminished as I allowed myself to abandon my insecurities and fully yield to my love for her. At the same time, I knew she'd better have an exceptional explanation for this shit.

The hole in my back and burning in my ears made me feel like my body temperature had risen ten degrees. My heart rate seemed to have doubled. Asia's clasp of my hand at my side caused my bodily organs to malfunction, as my stomach threatened to release violent waves of nausea on the oak wood pew. GET IT TOGETHER KYLA! DAMN! I screamed to myself the moment the congregation rose to celebrate the union of Mr. and Mrs. Jeffrey Terrence Oldham.

Were we being disrespectful or inappropriate in our hand-holding? Were Jeff 's parents cursing my mere presence and naked affection for a woman? Were the penetrating stares and inconspicuous whispers by Jeff 's cousins, aunts, and uncles deriving from shock, disgust, confusion, marvel, or admiration? Was Asia's intense grasp of my hand a proud proclamation of her role as the new love of my life, or the result of her own discomfort?

I felt as if I had been kicked in the stomach when the newly anointed couple strolled down the aisle and Jeff and I caught eyes for the first time in nearly three years. I could almost feel the tightening grip of his hand around Julie's in the same manner I nearly strangled Asia's palm, cutting off all circulation to her fingers.

A genuine look of surprise briefly cut through his still perfect smile and clouded his face. In a flash, his smile resumed, and he reclaimed his composed stance.

The walk to the rear of the church felt miles long. Shit. Why did he look surprised to see me? Was I not supposed to actually show up? Was my invitation to his wedding an act of retribution to show me that he found lasting love? Damn, didn't they receive my RSVP?

The heat waves from his family's side of the church were unbearable. Gradually, confused gawks turned into stares of recognition, timid waves of the hand, and nervous smiles.

Jeff's cousin, Coretta, whom I had spent a great amount of time chatting with at his holiday gatherings, was the first to break the ice and speak my name as Asia and I passed by the pew where she stood waiting her turn to greet the bride and groom.

Her excited eyes lingered on the grip I had of Asia's hand. She stepped forward. "How are you?" she asked after a brief embrace.

"Fine. Just fine," I squeaked. I cleared my throat to get rid of the anxiety my voice had so clearly revealed.

Coretta looked at Asia and then back at me.

"This here is, uh, Asia," I said.

In her easygoing, poised nature, Asia took hold of Coretta's hand with her free hand and shook it firmly. "Nice to meet you . . ." she said as a question, signaling that I hadn't mentioned Coretta's name.

"Coretta." Coretta looked to the floor.

Another one cast under Asia's spell. Line thrown, hooked, and reeled in, just from an introduction.

"See you both at the reception?"

"Yes," I responded.

"Good." She smiled. "We can talk more then."

As I approached the receiving line, I clutched my purse so tightly, I was sure to leave permanent fingerprints in the smooth leather.

Seven bouncy bridesmaids in burgundy dresses stood aligned, anxiously greeting each guest with an enthusiastic "Hello." They must have had a hell of a wedding coordinator and coach, all of them mimicking the same "Nice to meet you," as we shook hands down the line.

Fortunately, none of the faces was familiar, except for Kendra, the mother of Jeff's nephew, who, judging by the rock on her finger, had gone ahead and married his brother, Kent, despite their previous protest to such an occasion. Temporarily losing the Miss America stature each bridesmaid so graciously mastered, Kendra's face scrunched into a furious frown.

Damn, did Jeff tell anybody I was coming?

"H-hey, Kyla," she stammered, her eyes searching to meet Kent's farther down the row. Her struggle was apparent. Be kind to the lesbian ex-girlfriend of her husband's brother, or snub her for having the audacity to actually show her face at the joyous event?

Through her intense eyebrows, gentleness showed. Still, apprehensive and unsure what to do, she performed like most women do, suddenly pretending like something—anything—was more important than my presence in front of her.

I moved along after she began to concentrate on the ribbon around her bouquet, testing its durability by tightening the bow. Once I moved past, she politely greeted Asia.

A flowing veil adorned Julie's perfectly curled locks that hung well past her shoulders. Her flawless cream-colored skin glowed with tinted bronzer, and her blue-green eyes sparkled with glee with every greeting of "Congratulations." Puckered lips kissed the air when she embraced those who reached for her, an exaggerated "Mwah!" coming from her mouth.

Surely her fourth finger would break from the enormous diamond, which was at least twice the size of the diamond Jeff had offered me. No time for petty comparisons, Kyla, I thought, preparing myself for the introduction of my exfiancé's new bride.

"Congratulations," I said to her ecstatic smile. Baby-soft skin cupped my fingers delicately when I held out my hand.

"Thank you," she responded courteously.

After hurriedly cutting short his greeting with the talkative woman ahead of me, Jeff interjected in our conversation before it had hardly begun.

"Jules, this is Kyla," he said in the deep voice that used to coo sweet nothings in my ear.

I was stuck on "Jules." Jules? That was so . . . so My Best Friend's Wedding.

"Oh, Kyla," she said, literally taking a small step backward to give me a once-over.

Clearly feeling superior in this situation, with the ring, the dress, and the man, Jules leaned into the chest of her husband and clung for dear life. "We're so happy you could make it to OUR wedding."

The display of affection was amusing to me and did wonders to temporarily ease the jitters in my stomach.

Jeff accepted her snuggle and lightly kissed her forehead as I took my step in front of him. When I extended my hand for his, he tapped the back of it with his strong fingers.

"Don't even try it." He laughed and took me in his arms and squeezed tightly, planting a kiss on my forehead, just as he did with Julie.

Briefly I closed my eyes and relished in the gentle prickles left by his tapered five o'clock shadow.

"I wasn't sure if you'd really come," he said in my ear.

"Well, thanks for the invite," I whispered.

Perhaps the interaction lasted longer than I realized. When Jeff released me from his cradle, both Asia and Julie gawked incredulously in our direction.

Damn! It was just a hug. What did they expect? That we'd pretend we didn't know each other? Fix this, Kyla. Now!

I reached for Asia's waist and gathered her in my right arm. "Jeff, Julie, this is Asia." Should I have added my girlfriend to that, or was the hip-to-hip connection enough to convey who she was?

"It's very nice to meet you, Jeff, Julie," Asia replied to my introduction.

Julie stared at my hand resting on Asia's hipbone, and a satisfied grin surfaced on her lips. "Likewise."

Jeff put on charm thicker than honey, caressing Asia's hand in both of his. "So glad you could make it," he said, peering at her.

For once, the starstruck role seemed to reverse. Asia's brunette skin flushed a crimson hue, and she looked to the floor bashfully. I was slightly tickled by Asia's blushing face. Another part wondered why she was so taken. I mean, Jeff is a man. And she didn't like men.

Many weeks prior, on a quiet night while we watched a rented movie and ate stir-fry out of cartons with chopsticks, we agreed that neither she nor I felt the need to be with a man again. Ever. Neither of us was interested in being one of those lesbians that randomly slept with men here and there. At least, that's what she told me then.

Stop it, Kyla. Don't start distrusting her again. Hell, it could have been worse. They could have been yelling and screaming at each other, causing a ruckus the event. Thank goodness, they appear to like each other.

"See you both at the reception." Jeff smiled at both of us before moving on to the next guest in line.

"Kyla," Kent said.

Although his brother had moved on and was beginning a new life with someone else, I could feel Kent's bitterness. He didn't shake my hand. No "How are you?" or "Good to see you."

"Hi, Kent." I wasn't sure if I should say anything else or be just as frigid as he was, but I figured I'd give it a shot. "How are you?"

When he looked at me like I had just called his mama out of her name, I stiffened. The icy exchange hadn't gone without Jeff's notice.

"Come on, man." Jeff patted Kent's arm.

"I'm good. You?"

I could have said I had a massive brain tumor, five days to live, and my last dying wish was to see his brother get married, and I knew he wouldn't care. "I'm fine," I answered. "This is Asia." I tilted my head in her direction.

Asia almost looked paranoid, but Jeff eyed Kent once again and then sent Asia a soft smile.

She smiled back and appeared to relax. "Nice to meet you, Kent," she said.

Kent looked back and forth from me to Asia, shaking his head. "Yeah, likewise."

After that brief interaction, we were relieved to move on to the parents. Not like I gave a damn about Julie's hoitytoity mama and rich daddy.

What I most feared was the reaction of Mr. and Mrs. Oldham, my lovely "near in-laws." How did they feel about me now? After my breakup with Jeff, they were upset, to say the very least. With time, the anger subsided, and just prior to my move to Atlanta, Mrs. Oldham called to wish me well, assuring me it was best to allow time to learn about myself and experience life, rather than wind up in an unhappy marriage many years later. She wanted the best for her son, and if I couldn't be that to him, it was better that we both move on.

I wondered if she thought he'd found the best woman for him—a twenty-two-year-old recent college grad with no work history, no skills, other than organizing her walk-in closet, and a growing bank account, thanks to mom and dad. Who was I to talk though? During my stint as the woman in Jeff's life, I was a yet to be graduate, part-time employee in a department store.

A suffocating air of wealth engulfed my body when I approached the parents of the bride, Mr. and Mrs. Smarczyk. I wondered how a black woman felt about having the last name Smarczyk? I would've kept my maiden name.

"How do you do? Thank you for coming," Mrs. Smarczyk bellowed repeatedly to each guest in a deep, unflattering voice.

Bleached teeth as luminous as a midnight snowfall shined behind her burgundy colored lipstick. Taut skin, compliments of those weekly facials, crinkled only slightly at the corners of her eyes, giving the illusion of a much younger woman, perhaps one just a few years older than me. Not waiting nor desiring a response to her question, she didn't provide a chance for the guest to introduce himself or herself before moving on.

Not like I minded. I could just imagine telling her my name, and her recognizing it and booming to her husband, "Look, darling, this is Kyla, Jeff's gay ex-girlfriend. My, aren't we happy she's gay. Chuckle, chuckle."

Mr. Smarczyk was a bit more intimate, actually taking a brief moment to squeeze my hand upon shaking, as opposed to the short fingertip grasp from his wife. Maybe he had a thing for black women and was happy to be in a room full of them.

During my exchange with the Smarczyks, I could feel Mr. Oldham's eyes on me, carefully calculating and considering how to respond to our first encounter, his softhearted glance in my direction generating warmth.

"It's so good to see you," Mr. Oldham said with a quick hug.

An immediate lump in my throat surfaced as a result of his tender reception. "It's great to see you too."

"How have you been?"

"Wonderful. Thanks. And you?"

"Couldn't be better. Both my sons are settled down now. I'm feeling pretty good about that."

I wasn't sure how to respond.

Releasing me from his arms, he passed me on to his wife's open hands.

Taking mine in hers with a squeeze, she leaned forward and brushed my cheek with a light kiss. As she held my hands, she smiled generously at Asia. "You did the right thing," she said, keenly aware of the passion I felt for the woman at my side.

"Thank you," I replied humbly.

"See you later." She patted my hand. "You too my dear," she said to Asia.

As we walked through the glass doors of the church, pounds of anxiety and stress melted from my body like butter atop freshly popped popcorn.

"How are you doing?" Asia asked while we walked to the car.

"Relieved! But I think I should ask how you're doing, don't you think?"

Asia giggled and took hold of my hand. "At least now I know you have good taste in men and women."

"Yes, I do, or did rather."

"So what now? We don't have to be to the reception for a few hours."

"I know something we can do," I replied suggestively.

"Not after all that time I spent on my hair. Oh, hell no."

"What? I know we're not going through 'lesbian bed death' already, are we?"

"You know I can't resist you, sweetie. Just not right now. I need to look good later."

"Hmm, for who? Me? Or Jeff?" I laughed lightly.

Asia's expression hardened into a fiery scowl as we reached the car. "You better be playing with me, Kyla."

Damn. Why so defensive? "Yes, Asia, I was teasing. Don't get mad," I said when we both got into the car.

"Okay, I'm just making sure. I'm not thinking about your ex-man like that."

I muttered, "You could have fooled me."

"What was that?" she asked, fury dripping with each word.

"Well, you looked a bit flustered back there to me."

"So now you think I want to fuck you and your man?"

Now where in the hell was that shit coming from? "What are you talking about, Asia? And he's not my man."

"I don't like being accused of shit I'm not guilty of."

My remark had landed me in the middle of my first real argument with Asia, and a wicked side of her was emerging. "Asia, look," I said, leaning back into the cold leather interior, "I wasn't trying to upset you with what I said."

"You should've thought twice before opening your mouth then."

"I'm sorry," I said, trying again.

A sigh resembling a whimper slipped from Asia's lips, and she looked out of her window. "I wasn't lusting after your ex-fiancé, Kyla. For a moment I was overwhelmed by the fact that it was you that could have so easily been standing next to him. He's gorgeous, and he's charming, and I can see why you used to love him. It threw me off for a minute, Ky. I couldn't even look him in the eye, fearing I might see a bit of love he may still have for you. Maybe I overestimated my strength in this situation."

Shame on me for finding comfort in knowing I wasn't the only insecure one with an overactive imagination. For relishing in a moment in which Asia released her weaknesses. For finding joy that for once, even if only in my mind, I held the upper hand.

"I didn't know you felt that way, Asia. I should have been more careful with what I said."

Turning to me with glistening eyes, she asked, "Are you sure this is what you want, Kyla?"

Damn! How many times were we going to beat this horse? It was dead already. "Yes, Asia. I've said it before, and I'll say it again. This—you—you're what I want, no one else and nothing else."

"Really?"

We'd had this conversation three hours ago.

Rather than speak another word, I ran my fingers through her smooth hair and took hold of her chin. Kissing her quivering lips reminded me of the feminine vulnerability I craved and desired. Her captivating aura, combined with her statuesque beauty, lured me at first sight. Now, mixed with this tender, delicate element, I found myself fully drowning in the waves of her essence.

"You need not doubt from this moment forward that I'm dedicated to a life with you," I professed for the umpteenth time.

I vowed to myself to eliminate all actions that might contradict my commitment and love for her. I had found the ultimate love of my life and resolved to let go of my insecurities. A renewal of the confident Kyla was key to my relationship.

The drive back to the hotel was agonizingly long.

The stripping of each other's dresses from the doorway to the bed was intense. The fervor of our lovemaking sparked a raw, animalistic behavior in us, each seeking dominance and control of the other's body with fierce aggression, with nipples between teeth, fingernails carved into thighs, and the smacking of flesh.

Neither relenting to the other, we tussled for an hour, achieving multiple orgasms as we sat legs intertwined, grinding our hips together. As if orgasm conveyed submission, we took immediate control of the raging spasms and continued daring each other to come again. Resolving to an un-conquerable battle, we finally lay in streams of perspiration, a mixture of sweat, perfume, and femininity filling the air.

After the euphoric tidal waves had calmed, Asia groaned, "I don't even want to look in the mirror." Her silky straight strands turned kinky and clung like confetti against her face.

"Just wet it," I suggested.

"And then go out into this Arctic weather?"

"If you go real fast, you should have time to wash it. Hors d'oeuvres aren't until five."

"I'm getting you back for this." She smiled as she slowly rose from the bed, moving awkwardly from light muscle aches.

In less than two hours we were back on the road headed to the exquisite banquet hall downtown. Evelyn had told us that the lag between the morning ceremony and evening reception was because bridal party and closest family members would be spending the afternoon dining with the governor at a private country club and taking photos in the posh establishment.

Passing through the main street, Asia commented on the shining hanging wreaths attached to each light post, stating that it reminded her of a childhood trip to visit an elderly great-grandparent in Michigan.

"Y'all don't celebrate Christmas in Dallas?"

She looked at me sideways and laughed. "It's different up here. It's cold, and it snows. Sometimes it didn't really seem like Christmas when I was a kid because I'd watch all these TV specials with falling snow and people bundled up in winter coats, hats, and gloves. Then I'd look outside and people would be wearing spring jackets. It was confusing sometimes."

"Yeah, I suppose. It's different being in Atlanta and never having to think about a shovel or a snowblower."

"Never used one."

"You've never shoveled?" I asked, amazed by the thought.

"Nope. Why should I? I went from Texas to Georgia. Not a whole lot of snow happening in either place."

"So, what would you say if I wanted to move back up North?"

"Are you serious?" She searched my face for a sign of humor.

"What if?" I asked again, as poker-faced as possible.

"Hmph. We'll have to talk about that. I mean, I appreciate the beauty of a white Christmas and all, but I'm content to reminisce upon it fondly rather than live in it."

"Okay."

"One trip home and you're all ready to pack up and move back?"

"No, Asia, I was just asking. I have enough fond memories of home, but like you, I don't need to be here for it to hold a special place in my heart."

"So why did you ask?"

"I just wanted to know if you'd be willing to move with me, that's all," I said casually, sensing I was pissing her off.

"I'd probably be willing to do most anything for you, Kyla, but damn, two-month summers? That's rough."

"Don't worry. It would take a lot to get me back home," I said, recalling years of brutal winters. "I'm happy where I am. Sometimes I wish I wasn't so far from Yvonne, so I could be a better aunt. Not just an aunt who will send gifts from afar."

"Well, now that you've made the first trip back home, maybe it won't be so hard to come back more often."

"You're right. If I can make it through today, I can make it through anything."

"Yeah. And if our relationship can make it through today, we can make it through anything."

"We got this," I assured her. "It sure can't get any worse," I said, feeling we had survived three Mount Everest-size hurdles already.

"You had a life before me, Kyla, just as I had a life before you. I've just never experienced it firsthand and felt it the way I did today. But whatever happens inside there, I know that you're mine now." She nodded as we pulled up to the valet, alongside the Mercedes, Jaguars, and Volvos, Breathtaking in an egg-white floor-length silk gown with one shoulder strap decorated by small, beaded flowers that covered the butterfly tattoo on her back, Asia carefully exited the car. Her slender arms glowed with a light coating of bronze shimmer, illuminating random sparkles as we entered the ballroom and walked to our shared dining table.

Ivory-colored table covers were adorned with a foot-high heart-shaped vase filled with fresh red roses. Each setting contained a red dinner and salad plate, shining silverware, and a crystal flute. And a bottle of Piper-Heidsieck champagne sat on each side of the table. A velvet bag on each chair opened to reveal a personally engraved silver key chain, mine with a calligraphic K, Asia's with an A.

"Wow!" Asia whispered softly when we took our seats (at the ex-friend table, we later learned).

To my left were three childhood friends of Julie's. She had barely spoken a word to them, once she decided her biracial heritage put her two steps ahead of her darker-skinned companions, tossing them aside for a fresh set of running mates of equal hair length and fair skin.

Tanya, Gaylan, and Melinda each bandaged any unhealed wounds when they'd been gifted invitations to the highly anticipated nuptials of their "friend" and the older gentleman she'd snagged.

To Asia's right was Jason, a certified geek. His bowtie was so tightly wound around his neck, I prayed he wouldn't pass out from asphyxiation. A dependable obsession with Julie had earned him years of handholding her with homework, while she used him as an alibi for late-night arrivals home after high-school parties, saying she was studying with him.

Next to Jason were Ted and Tina, an older interracial couple that had returned to school in their forties and had the honor of sharing several courses with Jules. Not fortunate enough to bear children of their own, Julie soon took on the role as the child they never had, at least in their eyes.

Julie included them on the invite list, to avoid self-inflicted wounds and a spiral into depression.

Although outwardly well-groomed, it didn't take long to realize the couple would give their left arms and right feet to have Mr. and Mrs. Smarczyk killed, leaving Julie orphaned and in despair, seeking refuge in their arms.

A simultaneous round of "Oh!" circled the table when I answered the question of how I knew the married couple.

All eyes turned to Asia, questioning her presence. "I'm Asia, here to support Kyla," she said with a friendly pat to my shoulder.

"This is my girlfriend," I added coolly.

"Whaaaat?" Tanya, Gaylan, and Melinda questioned in unison, while Jason nearly did begin choking and gasping for air.

Ted and Tina were utterly dismayed by the announcement, suddenly calling to the tuxedo-dressed waiter assigned to our table, and ordering two double shots of scotch.

After the king-and-queen-style introduction and entrance of Jeff, Julie, and the wedding party, each table was delivered a fruit platter of grapes, watermelon, cantaloupe, strawberries, and pineapple, in addition to shrimp cocktail, individual Caesar salads, and bread so warm, it seemed to have just been removed from the oven.

As the tinkling of forks against glass interrupted the bride and groom's meal for light smooches in between bites, Asia and I attempted to control nausea from the endless babble between the three childhood castaways.

"Isn't Julie beautiful?"

"She's so lucky."

"I so envy her. She has it all now."

"I know. Isn't she just . . . fabulous?"

If I hadn't been chewing on probably the most tender filet mignon of my life, I would've gagged. Or even slapped one of them. When Julie's older sister, Erica, rose for the toast and spewed identical remarks in Julie's favor, I concluded that the sun did, in fact, rise and set at Julie's command. Ted and Tina's now bloodshot and glassy eyes gave way to tears of appreciation for Erica's well-spoken words.

During his toast to the couple, Kent threw a heart-shattering dagger when he praised Julie for being a "real" woman, who loved men and embraced the sanctity of traditional marriage. Could his resentment of me have been any more obvious? At any rate, I nodded and raised my glass in honor of Jeff and Julie with the rest of the crowd.

After plates were cleared, the four-tier cheese-cake was cut, andthe bride and groom shared their first dance to Taylor Dayne's "I'll Always Love You."

Asia and I observed the party under the glitzy disco ball and lights, tapping our feet against the floor and rapping painted fingernails on the table. The atmosphere grew lively when Jules and her MTV-generation friends, switching gears, requested the most frequently played song throughout all of 2003, "In Da Club" by 50 Cent, and turned up the volume. No Kelly Clarkson or Clay Aiken tunes drifted through the massive speakers.

Jules turned the elegant, swanky atmosphere straight hip-hop as she got low with Lil Jon and shook her tail feather with P. Diddy and Nelly. The scene was priceless. Asia and I watched black and white, young, old, and in-between, bounce left to right and up and down to the latest rap and R&B tracks.

Never failing to disappoint, Jeff proved he still had the moves as he and his new wife swayed side to side and against each other with the booming bass.

Finally we left our seats at the urging of the DJ, who called us out when we sat idle after all single women were summoned to the center of the dance floor. Under the twinkles of the flashing lights, Asia and I blended into the farthest corner away from Julie, fully anticipating the fall of the bouquet somewhere in the middle of the throng of women.

Edith, Jeff's unmarried, thirty-three-year-old, hard-up-for-a-man cousin, mercilessly toppled over two unsuspecting victims in her quest to retrieve the rose bouquet.

Just as the music started pumping again and I was in transit back to my table, a hand against my arm halted my steps. "Shall we?" Jeff asked, his other hand extended toward the floor.

I looked at Asia for an answer, and she smiled and walked back to the table alone.

Jeff's hand swallowed mine, a feeling I was no longer familiar with, as he guided me at his side. Falling into a natural rhythmic pace was easy, and I fondly recalled our Friday night ventures out to local nightclubs and dancing the night away. Surely, he dances the night away with Julie now. Stop it, Kyla. You both have new lives now.

Out of the corner of my eye I saw Coretta, who had taken a sideline seat at the edge of the dance floor, her head darting between Asia, me, Jeff, and Julie on the opposite side of the floor. In her imagination, she must have anticipated a snarling catfight between Julie and me, a jealous rage from Asia, or a rekindling kiss between me and Jeff. Surely none of the aforementioned would occur.

"How's Atlanta?" he yelled over the music, not losing his beat.

"I love it," I replied, trying to keep up.

"You seem happy."

"I am."

"She's beautiful."

I looked over at Asia, trapped in a conversation with Jason. They were the only two left at our table. Boredom filled her eyes, yet she smiled graciously. "Yes, she is," I responded. "You seem to be doing pretty well yourself."

"Jules is great. I couldn't be happier."

Both our attention turned to Julie, who, in a line with her friends, appeared to be mimicking choreographed moves from Beyonce's "Crazy in Love" video.

Before I could remark on the dancing, he commented, "She keeps me young at heart."

"As long as you're happy, Jeff, I'm happy for you."

"Me too, Kyla. Me too." He spun around in a 360 and faced me with a cocky grin.

Yeah, I know you still got it, Jeff.

We finished the remainder of the song as friends, former lovers, united on a day of celebration, each of us willing to let the past rest and wholeheartedly wishing the other well.

At the end of what would be our final good-bye, Jeff's satin lips rested on my cheek before breathing two velvety words into my ear. "Good-bye, Kyla."

"Good-bye, Jeff," I said, looking into his brown eyes for the last time. A warm smile concluded our grand finale as Jeff let go of my hand to take hold of his wife's.

I briskly walked to rescue Asia, cutting our evening short and leading her to the exit. My purpose had been completed. My life with Jeff was officially history, a finished chapter of my life. Pen in my hand, I was ready to stroke the paper with stories yet unfolded to write a new chapter.

***

The loud drone of the airplane swept many of the passengers into a comatose sleep, including Asia, who leaned her head against the closed window shade just moments after takeoff.

As I reached into my purse for my MP3 player, the movement of yellow stationery paper caught my eye. Opening the folded letter for the second time, I nestled under my shawl and re-read the letter that had been slipped under my hotel room door.

Dear Kyla,

Hey, girl, it's been a while, hasn't it? I'm doing well, and from what I hear, so are you. I have to say I was surprised to get a ring from your girl. When she called and told me you were in town, at first I wondered why in the hell she was telling me. Then she told me why you were here and asked if I'd be at Jeff's wedding too. I'm embarrassed to say I didn't get an invitation. The way I acted an ass back then, I'm not surprised and don't blame him for not sending me one. After what you did, knowing that you had the courage to face Jeff shocked me. I was sure you ran to hide in Atlanta, never to show your face around here again. How could a woman who left a

*fine-ass man for some chick redeem herself?
Yet, you did! I always knew, Kyla, even with
your indecisiveness with school and lack of
direction careerwise, that you would find the
one thing that defined you. I still can't believe
it's being a lesbian, but whatever rocks your
boat.*

*I'm saying all this to tell you that I wish I
hadn't treated you the way I did. I should have
been more supportive in what you were going
through. Don't get me wrong, girl, I'm not
saying I agree with female-female relationships, but after twenty years of friendship, I
shouldn't have left you hanging. You needed
someone, and I wasn't there for you. For that,
I'm sorry.*

*You take care of yourself in ATL. Asia
seems like cool peeps.*

*If you come back up north, stop by the
restaurant—drinks are on me.*

                                         Peace, Tori

P.S. Vanessa says hello.

Finally, I felt that all of the pieces to my
past had been put to rest. At last I could move
forward.

CHAPTER 8

What Shall Be Will Be

I had barely stepped foot into my apartment when my cell phone started ringing back to back. No time to lie down and reacquaint myself with my bed's down comforter. Not a moment to change into my pajamas, bundle up in front of the TV, and wind down from my rocky weekend. Not a second of quiet time to re-energize for my return to work.

"What's up, Nakia?" I answered, tired, but glad to hear from my friend. A loud groan, as if a beast were savagely eating away her flesh, greeted me on the other end.

"What's wrong?" I asked, startled by her disposition.

A duplicate moan repeated itself before she spoke. "I'm caught," she cried. "Huh?" "I'm caught!" she screamed. "Fred Jr. showed up at the house while Shanna was over. When I didn't answer the door, he used his key."

"What did he see?"

"He saw my big ass sprawled on the bed with Shanna's head between my legs, that's what he saw."

Damn! "Kia, I'm sorry. What happened?"

"He yelled something and ran out of the house."

"Did you go after him?"

"Hell no! I was too ashamed. Then I kicked Shanna out and haven't talked to her since."

This conversation required face-to-face contact. "Do you want to come over?"

She thought for a moment and then declined my invitation.

"Did he tell Fred Sr.?"

"I'm sure he has. He's been blowing up my phone, but I've been ignoring the phone since this happened on Friday. I can never face him again. I called in sick yesterday and today, just in case he showed up at work." She started to cry.

"Don't say that, Kia," I said in a soothing voice. "You don't have anything to be ashamed of. You discovered a new part of yourself, and there's nothing wrong with that."

"Well, you go tell your ex-husband you like eating out better than sucking dick."

Didn't ex-fiancés count?

"Oh, I'm sorry, Kyla."

She must have read my mind. "That's all right," I said. "But, really, face it, that's what you're going to have to do. You're going to have to fess up now or later."

"I just can't believe this shit."

"If you want me there with you, I'll go. I wouldn't desert you at a time like this," I said, recalling Tori's letter.

"You know they're going to think you turned me out."

"It wasn't my face between your legs," I replied, worried that Fred Sr. would think I had something to do with Nakia's discovery. Okay, well, so I did help her with the ad, but she brought her desires to me on her own. Would I have to take responsibility for that?

"I know. What should I do about Shanna? I like her so much."

"Then call her," I urged. "You might have found something good in being with her. Did you do anything besides have sex?"

"We talked a lot. I wasn't trying to go anywhere with her though, so we spent all the time at my house. That's about it."

"You make it sound like you would be outed just by being in public with her. That's probably not the case, Kia. What are you scared of?"

"People recognizing her and then thinking we're together."

"One, just because you're with a gay woman doesn't make you gay. And, two, how many times have we been out together? You never seemed uncomfortable."

"I know. But my interaction with Shanna could make it obvious. Don't tell me you've never been able to tell if two women are a couple just by the way they look at and joke with each other."

I considered the times I had been in public with a love interest and the lustful eye contact we'd share across the clothing rack while shopping or the way we leaned against one another while standing in line. "I guess you have a point," I said, trying my hardest to be understanding that she wanted to remain in the closet at this point. "Anyway, tell me more about Shanna. I already know she's got wonderful lovemaking practices, but tell me more about her."

"She's a teacher."

"A teacher?" I couldn't believe "Lickemlo" was aiding in the education of our children.

"Yes, a second grade teacher. Never married with an eighteen-year-old daughter at Spelman."

"For real?"

"For real."

"Damn! Maybe I should have tried hooking up with someone on the net before."

"Maybe not. Shanna's been meeting people through the Internet for a long time and told me some crazy-ass stories. One time she was getting kind of serious with this woman, hanging out, going to dinner, plays, shopping. You name it, they did it. Girl, one day Shanna went with a friend to this stud's house to chill for a while—"

"Look at you," I said, "Got the terminology down already."

"Whatever, Ky. I've been hanging with you for how long? Anyway, guess who strolls in singing, 'Baby, I'm home,' carrying some fish dinners? Shanna's girl. Shanna said the girl played it so cool like she didn't know her, never even seen her before. They all sat around with Shanna asking a million questions about them, and the whole time this girl was cuddled and snuggled up on the stud's lap. Come to find out, they had been together seven years, bought a house together, and were planning on having a baby. All the while this girl had a personal ad on the net and was fuckin' around with Shanna. Shanna kept her cool. Said she'll never fight over a woman or do anything to mess up her teaching career."

"Still, she could have busted the girl out at least," I said, unsure if I would have been able to remain as calm.

"Girl, yeah. I don't think I could have sat there the way she did." "Damn! That's crazy, Kia. That didn't scare her from meeting people online?"

"I thought the same thing. She doesn't club, and her friends never hook her up with a good match, so when she's done preparing projects for little seven-year olds, she chats online and meets people."

"So what did she like about your ad?"

Nakia giggled. "That I'm a first-timer. Said she wanted to make sure I had it done to me right."

"From what I can tell, you did."

"Yeah, I did. I'm really diggin' her, Ky. I need to figure out what to do about Fred Sr."

"Tell him," I suggested.

"You think he'll still let me see Fred Jr.?"

"I hope so. Call him and tell him you need to talk. If you want me to join you, I will."

"Cool. I'll do that. Hey, thanks for listening. See you tomorrow?"

"Yeah, if you bring your ass to work."

She laughed. A kitten's purr compared to her usual roar. Well, at least she tried.

"I'll be there."

"Okay."

"So you know," she added, "I'm calling Shanna right after I call Fred."

"Good. She's probably been sitting by the phone waiting." I was pleased with her emerging confidence.

"Say, Kyla, I'm sorry. How was the trip home?"

"It was, um"—I searched for the right word— "it was healing," I said with a smile and hung up.

Judy, a junior assistant buyer, stood next to me in the elevator as it rose to the third-level offices. She was the queen bee of investigation, with the keen ears of a bat and the fast lips of an auctioneer. If an employee was unclear of a new company policy, Judy could clarify. If there was a hint that someone might be let go, she knew who, and when the release would take place. If a job opening or promotion would soon take place, she was privy to all the details. Hyperactive as most busybodies were, Judy had practically pounced on me when I stepped onto the elevator. Her voice could near shatter glass with its squeaky tone and fast-paced outpouring of words.

"Hey, Kyla. Welcome back," she screeched just after the doors closed.

"Hey, Judy. How's it going?"

"Last week was crazy! Just crazy! Probably one of the busiest seasons I've ever seen. It was a madhouse downstairs. Josh, manager over boys, almost quit. Sue, Ashley's temp, walked out. And Amy was so busy with all her new work, she obviously proved worthy of a promotion," she said, barely able to contain her excitement.

Our mirrored reflections vanished when the elevator doors parted and opened. LALA promoted? What happened while I was gone?

Judy walked next to me, grinning, holding her breath and waiting for me to ask my next question. Her lips were pursed into a tight smirk, as if all the words were trapped inside, anxiously awaiting their escape through her clenched teeth.

"I'll see you later," I said, leaving her with no earhole to spill in. Rapidly I headed to my office, passing an empty desk where LALA should have been sitting, pretending to work. I set my belongings down, hung up my parka on the hanger behind the door, and sat behind my desk. Just as I reached to turn on the computer, I found a yellow Post-it note on the monitor.

Welcome back—settle in, then come see me. Gary. Without turning on my computer or checking my messages, I went directly to Gary's office, not worried about the changes that had taken place while I was gone, but most curious to know why I wasn't given a heads-up.

Gary motioned for me to enter while he wrapped up a phone call.

"How's my girl?" he asked excitedly.

"I'm doing great, Gary," I answered, standing before his desk, my arms folded across my chest.

Gary sensed my agitation. "Well, I guess you already heard," he started slowly. "There's no need to stand in front of me like you're about to attack me for what I'm about to say without knowing what it is first."

I was silent.

"An opportunity suddenly opened up that we needed to move quickly on. Amy expressed an interest, so we gave it to her."

"What in the hell happened that you didn't already know about two weeks ago?" I asked, finally taking a seat.

"It's confidential."

"Who's gone?"

"Martha."

Martha was a junior buyer over women's fragrances.

"Why?"

"I can't talk about it. Really. You know I would tell you if I could."

Office politics everywhere—the less you're informed, the better they figure you'll perform. If employees knew every messy detail that went on behind the scenes, they'd surely quit and find employment elsewhere, only to encounter the same "don't ask, we won't tell" policy and become frustrated all over again.

"Your job is secure, Kyla. I don't understand why you seem so agitated."

"I'm not agitated, Gary. Don't get me wrong, I'm happy for Amy. She's even luckier than I thought! What I want to know is why I wasn't made aware of the situation." Now Gary was silent.

"Okay then," I said, realizing he wasn't about to fess up. "What about a new assistant for me? Did anybody help out while I was gone?"

"Amy did everything you asked of her. Very well, I might add. And your assistant, well, that's already taken care of," he said slyly.

"Why are you smirking like that?"

Gary buzzed his secretary. "Becky, uh, has Andrea arrived yet?"

"She just got here, Gary. She's in the waiting area."

"Send for her." He then winked at me. Seconds later, knee-high patent leather boots, and fishnet stockings covering cinnamon skin circled the corner and walked through the door. A black dress with a silver linked chain belt the size of bracelets accentuated the small waist of her petite body. A pendant of some sort was lost between her protruding bustline that sparkled under a shimmer lotion. Dangling silver earrings hung underneath layers of thick, brunette hair with intense blonde highlights. Dark brown eyes were hidden behind coats of black eyeliner and mascara. A small beauty mark above her lip led to a wide mouth and sensuous lips colored in brick-red gloss. On her slender fingers she wore three rings on each hand, and her long nails were colored a deep, earth brown. Andrea, a fusion of beautiful Hispanic features and a fierce, dark exterior, stood in front of Gary's desk and waited for his introduction.

"Andrea," he said, standing and bringing her to me as if she were my belated Christmas gift, "This is Kyla. She's the buyer you'll be working for."

"Nice to meet you, Andrea," I said in turn, and shook her warm hand.

"Ahn-drrray-uh," she corrected in a heavy Spanish accent and a clack of her tongue piercing as she rolled the r when she spoke. "It is a pleasure to meet you, Kyla."

I winced, repeating the sounds she had just spoken in my head in an attempt to interpret what she had said.

"Ready to show her the ropes, Kyla?" Gary asked with a suggestive undertone only I understood.

"See you later, Gary," I said walking out, allowing "Ahndrrray-uh" to go ahead of me. I turned back to Gary to find him transfixed on Andrea's legs, lost in a brief fantasy world. A few whispers and a couple of impolite stares followed us as I walked Andrea to her desk.

"Why don't you put your things here and then come into my office."

Andrea stood motionless. "I don't understand." She had a perplexed look on her face. "Should I or should I not put my belongings here?"

Great. Just great. "Um, put your purse in the desk and then come sit here." I pointed to the chair in front of my desk through the glass window.

Silently I cursed Gary's perverted nature and waited for Andrea to take her seat. Just a moment passed before she came inside, pen and pad of paper in hand. She crossed her legs after she sat down and stared at me with intent eyes. Beneath the thick eye makeup, I could see that she was young, perhaps twenty-four.

"So let me tell you about myself."

"Ah, no need. Gary told me all about you." She smiled.

"He did? Well now, what did he say?"

"Yes, he says you are one of the best buyers here. You do your job well. Um, you are not demanding and easy to work for. He says I can learn from you a lot."

Such flattery. "Okay, well, why don't you—I mean, tell me about yourself."

"Sí. Okay. I'm Ahn-dray-uh," she told me again. "I moved here from Mexico six years ago after I graduated. Parts of mi familia were already here. I worked at Rich's part-time for last four years. I was referred by Matt from my old store, who is a friend to Gary. Matt said I was prepared to move to the next place, but because there was nowhere for me to go, he let Gary have me. And now you have me," she said brightly, displaying a sunny personality behind the dark appearance.

Scary she was not. Even with her severe coating, I detected a raging sensuality—the way she licked and bit her bottom lip while she searched for the next proper word—the gentle way she stroked the skin leading to her bosom while she spoke—the way her eyes bore into mine as if at tempting to extract my every thought before the words left my lips. If her interaction with Gary was similar to her interaction with me, I understood why he hired her on the spot.

"I think I will like working for you," she concluded with a penetrating stare into my eyes.

I shifted in my seat. "Yes, I'm sure we'll get along just fine."

Andrea and I worked together in my office throughout the morning, and I quickly realized that Gary did indeed find an exceptional assistant. She paid attention to every word I said and asked questions as needed. She was mindful of detail and visibly organized. And her positive disposition was refreshing.

Before I left for lunch, I stopped in Gary's office, just to give him grief anyway. "Gary," I said, closing the door behind me, "what's going on in that mind of yours?"

"Hmm?" he responded, playing dumb.

"Young. Cute. Sexy. It's your ultimate fantasy in the flesh."

"What was I supposed to do? Turn down Matt's offer? We needed someone quickly. You don't like her?"

"Of course, I like her. For a second I thought we'd need a translator, but besides that, she's outstanding."

"You two should mesh well together."

"Don't get any ideas. I'm in love now. My bed-hopping days are over," I stated proudly, yet wondered, Would I have taken a shot if I were single. Yeah, I would have.

"Aw, you don't mean that, do you?" he teased, realizing his lesbian fantasy tales were coming to an end.

"Yes, I do," I proclaimed once again before I walked out of the door, drowning out his laughter.

On my way down the hallway, I was stopped by a Psst! coming from the office supply room. Judy pretended to be searching madly for adding machine tape, but passed to me a small note held in the palm of her hand. It read: Cocaine—caught in the women's bathroom—was sent to rehab immediately by her family. She winked at me and went back to tossing aside pencils and pads of paper in her false portrayal of busyness. Damn, she was good.

As I approached Nakia waiting for me at her car in the parking structure, she looked like if she could miraculously drill herself into a hole in the ground, she would. The closer I neared her, I understood why.

At six feet five inches, Fred Sr. sat constrained in the back seat of Nakia's Volvo, his left hand tapping repeatedly against his knee. Despite his apparent anger, he was handsome in a peculiar way, though his brown baldhead was about a quarter-size larger than the average man's. His almond, angled eyes were mere slits as he cut a severe stare in my direction. I could almost see steam fuming from his nostrils with each exhale of pure agitation. Damn, why had I agreed to talk to him?

Nakia appeared ill—like she might throw up if she opened her mouth to speak. Lightning bolts of paranoia shot through her eyes like flashbulbs.

Jittery hands greeted mine when I reached her. "Kia, it's going to be all right," I said.

"He's so fucking pissed, Kyla. I don't know what to do. I couldn't get a word in last night, so I eventually hung up in the middle of his tirade. Then he was outside of my house this morning. Scared the shit out of me."

I looked at Fred Sr., near hyperventilation and foaming at the mouth. At least he still respected me enough to give me the front seat. As minor as that was, it kind of meant something, didn't it?

"Let's get in the car," I told her, guiding her in before I walked to the passenger side.

"Hi, Fred. How are you?" Should I have even asked?

"How in the fuck do you think I am?" he belted at me. "My son caught this . . . this bitch fucking another woman. What kind of muthafuckin' shit is that? This is someone I trusted to raise my son. Now she's just another pussy-eatin' dyke. Doesn't anybody have any fucking morals anymore?"

Just let him vent, Kyla, just let him vent. I looked at Nakia, who stared ahead, frozen stiff.

"Can't y'all dykes leave straight women alone? Y'all can't go fucking every goddamn body."

Again I looked at Nakia, this time seeking defense on my behalf, or at least an attempt to fess up to what the reality of her story was, yet I got nothing.

"Fred, look," I started, turning around in my seat, "you need to give Nakia a chance to explain."

"She ain't gotta explain nothing!" he yelled. "I know you did this."

So it was my fault after all. "If you feel like you have to blame this on me right now, then you go right ahead, but like I said, you need to hear what Nakia has to say," I said, hoping Nakia would open her mouth and say something. Was I going to have to tell on her myself?

"Yeah, whatever, man. I should have known you were hittin' that ass a long time ago, turning her out. I know all about you, Kyla."

"This is some bullshit," I mumbled and twisted face forward in my seat. "Just bullshit."

"Yeah, and now I'm supposed to let her spend time with my son? What can he learn from a dyke?"

"Nothing will change in the way Nakia treats Fred Jr.," I replied, upset but remaining calm.

"Maybe she can teach him to eat pussy right," he said bitterly.

"You're not giving her a chance, Fred."

Just as I was ready to continue speaking on Nakia's behalf, she cut me off.

"Stop it," she whispered.

Both Fred and I looked at her tense face.

"Stop it," she said again, a bit louder, placing her fingertips against her temples in frustration. "I got it, Kyla. This is crazy, Fred," she said in his direction. "First, you better stop blaming Kyla for this. This is not her fault, since you seem hell-bent on someone to blame. This is all me. All me. I wanted this. I wanted to experience being with a woman. And, to set the record straight, I've never been with Kyla. You don't fuck every woman you know, and neither does she. Don't patronize her like that."

"Hold on one muthafuckin' minute!" Fred's tight fist seemed ready to punch a hole through Nakia's tan leather seat. "You're trying to tell me that you've been wanting to screw other women? For how long, Kia?"

"I've been bisexual my whole life," she said calmly, "but I never acted on it until now."

Fred's eyes glassed over a murderous blood-shot red. "So the whole time we were married you were wishing I was a woman? Is that what you're saying?"

"That's not what I said."

"What kind of role model are you supposed to be for my son?"

"I'd never do anything to hurt Fred Jr. Never. You know I love him like my very own."

"I suggest you get over that right now, 'cause you ain't ever seeing him again. You just fucked that up, Nakia. Straight up."

"Please don't do that to me, Fred."

"Ha! Fuck you! I'm not letting him around you and your dyke friends no more."

"We can talk about this later," Nakia said.

"Ain't shit to talk about. Don't call me, and don't be trying to sneak and call my son either."

"Have you even asked him what he wants?"

"He don't know. He's confused as hell, thanks to you."

"Let me talk to him. Please."

"Hell no. I'm out," he said, fumbling with the door handle. Vibrations from the slam of the back door shook the car. Once outside, he smoothed his gray suit and walked to his black Mercedes like the composed businessman he was.

Nakia sat still, widened eyes not blinking, transfixed on an invisible object in front of her.

I sat mute and waited until she was ready, listening to the low drum of her idling car. Five minutes passed.

"You know, it's not like I believe I'll never be with a man again," she stated. "I do like men. The way I feel right now about Shanna is so much more than I expected though. So much more." She moaned and laid her head against the headrest. "But is something that feels good worth losing the people I love?"

"You're right, Kia. It's hard to lose the ones you love because of something you feel."

"I can't lose Fred Jr., I really can't, Kyla. What I can do is tuck this feeling away, back to the place it's been this whole time. I'll get over it," she said uncertainly.

"You're saying you'd let Shanna go in order to see Fred Jr.? That's a hard decision you have to make."

"I don't know if he'll let me see Fred Jr. now either way."

"It might take some time."

"I don't know what to do." She leaned her head against the steering wheel. "When I talked to Shanna last night, it was wonderful. She was so supportive and said she understood why I reacted the way I did. She didn't seem angry at all."

"How did you end the conversation?"

"She told me to call her when I was ready."

"Can you not call her? Can you never see her again?"

"I like her a lot. I know it would be hard."

"Can you not see or talk to Fred Jr.?"

"No. Now, that I cannot do."

We sat, choked by the idea that Kia would suppress, once more, desires that were to her a natural part of her being. Swallowing that reality was a challenge for her. A generous tide of tears streaked her face, creating small rivers in her foundation. She cried while I held her hand.

"I can do it," she chanted quietly to herself over and over.

I didn't say anything, although I wanted to scream. Scream at Nakia for not fighting for both her wishes. To express a part of herself, and to love Fred Jr. at the same time. But it was Nakia's life and not mine. The last place I wanted to find myself was guilty of encouraging her down the wrong path.

"I love you, Kia, no matter what you do."

"Thanks, girl," she said, adjusting her rearview mirror to begin wiping her tears away. After reapplying pressed powder she smiled reassuringly at her reflection.

She picked up her phone and dialed a number. She then lowered her head and scrunched her eyebrows between her fingers in frustration at what she was about to do.

"Hey, Shanna, it's Kia," she said. "I'm okay . . . yeah, I know you didn't expect to hear from me so soon . . . well, I was wondering if you could stop by tonight . . . um, no not for that." Kia looked at me with sadness in her eyes. "I need to talk to you about something . . . um, I'd rather talk about it in person . . . sure, yes, eight o'clock is good . . . all right, I'll see you then . . . bye."

"I hope it goes well tonight, Kia."

"It will. This is so much bigger than just Shanna. That's just the first step."

"I know. I'm here if you need me."

"I know that. Right now, let's go eat," she said, attempting to sound cheery.

"You sure?"

"Yeah. No time to sulk. I may as well adjust back into my old life and get Fred Jr. back. But I'll tell you this—that was the best fuckin' Christmas gift of my life," she said, releasing one of her harking laughs that I hadn't heard since I got back to Atlanta.

"It's yours forever. No one can ever take that gift away from you."

"Christmas two thousand three, it's a season I'll never forget!"

Nakia set her car in reverse, and we exited the dark ramp and welcomed the bright rays of light through a sun floating atop the clouds.

***

"Kyla speaking," I said, answering my work line, fatigued and irritable. It was late Friday afternoon, and I was ready to go home and slip under my covers. Every night of the week I had been up until wee hours of the morning with Nakia, consoling her through her U-turn back to straight life after the brief turn in her life's road.

"Kyla, this is Monica from the Big Brothers Big Sisters program."

"Hi, Monica," I said, recalling her as the head of recruitment who gave her final stamp of approval on my application.

"Yes, hi. Well, I'm not sure how to tell you this," she began.

"What is it?" I asked, worried something had happened to Lisa.

"Well, we received a phone call this morning from a very irate man regarding your participation in this program. He suggests that your character is unfit to mentor teen girls."

"And why is that?" I asked, even though I knew the answer and knew who was behind the phone call. Fuck! It wasn't my fault that his ex-wife was into women.

"He stated your sexual orientation and promiscuity is a bad influence to an impressionable youth."

"Is there any clause in our agreement that required me to disclose my sexual orientation?"

"No."

"Wouldn't that be considered discrimination?"

"Yes, it would."

"Then I don't understand why we're having this conversation."

"Because this kind of information does get added to your file, Ms. Thomas."

Oh, now I was Ms. Thomas. "Wait a second. I didn't break the law. I didn't kill anybody or rob a bank, and I haven't been convicted of a felony. That's the kind of information that should be in my file, not some he-said conversation."

"I understand why you're frustrated, Ms. Thomas. However, you must look at it from our point of view as well. This caller tells us that you've been bringing your lesbian friends with you on outings with Lisa."

"Monica, I don't believe there is an issue with my bringing a friend along. She's not my girlfriend, if you must know. And I would never expose Lisa to an inappropriate situation."

"Ms. Thomas, I'm not trying to put you on the defense. Although I must let you know that after your next visit with Lisa this Sunday, we will be doing a review with her and reevaluating your position."

"Lisa and I have made wonderful progress together." I felt the need to state my case before my relationship with Lisa crumbled right in front of me.

"I see that. You've been with her longer than her previous big sister."

"Please don't take that away from us," I requested, similar to Nakia's pleas to Fred Sr.

"We'll have to leave that up to Lisa. Have a good day, Ms. Thomas."

Before I could reply, she hung up the phone. I wondered what to do next. Seek legal advice? Get Asia's opinion? Call Nakia and tell her what her ex-husband was doing? Call Fred Sr. and ask him to leave me the hell alone? Yet I knew calling him would be of no help. It had been several days since our conversation in the car, and he was still determined to slander my character. Nakia had had no success in her attempts to speak with him rationally. He either ignored her calls when her number appeared on the caller ID, or he went to the opposite extremity and screamed at her through the phone, reiterating to her how she was now worth no more to him and Fred Jr. than a lost penny under the sofa pillow.

Andrea interrupted my internal debate while I stared at the receiver, contemplating my next move.

"Kyla, it is five o'clock on Friday and I am prepared to go home. Do you need something from me?"

For the first time during her week as my assistant, Andrea veered from a monotonous all-black attire and wore a deep fuchsia sweater with a neckline so daring, I could see the small brown speckles leading to her nipples.

"No, Andrea, I'm fine. Thanks for asking. Have a nice weekend," I said, ready for her to leave me alone with my thoughts.

Rather than scurry out of the office as most dismissed employees would, Andrea took the seat in front of me. "Something is bothering you, Kyla."

"Yes, there is." And I'm not interested in sharing it with you.

"Sometimes people on the outside can help."

I didn't say anything in return.

"No hay mal que por bien no venga. That means, there is no bad that something good does not come from it."

Still I was unable to respond, confused by Andrea's desire to uplift.

"I have a gift, Kyla. I see things and I see you. For you, what may seem bad has turned good. That will continue in your life. Do not worry." She lifted herself from the chair. "As you all say, every cloud has a silver lining. You will find it."

Tempted between laughter and marvel, I opted instead to wish Andrea a good weekend again before she left my office. Had Gary hired the oracle? Finally, I did laugh despite my sincere appreciation of her soothing words.

Out of high heels and relaxed in a new pair of K-Swiss, my feet sang songs of gratitude while I strolled through the Atlanta History Center Sunday afternoon. Nearing The Turning Point exhibition, my conversation with Lisa turned to Fred Jr. She informed me that Fred. Jr. told her exactly what he had witnessed when he arrived unannounced to Nakia's. He also told her that Fred Sr. gave him strict instructions not to contact Nakia, me, or Lisa under any circumstances.

"He sneaks to call me every night, waiting until his dad falls asleep or goes out for a while. It's like I'm the only person he has to talk to right now."

"You might be, Lisa. It's probably difficult for him to talk to his friends about this."

"His boys would talk about him real bad."

"Yes, unfortunately that might be true. Kids can be cruel."

"Kyla, he said he threw up on the way home."

"He was that sickened by it?"

"Well, kind of. I mean, no one really wants to catch their parents having sex. Ever. But then to see that by someone you consider your mom, well, a second mom . . . it was too much. He kept trying to get it out of his head but couldn't."

"So how does he feel about Nakia now?"

We stopped to view a display case filled with guns and rifles used during the battle between northern and southern states of the Civil War. We were silent for a moment as we studied the equipment.

"At first he was kind of, like, not sure what to do, but he still loves her. It's his dad that won't let him talk to her."

"He told his dad he wanted to talk to her?"

"Yep. He won't let him though. Can you get them together, Kyla? He wanted me to ask you."

"Lisa, it wouldn't be right for me to get in the middle of this," I answered, knowing it best not to meddle with an angry black man. "There's nothing more I'd like than for Fred and Nakia to be able to see each other, but if Fred Sr. found out I got them together . . . "

Lisa appeared disappointed by her unsuccessful attempt to help Fred. Jr.

"Do you understand that technically Nakia has no right? Fred Sr. can use that against all of us. We just have to wait for him to come around and pray that he does." If Tori can have a change of heart, anyone can, I thought to myself. I just hoped it didn't take as long.

"I'll tell him you can't help."

"Lisa, do you have any questions you'd like to ask me?"

Lisa took a moment to trace her finger down the crease between two pieces of glass.

"Um, well, I don't know," she said, visibly nervous for the first time since I'd picked her up that morning. "It's like I'm trying not to see you differently, but it's like I can't help it. There are a few kids at school that people say are gay, and every time I see them, it's like that's the first thing I think about. You know, like, there's a gay person."

Her response was exactly the answer I expected and had grown accustomed to.

"I'm glad you're trying not to focus on it, Lisa. When you see people you know are gay, just remember that's not all there is to them—that there is so much more than just that part of who they are. Now that you know about me, it doesn't mean I'm going to treat you any differently. I hope you feel the same."

"Yeah, after my dad told me that the lady from the club called to see if I had any problems with you, I was like, 'No.' Then he told me why she asked, and I was surprised. I mean, you don't look like you're gay or anything." She finally turned to face me. "Why are you?"

"Why am I gay?"

She nodded.

I took a deep breath. "I fell in love with a woman. For me, later in life I learned that's what feels best for me and makes me happy."

"Well, honestly, I have this friend—not me," she clarified. "I have this friend who told me that she thinks she's gay. I asked her how she knew, and she said she doesn't like boys at all. I know we're only twelve, but I know I like boys, so I guess it's not too early for her to know she likes girls. I was thinking that, maybe if she has questions, she can talk to you."

"Has she talked to her parents?" I asked, fearing a female version of Fred Sr. hiring a hitman after learning a lesbian spoke with her daughter about exploring her inner feelings.

"Kind of. I mean, they wouldn't let her say much when she tried to explain. They said she was young and would grow out of it."

"That was pretty brave of her to tell them already."

"You know, it was."

"If we get an okay with Monica and your friend's parents, maybe you can invite her with us sometime."

"That would be cool! So you'll tell Nakia that Fred isn't mad at her?" she asked, switching the subject back to her crush.

"Definitely. I know she'll be glad to hear that."

Lisa stopped and gave me the briefest hug. "Thanks, Kyla. So you know, I'm going to tell Monica that I don't want anyone else as my big sister." She smiled.

"I'm so glad, Lisa. Thank you." I gave her a tight squeeze in return.

Lisa pulled out the new lip-gloss we'd purchased earlier and applied it to her lips. Then we continued on with the rest of our afternoon walk through the center.

"How'd it go?" Gene asked after I dropped Lisa off and she was in her bedroom, door closed, with music blaring from the speakers.

"It went well. She had a few questions, as I expected she would, but she said she plans to give Monica a thumbs-up."

"That's my girl" He patted me on the shoulder. I suppose because Lisa wasn't there to pat hers. "Her mom would be proud."

"She would be."

"To ease your mind, Kyla, it was never a concern of mine. When Monica called with this so-called information, I asked her why she was telling me. I know my daughter, and if anything felt wrong to her, she would have told me."

"Thanks, Gene. I've calmed down since her phone call. I understand it's her job to investigate."

"True, true," Gene said with a faraway look, his attention fading as he began to tune me out like he did in most our conversations. It seemed like every few minutes the ghost of his wife circled in his midst, seizing hold of his awareness and erasing the object that held his concentration, even for the briefest moment.

"Gene, um, please tell me if I'm out of line for asking you this, but do you date at all?"

The shock of the sudden interruption of his reminiscent state caused his eyes to widen.

"I'm sorry if that's too personal."

"No, no, Kyla, that's fine. Well, no, I haven't dated since my wife's passing. Colleagues have offered to set me up on dates, but nothing ever manifested. Why? You interested?" He laughed.

Is this a bad idea? I asked myself ten times over the next few seconds. Could she really abandon the explored intimate moments she had shared? Tuck them away into a corner of her mind, suppressing that which came natural to her? Could this be the destiny of two like spirits?

Both in love with what they could not have. Nakia sacrificing a part of her being, leaving behind the chance to love another woman in order to actively participate in the life of a young man she loved as her own child. Gene, lost in love with his departed wife, succumbing to haunted illusions of her presence each time he blinked his eyes. Both capable of love, yet both sheltering a piece of their heart, its contents filled with memories of what may have been.

"I have a friend I'd like you to meet."

"Oh yeah?" he questioned, half-wary, half-interested.

"You may have some things in common."

"I don't know, Kyla. That's kind of Alicia Silverstone Clueless, don't you think?" Asia frowned while she searched airfares through various websites offering the highest discounted tickets available.

"Don't you think the kids will be upset, considering they got the hots for one another?"

"I thought about that, but I'm talking about two adults who need love in their lives, not two kids who have their first crushes. They'll get over it."

"I suppose," she said, clicking on another promising link. "The Fresh Prince got over it."

"Huh?"

"On the show. Remember he was about to marry Nia Long, and then he didn't, so his mom and her dad got married. Didn't you watch that show, girl?"

"Yeah, I did, Asia, but damn!" I wondered where her brilliant, educated mind drifted off to at times. We were positively a perfect match.

"I have to find a way to bring it to Kia. Should I tell her in advance or set her up?"

"Oh, you mean the way you set me up?" Asia grinned.

"Worked like a charm, didn't it?"

"I say tell her and let her decide. She's just getting over someone, even how short-lived it was. You sure you wouldn't be setting Gene up to get his feelings hurt? I mean, she's bisexual. Will she ever be truly satisfied with just him? Especially after having finally experienced being with a woman."

"I know. I thought about that. But even though she's sad, every time I've talked to Kia, she assures me that she's willing to sacrifice her desire for a woman, if that means she can have Fred Jr. in her life. Some days she handles it okay, and other days she struggles pretty bad. She's adamant that she's leaving women alone though. She took her ad off the dating site a while ago, she deleted

Shanna's number from her cell phone, and she's gradually breaking Fred Sr. down."

"For real?" Asia asked.

"Yeah. She said he actually listens to her side of the story now. Still doesn't say much, but at least he's not cussing her out anymore."

"That's a start. She must really love that boy."

"Yes, she does. It's awesome."

"Do you think you could love another woman's child like that?" Asia asked.

Jaron's delightful brown eyes sparkled in my head. "Sure, I could. I'd like to have a family of my own someday," I said, massaging her shoulders.

She turned from the computer screen and looked up at me standing behind her.

"I might not be able to legally marry, but no one can tell me I can't have a child and have a family."

She spun on the stool to wrap her hands around my waist and rest her head on my belly. "So, who's going to have the baby? Me or you?"

"You'd be beautiful pregnant," I said, imagining her heavenly glow emphasized by the growing life inside of her. Were we actually having this conversation already?

"So would you."

"We can flip a coin."

Asia reached for the cup of change next to her computer and retrieved a quarter. "What are you?"

"Tails," I said, wondering if she was really serious.

"Okay."

With a flip of her thumb, the quarter shot airbound above our heads, twirling in circles, finally landing secure in the palm of Asia's hand.

"Let me see."

Slowly she unwrapped her fingers from around the coin to reveal the profile of George Washington. "Yes!" she squealed, clapping her hands in the air.

"Mama Asia," I said and bent to kiss her forehead.

"I like the sound of that. Mama Kyla sounds pretty good too."

"I'll be his or her mom too."

"I know you will," she said. "But, hey, I have an idea. Why don't we each have a child? I can have the first, and you can have our second child. Then we both can experience pregnancy. I want to rub your belly and feel the baby you'd be bringing into our lives."

If it were possible for me to fall deeper in love with her, I did that very second. "I love that idea."

"Who will be the father? They should have the same dad."

I stopped myself from visualizing a child with Jeff before the idea had time to fully manifest in my imagination. "I don't know," I said, "but whoever he is, he'll be one of the luckiest men in the world."

Asia spun back around in her stool and went back to the computer screen. "Now that that's settled, let's solve the immediate problem at hand and find some flights. I want you to hang with me and my family for a few days."

"Me too. Let's book the flights, and then I'll talk to Gary. With the stunt he pulled with Andrea, I know he won't trip on me."

"Good. Everyone is anxious to meet you."

"I'm excited too. You sure there's no psycho ex-girlfriends or secret boyfriends I need to worry about?"

"Hell no. My name is not Kyla," she joked.

"No heartbroken ex-loves?"

"Nope."

"No ax-murdering crazy girls who can't get over your fine ass?"

"Well . . ."

"No stalking men determined to turn you out?"

"Oh hell no!"

"All right, I suppose I'm convinced it's safe to go visit."

"My mom and dad have the guest room all set. Oh, I e-mailed them a photo of us from the wedding."

"Jeff's wedding?"

"Who else, Kyla?"

"Do they know whose wedding it was?"

"Yes, sweetie."

"So your mom knows I almost got married once?"

"Yep."

"What did she say?"

"Don't worry, darling, she didn't say anything about that, really. My mom has grown to be very understanding. She feels a person can alternate between relationships, loving a man and then a woman, and she doesn't care, so long as they're happy. If you're asking if she formed an opinion of you because you were once engaged, the answer is yes." Asia didn't elaborate and left me hanging.

"What, Asia, what?" I asked, paranoia simmering through my veins.

Asia smiled smugly and let me wait a minute before she responded. "She said you must be a person who doesn't want to make mistakes in relationships. She said I'm lucky because you seem to commit only when it's right."

"Really?" I asked, flattered.

"Yeah. She already likes you, Kyla. We talk about you all the time. Now you just have to live up to all the praise I've given you," she said with a wink.

"I'm learning from the master. You won my mother over, which was a huge task. I'll try to follow suit."

"Just be you."

"I am. That's what you did," I said with another kiss to her forehead.

"You'll be fabulous. Now, when is this peculiar date going to take place?"

"Don't say it's strange. We're going out Saturday, if Nakia agrees to it. I guess I won't try to set her up blindly."

"Be careful, honey. You're already on thin ice. Gene might have Monica get rid of you if this backfires."

"Asia, Gene is not going to stop letting me see Lisa just because he and Nakia bomb. If they bomb."

"All right," she said. "I'll let you do your thing. I hope you know what you're doing."

"I knew what I was doing with you."

"Yeah, but what was your track record before that?"

Ouch.

"I'm sorry," she said before I could defend myself or act like my feelings were hurt. "Let me make it up to you." She took my hand and led me toward her bedroom, leaving the task of finding airfare for another time.

I didn't dwell on her comment. We both knew my past was all but pretty, and to believe that it wouldn't have resurfaced on occasion would've been foolish on my part. That was then. She was my now, my present, my future, my everything.

Loaded with anticipation, I followed her, making a pit stop in the kitchen for a can of whipped cream.

CHAPTER 9

New Beginnings

Radiant in a satin bustier and black skirt, Nakia twirled in the arms of Gene while they danced to the upbeat live jazz band performing at one of Atlanta's hotspots. She laughed—loud—as he released her into spinning circles once again, not once letting go of her hand. Back in his arms she cuddled her short blonde curls into his neck, closed her eyes and smiled, a sight that nearly brought me to digging through my purse for tissue.

Gene, once distant and removed, beamed with happiness, and seemed to embrace life once again. Though recognizable lapses back into time flashed over his face from time to time, the occurrences were far less frequent, and were immediately erased at the sight or mention of Nakia.

Nakia, still fragile from her life change, gained strength with each passing day. During private conversations between the two of us, she confided that she'd find herself suddenly astray in a daydream of Shanna, recalling the touches they shared. Yet greater than her desire to be with Shanna was her wish to share in the life of Fred Jr. Winning him back had become her primary focus.

Side to side, Gene and Kia swayed to the beat, Gene brushing his cheek against Kia's soft mane, with them often breaking apart to glance at one another for proof that they were indeed not lost in a dream.

"I have to tell you," Asia said, stroking my thigh under the table, "you really did it."

I leaned against the cushioned seat in the oversized booth. "I did, didn't I?"

"I'm surprised."

"You shouldn't be. You saw the way they looked at each other when we went to dinner."

"Like we had disappeared and weren't even there."

Gene and Nakia, each rattled by the instant attraction, had stood eye to eye in Nakia's three-inch stilettos. Their gaze into each other's wounded spirits was, for them, like finding a cure for the common cold, each the remedy the other required on a path to wellness and wholeness.

Asia and I spent the dinner politely ignored, while Gene and Nakia engaged in exclusive conversation. Our interjections fell on deaf ears or were replied to with curious stares in our direction, followed by an exchanged look between the two that said, "Did you hear something?"

So we sat and listened to them talk about work, children, travels, music, religion, politics, and any and every other topic that crossed their minds in the two-hour period we were there.

Not only were we not spoken to, their body language shut us out as well. Nakia leaned forward, her chin resting atop her clasped fingers, while Gene turned sideways, his arm resting on the back of Kia's chair.

Although pleased with their connection, I could only take so much rejection. Asia signaled the waitress, we paid the bill, and said goodbye. Again, we were met with eyes that seemed stunned that we were even still there.

A month later, celebrating Valentine's Day as a foursome, Asia and I still spent the evening alone, observing two people so engrossed in one another that the rest of the world seemed to fade into a canvas backdrop as they painted the story of their new beginnings.

What was right for me proved opposite for Nakia.

Once Kia made the decision to sacrifice herself for the love of another, gradually, positive events followed. First, she fell in love. A love that nurtured and revitalized her injured heart. Upon learning of his ex-wife's reclaimed love for men, Fred Sr. developed a renewed willingness to establish and maintain a cordial relationship with her. In perfect alignment, a reuniting of Fred Jr. and Nakia followed. Fred Jr. released hold of his crush for Lisa, considering it was her father who unintentionally contributed to his ability to have Kia back in his life.

Appreciating her father's newfound happiness, Lisa, in turn, transferred her infatuation with Fred Jr. into that of loving adoration for a big brother. A new family was born.

"Let's dance," I said, standing up and offering my hand to Asia.

"My pleasure," she replied, stretching her long legs from underneath the table.

We strolled into the crowd and blended in with the couples stepping to the rhythm of the drum. Holding hands, Asia and I tapped our feet front to back and side to side, her laughing at my concentrated efforts to stay on beat.

When our bodies met, just for a pulsating moment, her lips touched my ear. "I love you so much," she whispered, and backed away for a spin.

Without losing a step, when she returned, I replied, "And I love you."

When the band took a short break, Kia and Gene headed toward our seats, with Asia and I in tow. I stopped when I heard a familiar voice.

"Hey, Kyla."

I turned around and saw Angie, dressed in her usual jacket and slacks, holding hands with a lovely lady wearing a short-length shimmering party dress.

"Asia!" the woman exclaimed before I could respond.

"Oh my God, Deidra," Asia responded with a swift hug to the woman. "How are you?"

"Great, just great."

"How have you been, Angie?" I said, finally able to ask.

"Hanging in there," she said, her eyes on Asia, visibly curious as to Asia's connection with the woman at her side.

"That's good to hear," I replied.

Asia and I stood before our exes for a few moments of uncomfortable silence. The woman was a hyperactive thing, visibly jittery and excited, smiling widely, her eyes dancing wildly between Angie, Asia and me.

"Okay, well, Kyla, this is Deidra, my friend from Columbus that I told you about," Asia said, introducing us.

Deidra rushed her hand into mine and shook it with vigor.

"Hey, Deidra, it's nice to meet you," I said.

"Same to you. But, Asia, guess what? I'll be relocating to Atlanta in a month."

"Is that so?"

"Yep! My baby here wants me closer to her." Deidra snuggled against Angie.

"That's so nice," Asia said a bit icily.

I knew she was recalling the many miles she put on her truck to visit Deidra, who was now ready to pack a U-Haul and move to the city with Angie. Deidra didn't appear to notice.

"I'm so crazy about this girl, I'll do anything for her." Deidra kissed Angie's cheek. "Angie's going to help me get my cosmetology license and connect me with some owners of salons that she knows."

I smiled at Angie, who returned one as well. She had found exactly what she was looking for, someone she could care for and who allowed her to be the nurturer and caregiver.

"That's fabulous, Deidra," Asia said.

Angie cleared her throat.

"Oh, Angie, I'm sorry," I said. "Angie, this is my Asia."

Angie took hold of Asia's hand. "So good to meet you," she said.

"Likewise," Asia replied coolly.

"You two here alone?" Angie asked.

"No, actually, we're here with Kia and Gene, Lisa's dad."

"They're dating?" Angie asked, puzzled.

"Yes, they are. Isn't that something?" I answered.

"Do you mind if I say hello to her?" Angie asked.

"No, no, not at all. Come this way." I took Asia's hand and led the group back to our table.

The look on Kia's face was priceless as we neared the table. She looked at me like, Damn! Haven't you been through enough? She stood for an embrace.

"Hi, Nakia," Angie said. "Long time no see."

Though Angie and Kia had heard much about the other, they'd only met on two occasions, the last being an evening Kia was visiting when Angie arrived to pick me up for one of our dinner dates.

"I know," Kia responded. "You look well."

"I am, thank you."

Deidra spied the spacious, oversized booth where we were seated. "Asia! Can we sit with you?"

Asia exhaled. "Absolutely."

Once seated, Angie was formally introduced to Gene, whom she had only heard about through my stories of Lisa.

"So tell me, did Kyla hook the two of you together?" Angie asked, already knowing the answer.

"You know she did! She did a good job though." Nakia winked at me.

"Yeah, I'm not complaining either," Gene said.

"What about you two?" Kia asked, referring to Angie and Deidra.

Deidra replied, "Well, I was in the city visiting my cousin who was trying to get his computers set up in his new real estate office, and who walks in to assist him but this fine woman right here. When I saw her I was like, I have got to have her." She squeezed Angie's arm. "At first she was playing me real cool, but then she started giving me some time, and we've been going strong for about eight months."

Mentally, both Asia and I did the math in our heads and realized Deidra had met Angie prior

to their breakup. And Angie was already court-
ing Deidra at the time of our final dinner. Angie
eyed me curiously, possibly for a reaction. Hell,
she wasn't my woman then, so I didn't care. But
it was a different story for Asia.

"Wow! That long ago," Asia commented.

I discreetly tapped her lightly underneath the
table, advising her to let it go. We were in a new
time and a new place, and it wasn't necessary to
make Deidra feel bad for her cheating heart. It
was difficult for Asia, I could tell, not wanting
to be made a fool of by her ex in front of her
new girlfriend. It was kind of funny when I
thought about it, the four of us sitting there, all
having slept together in an indirect way. Briefly,
I wondered if Asia's intimate affections toward
me were similar to those to Deidra, and if Angie
had whipped it on Deidra the same way she had
whipped it on me.

"Let's order a round of drinks," Gene suggested, taking the initiative to liven up the moment. He signaled for our waiter.

We all ordered and received a fresh beverage,
which helped to soothe Asia's slightly injured
ego. Soon we were all telling funny tales about
each other's partners, the first time we'd heard
them sing (no one had a bearable voice, except
Gene), and better yet, the first time someone

slipped and passed gas. It was a hilarious conversation that left us bent over in laughter and tears. Though it was an unexpected twist to our evening, it was the perfect way to spend our first Valentine's Day.

After our joyous time ended and we were in Asia's truck en route to her apartment, Asia said, "I can't believe that shit."

"Believe what?" I asked, unsure what she was referring to.

"Deidra and Angie. She was cheating on me with your woman," she answered, gripping the steering wheel tightly.

"Asia, you're still on that?"

"Yes."

"Why can't you let it go? We just had a really good time. Why is it still bothering you?"

She was quiet for a moment as she exited at Covington Highway headed to Decatur. Finally she said, "I don't know." She shrugged her shoulders. "I guess I really don't like feeling like someone has gotten over on me."

"Asia, I know what you're saying, but she wasn't like your other ex who took advantage of you financially."

"No, she didn't. But she took advantage of my time with all those trips out there to see her, and now she's all ready to pack up and move here with Angie. I could hardly get that girl to drive to Atlanta to see me. There I was trying to be with her, and she had already moved on to Angie."

"Babe, I know you don't like to feel like someone has gotten over on you. No one would like that. But look at it this way. If they hadn't gotten together, we may not have gotten together. You still would have been seeing her when I was trying to connect with you, so it all worked out, right?"

"Still."

"Still what?"

"I don't know. Maybe it bothers me because I know who she left me for. Your ex."

"Well, I left her for you."

"But you didn't even know me, and you and Angie were only fuck buddies anyway."

Damn! "You're lucky I'm still buzzed, Asia, 'cause I'm going to let that one slide." I granted myself the moment needed to cast aside her statement. "Anyway, you're acting like you really had something for this girl. If I didn't know better, I'd think you preferred her over me, by the way you're acting."

"Kyla, please, that's not what this is about."

"Well, listen to you. You're in the car with me, the woman you love so much, but you're whining about your ex having cheated on you. What difference does it make at this point?"

"First of all, I'm not whining, and second, it doesn't matter. But how would you like it if you found out one of your exes cheated on you? Wait, never mind. You were always the one doing the cheating."

Should I let that one slide too? Why ruin an almost perfect evening?

"Look, Asia, I don't know why you're so upset, but I'm not going to keep talking about this. If you want to stay mad about Deidra, then you can stay mad on your own." I turned my attention to the line of trees we were passing.

"I'm not mad," she said, looking at me. "It's just weird, that's all . . . me, her, you, Angie, and how we're all connected. And to know that my ex left me for my girlfriend's ex is just crazy annoying."

"What happened with you and Deidra is done, and what happened with me and Angie is over, so who really cares if they're together? I'm kind of happy she left you, 'cause that made room for me." I smiled.

"All right, all right, forget it. It doesn't matter."

We pulled into her apartment complex, and she punched in the code to open the iron gates. We passed the pool on our right and pulled into a parking space just outside her one-bedroom unit.

I followed Asia into the apartment, and when I turned to bolt the door, she was behind me, pressing into my backside, my trench coat crunching between us. I leaned against the door, collapsing my weight forward.

Asia ran her fingers up and down the sides of my thighs and grinded her body into my hips. She began with a slow grind that intensified until my body began to sweat underneath my dress.

"I'm hot," I said, my eyes closed, and the side of my face and palms pressed to the door.

"Good! That's how I like it."

Asia began to remove my coat, which she laid on the runner in the hallway where we stood. She smiled deviously and reached into her purse to retrieve our favorite strap-on. This was the first time she'd surprised me by pulling one of my numbers, carrying it with her.

"Lay down. I want to fuck you, Kyla."

I had already come to know that the only time Asia spoke even slightly dirty to me was after she had been drinking. I had never seen her drunk, but even a light buzz caused a brassier and bolder side of her to emerge. Otherwise, our lovemaking was generally exciting and thrilling, yet tender, with only sweet words spoken.

I lowered myself to the floor and positioned my body comfortably on the coat.

Asia stood over me, lifted her dress, and stepped her four-inch heels into each side of the strap. She tightened it to her comfort level before meeting me on the floor. "Open your legs," she said.

I spread my legs, and she placed her body between them. With her right hand, she parted my lips, and with her left, she stroked my hair, nibbling her teeth into my neck. She glided the strap-on inside of me and moved her hips slowly until I was comfortable and adjusted to the pressure. Then I let her fuck me on the floor, just like she wanted to.

BUZZ!

The annoying tone from my laptop interrupted my late-night reading. I lifted my glasses to my forehead and crawled out of bed to my desk.

    bottomsup: HELLO?????
    kyla69: hey cuz
    bottomsup: hey baby doll. what r u doing?
    kyla69: reading. u? not working i c
    bottomsup: don't forget who's the HNIC
    kyla69: LOL
    bottomsup: sweetie, we need to chat.
    kyla69: we are
    bottomsup: u sitting down?
    kyla69: of course, what's up?
    bottomsup: u know i luv u, right?

kyla69: spill it david

bottomsup: well . . .

kyla9: yes???

bottomsup: i'm moving in with marlon

Swiftly I moved my glasses to the bridge of my nose, just to make sure my eyes weren't deceiving me.

kyla69: u're moving out?

bottomsup: yes baby

kyla69: i don't know what 2 say

bottomsup: just be happy 4 me

kyla69: i am david. for real. when r u leaving?

bottomsup: as soon as u're able to take things over urself

kyla69: myself?

bottomsup: i'm not paying rent in 2 places darling

kyla69: i know, it just came out

bottomsup: u've lived on ur own before, did ya 4get?

kyla69: no, of course not.

bottomsup: it's not like i'm ever there babe. i'm ready to move officially with marlon

kyla69: that's great. really. i should have known this day would come bottomsup: sooner or later sugarplum

kyla69: april good 4 u?

bottomsup: don't rush it—go over ur stuff

kyla69: don't worry about me boy

bottomsup: all right big baller

kyla69: u got that right

bottomsup: shoulda known u were one of those women keeping a stash

kyla69: mama didn't raise no fool!

bottomsup: u're right. aunt gladyce don't play

kyla69: thx 4 letting me know david

bottomsup: no...thank u 4 being a confused-ass girl and moving to atl

kyla69: huh?

bottomsup: if it weren't 4 me following u down here, i never would have met marlon

kyla69: gotcha

bottomsup: there goes my two way. this guard always thinks he seen a ghost on the 16th floor—ain't shit up there.

kyla69: take care of ur business

bottomsup: later babe

kyla69: bye sweetness

After logging off and shutting down my laptop, I nestled under the covers with my all-time favorite book authored by Alice Walker. Yet

I could no longer focus on Celie's terrorizing husband. My mind wandered to days ahead, after David would be gone and the place would be all mine. I'd be by myself. Alone. Did it have to be that way?

"I'm away for only three days, Andrea. Everything around here looks good. Tomorrow just process the orders on the list I gave you."

"*Sí*. I will."

"Thanks." I smiled at the neatness of my desk. Promoting LALA had been a blessing. Aside from his lustful intentions, Gary's praise of Andrea had proven accurate. She was efficient, detailed, and a positive asset to the work environment.

The rest of the office had taken to her charming smile and calm demeanor, and I often found her chummed up with the other assistant buyers headed out to the mall for lunch.

Before she left the office in her skintight leather pants and painted-on sheer blouse, I called her back. "Hey, I just wanted to thank you, Andrea."

"*¿Por qué?*"

"For your words to me that day a while back when I was frazzled, when I was upset about some things."

She appeared pleased. "So everything is good?"

I thought of Nakia and Gene, and their relationship growing stronger with each day. I thought of David, just a couple of weeks away from moving in with his lover and stepson. I thought of Lisa and the okay from Monica to continue mentoring her. And finally my thoughts landed on Asia and I boarding a plane in just a few hours so I could meet her family for the first time. I touched my pocket and felt the gift box I had been waiting to give to her.

"Yes, Andrea, everything is definitely good."

"I knew it would be."

"See you next week."

"Enjoy your time, Kyla," she said and left the office.

Softly I whistled while walking down the hall, passing Gary's office on my way out. He managed a thumbs-up and a smile, although he was on the phone intent on securing tickets to a Kelly Clarkson concert. Tickets had gone on sale at ten a.m., and it was 10:05.

"Good luck," he mouthed with a wink and a grin.

Finally, after my repeated testimonials that my flagrant sex tales were over, Gary had accepted the fact that I was in love with Asia. Still, he'd kid about Andrea and I hooking up late nights in my office, if only to indulge his aroused imagination.

Nakia scooted a customer off toward a clearance rack then rushed in my direction. She grabbed my shoulders and kissed my cheek. "Have a good time," she said.

"Thanks, Kia. I'll call you Sunday when I get back."

"Call my cell. You know where I'll be," she said, referring to Gene's house in Marietta.

"Of course." I smiled. "Tell Lisa I'll see her in a couple of weeks."

Nakia dramatically blew me a kiss, superstar-style, and headed back to assist the clearance shopper, undoubtedly searching and praying to find a winter garment among the spring and summer wear that filled the store.

The drive to the floral shop, where a dozen yellow roses were waiting for my two o'clock pickup, granted me time to reflect upon the last few years of my life. All of the pleasures I had experienced with various relationships and encounters. The genuine and unconditional love received from Jeff, the intoxicating passions I shared with Steph, and even the short-lived trysts with countless women were irreplaceable moments I held close to my heart, though I hoped the majority of those skeletons remained in the closet.

Despite the pain of my devasting loss of Steph, and the scandalous end of my engagement to Jeff, I had once again found happiness. Although Asia and I had not yet had a year together, there was no refuting the fact that I was ready to take our relationship to the next level.

When I arrived, I inhaled the aroma of fresh flowers in the air.

"Would you like a card?" the clerk asked me

"No. No card," I said and left with a huge grin on my face.

After punching in the code Asia had given me, I entered her gated apartment complex, parked outside her unit, and grabbed my luggage. Yep, the Louis again. The front door was ajar.

I found Asia pacing back and forth in the kitchen.

"Oh, she's here now. I'll see you soon, Mom." Asia hung up the phone on the wall-mounted base. "You don't want to miss the plane, do you?"

"We have plenty of time."

"No, not really. Let's go." She was ready to take hold of a suitcase to load into her truck.

"Wait, Asia, wait a minute." I gently took hold of her arm.

"Kyla," she said impatiently.

"Have a seat." I sat her on the blue kitchen stool. From behind my suitcase, I retrieved the roses and handed them to her.

"Oh, they're beautiful, sweetie." She sniffed the soft aroma. "But we're about to leave. Who's going to take care of them?"

"Ssshhh. That doesn't really matter. I only wanted to give them to you on this occasion. There's, um, there's something I want to ask you."

Asia peered at the ticking clock over my head, yet curiosity lured her eyes back to mine.

"Asia, you are everything I've hoped and wished for in a woman. You're ambitious, smart, beautiful, loving, honest, and genuine. You make me smile at the end of a long day. I look forward to hearing your voice each morning and can't wait to see your face every night. So I was thinking . . . can I have your hand please?" I reached for her fingers. I claimed the silver ring from the box I'd been holding. "I'm ready to take the next step, Asia. You are the love of my life, and I don't want to wait any longer to begin sharing that life with you every single day." I slid the silver ring on her finger and closed her hand around it. "Please say yes."

"To what?"

"Open."

Asia slowly opened her hand one finger at a time, revealing a shiny new key attached to a silver keychain around her finger.

"Will you move in with me?"

A baffled expression crossed her face. "Move in with you? What about David?"

"David's moving out in two weeks. I want you to move in."

"Oh, baby." She smiled, taking me in her arms. "I can't believe you didn't tell me before! There's nothing more I'd love than to wake up each morning to your body next to mine."

"So that's a yes, I take it."

"Of course, it's a yes." She kissed me open-mouthed, her tongue on mine, and nibbled on my bottom lip. She wiped lipstick from my chin. "Can't let my mom know I've been slobbering all over you."

"I guess you better not tell her what else you've been kissing." I laughed as I wiped her face.

"Mmm, so nasty. That's why I'm crazy about you," she said, placing the roses on the counter and the key inside a jar. "But right now, Miss Kyla, we have to go, or that whole love scene isn't going to mean a thing if we miss our flight."

"Yes, ma'am," I said with a salute, allowing her to rush me out of the door and into her truck.

CHAPTER 10

Texas Heat

The temperature was a fiery 88 degrees when we exited the Dallas-Fort Worth International Airport. I was sure I burned my throat after I'd inhaled my first breath of the hot, suffocating air.

"Shit!" I gagged, and tried to gain control of my breathing. "It's only April."

Asia slid on a pair of Gucci sunglasses and shielded her eyes from the sizzling sun. "Yeah, it's hot here, but not usually this hot already. Don't be a wimp. We checked the weather before we left; you knew it was hot." She smiled at me.

I frowned back.

"All right, let me get you cooled off."

We strolled with our luggage and found temporary shade in the seating area at the shuttle bus stop. Asia retrieved her cell phone from her purse and dialed while I sat down and rested.

"Hey, Mom, we're here. Where are you?" Asia then spun to her right and peered at the long line of cars crawling toward us. "Oh, I see you!" She waved her hand above her head.

I stood and smoothed my sleeveless, tie-front sundress, and pressed the edges of my hair smooth with my fingertips.

When a black shiny Mercedes-Benz E320 slowed and then stopped before us, Asia darted to the curb, leaving her luggage behind. The driver side door opened, and a tall man, at least six foot four inches, dressed in tan dress slacks and a white button-down short-sleeve top exited. He was the color of an almond, with a head of mostly gray, short curly hair that matched his perfectly trimmed mustache. He wore mirrored sunglasses, a pinky ring on his right hand, and a sparkling gold watch on his left wrist. He smiled warmly and opened his arms to Asia. She reached back.

"Hi!" she exclaimed.

"Hey, Angel." He then kissed her on the cheek. "Let me get your mom." He released her and walked to the passenger side of the car.

Asia hadn't stopped smiling since the car pulled up. She turned her head and gestured for me to step forward next to her. She grasped my hand tightly while we waited.

After opening the car door, Asia's father took hold of her mom's hand and assisted her out of the car.

My mouth literally fell open. Asia's mom was about an inch taller than her and had the same slim figure, and long, dark hair. Her skin was dark brown, and her eyes the color of black opal. She wore stylish, wide-leg crop pants with a cap-sleeve tee. She smiled delicately at her daughter, displaying gentle laugh lines around her mouth and eyes.

Asia let go off my hand and hugged her mom then laid her head against her shoulder. Her mom stroked her hair and closed her eyes. I felt like crying just watching the tenderness of their hold.

"My Angel."

Asia lifted her headed and pecked her mom on the cheek. She stepped back. "Mom, Dad, this is Kyla."

My nerves were amazingly calm. "Hello, Mr. and Mrs. Harris." I shook her father's hand.

Asia's mom took me in her arms. "It's so nice to meet you."

"Let's get you out of this heat." Mr. Harris opened the trunk and placed our luggage inside.

Both Asia and I sank into the cool, black leather interior of the car.

After fastening her seat belt, Mrs. Harris turned to me. "That sure is a pretty dress you have on, Kyla."

I touched the print design of the cotton dress. "Thank you. I got it at work."

"You're a buyer, right?"

"Yes, I am."

"I had a friend who was a buyer at Dillard's for years," Mrs. Harris responded. Then she proceeded to tell me that, despite the long hours, her friend loved the job and its perks. "She always had first pick of new season clothes." She smiled.

"Yeah, Kyla always dresses beautiful."

"She's a beautiful lady, isn't she, William?"

Mr. Harris peeked at me through the rearview mirror. "She certainly is."

Asia leaned over and playfully tweaked my nose. "Magnificent," she whispered.

I smiled.

We headed on U.S. 75 toward Plano, where Mr. and Mrs. Harris moved after Asia had relocated to Georgia. During the drive the conversation shifted from Asia's work, to her dad's upcoming retirement, to her parents summer trip to the Caribbean.

"There's room at the condo," Mr. Harris said. "We're going in August, and it'll be hot, but if you girls are up to it, we'd love to have you join us."

"Jason might join us too. He's got a new girl-friend, Asia. Did I tell you?"

"Please tell me he doesn't already." Asia shook her head in disbelief.

"Yes, he certainly does. That brother of yours . . ." Mrs. Harris sighed. She turned to me. "My son seems to be having a hard time settling down. Every other week, he calls me and tells me about a woman he met. 'This might be the one,' he says each time. I know there are plenty of lovely women in Texas. I don't know why he can't settle on one."

"He doesn't want to, Mom, that's why. He's en-joying making his rounds from Dallas to Houston to San Antonio."

"You make him sound like some kind of pimp, or mack daddy, whatever they're called."

"Well . . . " Asia grinned, teasing her mom.

"William, talk to your son."

Mr. Harris exited the interstate and turned left. "Of course, I will, Charlene," he said devi-ously. "But he's learned everything he knows from me, don't you know that?" He chuckled.

We all laughed.

For the second time in an hour, my mouth gaped open as we pulled into a beautiful subdivi-sion comprised of two-and three-story brick homes with deep-green, manicured lawns with flowered landscaping. Mr. Harris pulled into the half-circle driveway of a maroon-colored home that was at least three times the size of my mom's house.

Dazzled, I gawked in Asia's direction.

She smirked. "What?"

I didn't answer. I was too spellbound by the sculptured angel water fountain to my right.

"Mom, Dad, I'm going to take Kyla for lunch, okay. We didn't eat before we left. We'll be back in a little bit."

"Sure, sweetie," Mrs. Harris replied.

Mr. Harris retrieved the luggage from the trunk. "I'll put these in the guest room."

Asia and I got out of the car. She took the driver's seat, while I sat on the passenger side. Mr. and Mrs. Harris stood at the edge of the cement stairs leading to the massive doorway of their home. They waved as Asia pulled off.

"It's absolutely gorgeous here. And your mom . . . Damn, girl! You're lucky I met you first."

"I know, she's beautiful. She keeps that gray covered up." Asia laughed. "Even with it, she's stunning."

"You look just like her."

"Yeah, everybody says that." Asia glanced in the mirror, as if checking for herself. "What are you hungry for?"

"Umm, you." I bit my bottom lip and moaned, my attempt at sexiness.

We laughed.

"Later, promise," she said then kissed the air in my direction.

"Okay. In that case, let's have some Japanese. Any good restaurants around here?"

She thought for a moment. "Yep. There's this place called Sushi Rock my mom and dad told me about. Let me see." She began fumbling with the navigation system.

Once she located the restaurant, we sat back and allowed the computer voice to guide us through the streets of Plano.

"So what's on the agenda while we're here? I know you have it all set."

Asia smiled. She was the queen of planning.

"Yes, I certainly do."

She started to run down our Dallas itinerary: dining that evening with her parents, brunch with her brother the following morning, a visit to Fair Park that afternoon, etc, etc.

I closed my eyes and listened to the sweet tone of each word she spoke as she continued on with details of our packed, three-day vacation.

"You're going to love Dallas. We won't be staying in the burbs the whole time."

"Doesn't matter where we are, so long as I'm with you."

"Aw. I'm so happy you're here to meet my family."

"Me too."

We rode quietly until we reached our destination. Asia quickly hopped out of the car and started toward the door.

She must be real hungry. I laughed to myself.

She stopped in the middle of the parking lot and turned around, surprised that I wasn't behind her. She leaned on one hip. "Come on, Kyla, I'm hungry!"

I got out of the car and walked toward her, silently thanking each person I had met and each path I had crossed, for I knew that, in some way, every encounter had helped guide me toward my destiny: Asia.

For me, Asia was the ultimate love of my life. She was, after all, the person who made me want to be a better me. I only hoped that for the rest of our lives together, I'd make her better too.

Epilogue

Four years later

This-is-gorgeous," Angie said, taking a step inside my bedroom. It was truly the master suite of the house, decorated in colors and flavors of my taste. Sitting alongside one of the walls was a grand, king-size four-post canopy bed in red mahogany, covered in pillows, and a comforter in shades of cream and rust. A chaise lounge sat next to the gas fireplace that warmed the room on chilly nights. A matching dresser and chest in the same red mahogany sat along two separate walls, distanced by another matching entertainment center that encased the television and stereo system.

Through the bedroom was the suite's bathroom, fully equipped with a whirlpool tub, stand-alone shower, two sink basins and separate lighted vanity tables. And, still, beyond the bathroom was the enormous walk-in closet, which could have served as a seating area of its own.

"Girl, this is serious," Angie said, admiring the closet. "You needed some space to put all those pretty work suits of yours."

"Tell me about it. There's more than enough room now," I said, spying an entire empty hanging rack.

Before we exited back through the bedroom, Angie took a seat on the edge of the bed. "Ahh, nice and comfy." She grinned.

"Yes, it is," I replied with a small chuckle. I then led her out of the room and into the guest bedroom next door.

After our tour, we headed down the split staircase to greet the other guests in the open family room with a ceiling that reached the height of the second level.

"I'm moving in," she said with a wink and a smile.

"Yeah, okay." I laughed.

We joined the others, who were sitting and standing about the room chatting.

"It's fabulous, isn't it?" Nakia asked Angie when we returned.

"It sure is. Even better than I heard."

"Yes, you did well for yourself." Gary gave a thumbs-up, and his wife Mary nodded.

"Why, thank you," I replied. "I'm glad you all could make it."

David laughed. "Make it? Girl, we aren't leaving. Me, Marlon, and MJ have our bags packed and in the car."

Before I could respond, we heard the garage door open, and through the mudroom came Asia and Deidra, lugging two large bags of ice.

"Let me help you," Angie said, already in motion toward Deidra.

"Thanks, sweetie." Deidra exhaled after Angie took the ice from her arms and set it on the granite countertop.

"Finally, time for drinks!" Asia exclaimed with the same enthusiasm I have when about to have a martini.

Just as she was about to add ice to the cooler, the doorbell rang.

"I'll do this," I told Asia, and watched her walk through the foyer to answer the door.

She was still a spectacular sight, simply beautiful in my eyes. Tonight she wore all black, her shiny black hair lying against her blouse. Her frame was still slim, and her walk ladylike.

She opened the door, smiling graciously, and greeted Grace, her coworker, and her husband, Stanford, who both complimented the welcoming décor of the foyer.

***

From the first month Asia moved into my apartment with me, we began a savings account, each depositing equal portions of the amount Asia would no longer be paying in rent. Initially, the joint account was somewhat challenging for her, having been taken advantage of in the past. However, I reassured her that I would never take from her, and that I still had a separate savings account of my own. She was comfortable with that and maintained her own stash as well.

Our fierce dedication to saving more than we budgeted allowed us to place a rather decent down payment on our new luxurious home in a Stone Mountain subdivision. Did we need 4,000 square feet? Not necessarily. But we wanted it.

In recent months, we had been discussing adopting a daughter. We weren't one hundred percent set on the idea, but were weighing our options of adoption against artificial insemination. If we opted against adoption, we hadn't decided if we wanted to select the father of our child from a catalog of men, or solicit a friend for the honor. (Gary jokingly accepted the role when I told him of our consideration.) Either way, after four years of a solid relationship, we were ready to take the next leap.

Asia and I hadn't had to overcome many bumps or jump major hurdles in our relationship. We had

successfully reached the point of genuine content-
ment and were proud of the strength of our union.
Occasionally we would suffer moments of frustration after we both worked a string of long days, and
tempers shortened and patience disappeared over
the simplest things.

Exhausted and overtired, one night I angrily
stomped out of the room to sleep on the couch
after she kept rolling up in the comforter, taking
it from my side of the bed.

She'd snapped at me when I reminded her
that it was her job, after she was awaken at four
a.m. to tend to an ailing patient. She was clearly
envious and annoyed as I snuggled with my pillow while she hurriedly dressed. But, aside from
random incidents such as those, we were living
the ideal relationship I always knew I could have.

I must add, even though we worked crazy long
hours and were frequently spent, we still find
time for each other. Some nights, depending
upon who arrived home first, a hot bubble bath
would await the other. Sometimes one of us
would be waiting in it, other times we'd grant
that solitary time to unwind. Though many
nights were spent sleeping comfortably in each
other's arms, many additional nights (and morn-
ings) were spent making love. We had not tired
of pleasing each other in every creative way.

Our circle of friends remained fairly small. Of course, Nakia remained my closest comrade, sharing lively conversation over lunch and hanging out with Lisa, now an outgoing high school junior, and Fred Jr., who was headed to Morehouse in the fall. Each had fallen happily into the roles of big brother and sister to Gene and Nakia's two-year-old son, Aidyn Gene, a delightful addition to their family, and part of the inspiration Asia and I felt in our increased desire for a child of our own.

Andrea and I had formed a great business relationship that bloomed into a sweet friendship as well. She remained my assistant, very comfortable in her position and still offering random moments of clarity on busy days. Her dress remained primarily black, though her makeup had lightened a bit since the arrival of Santino, her boyfriend of one year. Twice Santino and Asia met me and Andrea at the mall for a friendly lunch.

After bumping into Angie and Deidra years back, Deidra and Asia found that although they were unsuccessful in a romantic relationship, they swiftly blossomed into the all too common friendship with an ex. Deidra had sent Asia a jolly email telling her how nice it had been to bump into her like that and how odd it was that each of our ex's were connected. Asia responded in a joking, semi-serious manner that Deidra had come across my ex well before their relationship had officially terminated. Deidra apologized repeatedly, saying she couldn't help it; that it had felt like love at first sight and she just had to be with Angie. Asia recalled my having said those exact same words in reference to her and acquiesced to the fact that perhaps it was all simply meant to be.

Still, initially I was slightly disturbed by the newfound friendship, unsure if Deidra's intentions were sincere. Especially with Angie as her partner. I mean, Angie was into some freaky shit, and my days of bed-hopping and threesomes were over. I prayed neither of them was hinting around to a four-party orgy. Asia assured me that there was nothing to worry about, and that I need not concern myself with Deidra, and she could handle herself if Deidra ever attempted to cross a line.

We soon realized that our frets were futile, as Deidra and Angie's relationship proved just as strong as ours. The four of us gathered for outings, attended plays and frequented Pride events. In the beginning I found myself uncomfortable in some moments, when Angie and I would speak eye to eye and my mind would randomly perform brief flashbacks of those same eyes devouring my body during moments of heated pleasure. I wondered if that happened to her as well. But as quickly as the reminiscent moment occurred, it was just an afterthought.

"Hey, Kyla," Grace said, giving me a hug.

Stanford and I hugged also.

"What would you like to drink?" Asia asked them both.

"Brandy and Coke for me," Stanford said.

Grace asked, "Do you have red wine?"

"Of course. Please, go ahead and join the others. Kyla and I will get this."

Asia and I began preparing drinks as our guests mingled about the room, which was in our view. David entertained them all: Marlon, Gene, Kia, Gary, Mary, Angie, Deidra, Grace, Stanford, Andrea, and Santino, our closest friends we'd asked to join us in the celebration of our new home.

"I've been dreaming about this day for so long," Asia said, retrieving the martini shaker from the cabinet.

"So have I. I'm so happy it's here."

I mixed gin with juice and vodka with cranberry and Bacardi with lemonade. Asia concocted an apple martini with a splash of Sprite.

When the drinks were ready, we placed them on trays and delivered them to our guests, the both of us each having a glass of white wine. We gathered around the center of the room for a toast.

"Asia and I want to thank each of you for coming tonight. We're so glad this day has arrived, and I'm sure you are too, after having had to listen to I don't know how many stories during our search for the perfect home."

They all laughed and nodded in agreement.

"We want you to know that we appreciate you and that we treasure each and every one of you. You each bless our lives with something very special. Here's to all of you," I said, raising my arm.

"Wait, wait, wait," Nakia said.

Her voice had softened greatly since Aidyn, thank goodness, because I feared she'd scare that baby back into the womb with that raucous voice of hers.

"Kyla, Asia, I have to take this opportunity to say that the two of you exemplify love in its greatest form. It's genuine, it's sincere, it's honest, and it's strong. And you complement each other in ways I've never seen. I can see that you two have mastered one of the greatest feats in relationships, and that's being friends. You two are truly friends, the through-thick-and-thin kind of friendship that's needed for relationships to survive. You not only love each other, but you like each other, and I admire the both of you so much. I'm sure I speak for all of us when I say we're blessed for what you bring to our lives as well," she said, choking up a bit on her last words.

My lips quivered slightly also. "Thanks, Nakia," I whispered, as we all clinked our glasses together.

My glass touched Asia's glass last, and our eyes met. We lingered before taking a sip of our wine.

"She said it all, didn't she?"

"Well, she missed one thing," I said.

"Oh yeah? And what is that?" Asia pulled me closer, her arm around my waist.

I leaned close to her ear. "She didn't say all the beautiful things I'm going to do to you as soon as they leave tonight."

Asia tilted her head back in light laughter. "Hmm. Like what?"

"You know, that thing with my fingers and tongue from the back."

She moaned softly. "All right, we can make them leave now." She kissed me on the lips.

"Hey, hey, now, ladies," David said, "you still have company here."

"Okay, okay. I guess we can wait," I said, and everyone chuckled.

"Let's get this party started!" Asia squealed, releasing me and heading to the Bose system.

"Cool," Gary said. "Got any Carrie Underwood?"

Mary rolled her eyes, and Asia grinned at me as she fingered over the CD tower, leaving Santino looking confused and Andrea smiling.

"Sure, Gary. I think I do."

ORDER FORM
URBAN BOOKS, LLC
97 N18th Street
Wyandanch, NY 11798

Name (please print):_____

Address:_____

City/State:_____

Zip:_____

QTY	TITLES	PRICE
	16 On The Block	$14.95
	A Girl From Flint	$14.95
	A Pimp's Life	$14.95
	Baltimore Chronicles	$14.95
	Baltimore Chronicles 2	$14.95
	Betrayal	$14.95
	Black Diamond	$14.95

Shipping and handling-add $3.50 for 1st book, then $1.75 for each additional book.

Please send a check payable to:

Urban Books, LLC

Please allow 4-6 weeks for delivery

ORDER FORM
URBAN BOOKS, LLC
97 N18th Street
Wyandanch, NY 11798

Name (please print):_____

Address:_____

City/State:_____

Zip:_____

QTY	TITLES	PRICE
	Black Diamond 2	$14.95
	Black Friday	$14.95
	Both Sides Of The Fence	$14.95
	Both Sides Of The Fence 2	$14.95
	California Connection	$14.95
	California Connection 2	$14.95

Shipping and handling-add $3.50 for 1st book, then $1.75 for each additional book.

Please send a check payable to:

Urban Books, LLC

Please allow 4-6 weeks for delivery

ORDER FORM
URBAN BOOKS, LLC
97 N18th Street
Wyandanch, NY 11798

Name (please print):_____.

Address:_____/_____

City/State:_____

Zip:_____

QTY	TITLES	PRICE
	Cheesecake And Teardrops	$14.95
	Congratulations	$14.95
	Crazy In Love	$14.95
	Cyber Case	$14.95
	Denim Diaries	$14.95
	Diary Of A Mad First Lady	$14.95
	Diary Of A Stalker	$14.95

Shipping and handling-add $3.50 for 1st book, then $1.75 for each additional book.

Please send a check payable to:

Urban Books, LLC

Please allow 4-6 weeks for delivery